"HAVE

"Yes," Tokaido said.

He showed a montage of the suspect vehicle picked up by various traffic cams. After a few miles it turned onto a wide parking lot adjacent to a truck stop. The monitor showed the vehicle swing around and vanish from sight behind lined-up rigs and road trailers.

"Great," Brognola snapped.

"Not over yet," Tokaido said.

The view of the truck stop continued for a long few minutes before the suspect car came back into sight. Passing traffic forced it to wait before it swung right and drove away.

Brognola sighed. "So they stopped for a few minutes to use the toilet. Maybe pick up some coffee."

Kurtzman chuckled. "He doesn't see it."

"See what?"

Tokaido zoomed in on the image of the car waiting to merge into traffic.

There had been five men in the car when it arrived, but there were only four when it departed. Only two passengers in the rear instead of three.

"They lost one," Brognola said. "Son of a bitch."

Other titles in this series:

#73 COLD OBJECTIVE	#106 HIGH ASSAULT
#74 THE CHAMELEON FACTOR	#107 WAR TIDES
#75 SILENT ARSENAL	#108 EXTREME INSTINCT
#76 GATHERING STORM	#109 TARGET ACQUISITION
#77 FULL BLAST	#110 UNIFIED ACTION
#78 MAELSTROM	#111 CRITICAL INTELLIGENCE
#79 PROMISE TO DEFEND	#112 ORBITAL VELOCITY
#80 DOOMSDAY CONQUEST	#113 POWER GRAB
#81 SKY HAMMER	#114 UNCONVENTIONAL WARFARE
#82 VANISHING POINT	#115 EXTERMINATION
#83 DOOM PROPHECY	#116 TERMINAL GUIDANCE
#84 SENSOR SWEEP	#117 ARMED RESISTANCE
#85 HELL DAWN	#118 TERROR TRAIL
#86 OCEANS OF FIRE	#119 CLOSE QUARTERS
#87 EXTREME ARSENAL	#120 INCENDIARY DISPATCH
#88 STARFIRE	#121 SEISMIC SURGE
#89 NEUTRON FORCE	#122 CHOKE POINT
#90 RED FROST	#123 PERILOUS SKIES
#91 CHINA CRISIS	#124 NUCLEAR INTENT
#92 CAPITAL OFFENSIVE	#125 COUNTER FORCE
#93 DEADLY PAYLOAD	#126 PRECIPICE
#94 ACT OF WAR	#127 PRODIGY EFFECT
#95 CRITICAL EFFECT	#128 REVOLUTION DEVICE
#96 DARK STAR	#129 PULSE POINT
#97 SPLINTERED SKY	#130 ATOMIC FRACTURE
#98 PRIMARY DIRECTIVE	#131 TRIPLECROSS
#99 SHADOW WAR	#132 COLD SNAP
#100 HOSTILE DAWN	#133 DOMINATION BID
#101 DRAWPOINT	#134 DEATH DEALERS
#102 TERROR DESCENDING	#135 MIND BOMB
#103 SKY SENTINELS	#136 DOUBLE BLINDSIDE
#104 EXTINCTION CRISIS	#137 CITADEL OF FEAR
#105 SEASON OF HARM	#138 WAR TACTIC

DON PENDLETON'S

STONY

AMERICA'S ULTRA-COVERT INTELLIGENCE AGENCY

MAN®

DEATH MINUS ZERO

A GOLD EAGLE BOOK FROM

W🌐RLDWIDE®

TORONTO • NEW YORK • LONDON
AMSTERDAM • PARIS • SYDNEY • HAMBURG
STOCKHOLM • ATHENS • TOKYO • MILAN
MADRID • WARSAW • BUDAPEST • AUCKLAND

Recycling programs
for this product may
not exist in your area.

First edition October 2015

ISBN-13: 978-0-373-80453-5

Death Minus Zero

Special thanks and acknowledgment to
Mike Linaker for his contribution to this work.

Printed in U.S.A.

DEATH MINUS ZERO

CHAPTER ONE

Virginia

As he did every morning, Saul Kaplan stepped out of his town house and approached the waiting car. As he also did every day, he dropped his briefcase on the seat, climbed inside and took his place in the vehicle. The driver, a uniformed US Air Force sergeant, waited until Kaplan was settled. He glanced in the rearview mirror.

"Morning, Doc," Sergeant Steven Kessler greeted Kaplan.

"Good day, Steven. I think it is going to be a pleasant day."

"You sit back and enjoy the ride, Doc."

Kaplan smiled at the title he had been awarded by those he worked with. In truth Saul Kaplan was neither a professor nor a doctor, though he had been granted honorary degrees as he'd risen through the levels. But he barely recognized them and refused to use the titles; he recognized his skills in his chosen profession and was happy simply to develop his craft, seeing no advantage to having paper titles. Kaplan saw no need for aggrandizement. He was simply Saul Kaplan. That was enough for him. He was at the top of his game.

Kaplan was the man who had created and designed the Zero Platform and the human technology that went with it. It was through his determination and drive that the orbiting satellite had been approved and built. His sheer persistence had pushed Zero through the seemingly insurmountable barriers initially placed in his way. The US Air Force, the branch of the American defense services that had taken on Zero, held Kaplan in great esteem. His creation had already proved itself, and Kaplan's dream had stepped away from being a flight of fancy to become a solid reality that was continuing to prove itself in more ways than even Kaplan might have envisaged. "Doc" was simply something people called him out of respect for his skill and dedication to the work he did and Kaplan accepted it in the spirit it was given.

The Zero Platform was an orbiting defensive-offensive machine providing observation and analysis, though it also carried an array of weaponry capable of offering destructive potential. Currently that ordnance comprised powerful long- and short-range explosive-warhead missiles that could be used in an aggressive manner if the United States so decided. Weapons planned for future use—laser and particle beam—were still under development, though the complexities of putting them into action was proving frustrating, especially for Saul Kaplan. He was still working out the mechanics of the weapons. His expertise was being tested to the limit as he and the Air Force techs at Zero Command spent their days wrestling with the math and the applications of the weapons. Kaplan was confident they would succeed. The Air Force, always wanting everything by tomorrow, had been forced to step back and allow Kaplan his space.

During Zero's early days the USAF had made it difficult for him, and Kaplan had walked away. His return to a full-time commitment to the Zero Project had come after an attempted takeover by rogue elements in the US and an aborted attempt by the Chinese to destroy the project. Kaplan had, in the end, come back to the fold after he had deliberated the point of his involvement with the man he knew as Matt Cooper. It had been Cooper, drawn into the affair, who'd convinced Kaplan that America would be better off having Zero and making sure it was the best. Cooper had also made the point that Doug Buchanan, the human part of Zero, had committed himself to the project and the two men needed each other. Kaplan had capitulated and had returned to the Zero group, determined to carry on his work.

Zero held state-of-the-art communication equipment and was also able to produce pinpoint, bird's-eye views of the Earth. America did not publicly announce Zero's existence and most of the nation had no idea that it was orbiting the Earth, monitoring and watching. It had, by nature, been identified, but only as an orbiting information platform. Its full operating capability had not been released. The platform served its purpose and the Air Force considered it one of their most important assets. Unfortunately, Zero's secrets had been discovered by elements within the upper echelons of the People's Republic of China, which had long harbored a desire to wrest Zero from the Americans.

ZERO'S ATTRIBUTES WERE controlled through a unique partnership between Zero, the machine, and Air Force Major Doug Buchanan, the human element within Zero. The uniqueness was in the coupling of man and machine via Kaplan's genius—more specifically, his creation of the biocouch that fused Zero with Buchanan.

The implants within Buchanan's cancer-ridden body allowed the man to resist his illness; the coupling kept the cancer under control while generating the symbiosis of man and machine. The biocouch constantly fed him with controlling drugs that held his cancer at bay and with regenerating elements that kept him alive and well.

Since the initial connection Zero and Buchanan had successfully operated the platform, and with each passing year the partnership had grown and proved itself on a number of occasions. Kaplan had labored ceaselessly to improve the setup, making adjustments to Zero's electronic systems as well as working on ways to reduce the advance of cancerous cells within Buchanan's system.

While Zero Command's medical team monitored Buchanan's physical well-being, Air Force psychologists watched over his mental health. Their counseling sessions found that Buchanan was handling that part of his health far better than they could have expected. They were unable to find any undue stress. No deep-rooted psychological problems. Doug Buchanan passed their probing analysis with ease, leaving them with little to do in that area.

The Crown Victoria eased away from the curb and merged with the light traffic. It was barely 7:30 a.m., the day bright and holding a sharp chill in the air. The forty-minute drive to the facility would take them out of the city and through the countryside. The drive to the Zero Command Center was something Kaplan enjoyed. A relaxing start to the day, allowing him time to gather his thoughts for what lay ahead.

The route they traveled was one of three that could

be chosen. Kaplan knew alternate runs were not announced and were picked randomly just before each journey. There had been no problems with the routing since the creation of Zero Command. Sometimes, though, he wondered if the lack of anything but uniformity would lead to complacency.

The Crown Victoria cruised steadily, maintaining a smooth ride along the quiet back road. The single-lane blacktop was bordered by trees and a wide grass verge on each side. It was a pleasant run along a peaceful scene.

Until a car sped into view, swinging in close and causing Kessler to swerve to avoid a collision. The pressing closeness of the vehicle forced him to run off the road and across the grass, narrowly missing the close-standing trees. Kessler stood on the brakes, bringing the Vic to stop. Something about the intimidating presence of the other car alerted Kaplan that something was not right.

"Doc, stay in the car," Kessler said. "Let me check this out."

Kessler pushed open his door as he reached to open the glove box where he kept his service automatic.

As fast as he was, Kessler failed to stay ahead of the moment. Kaplan saw the passenger door being yanked open behind his driver, and a dark shape leaned in. Kessler stood no chance. The hand extended toward him held an automatic pistol. The weapon fired a single shot, sending a slug into the back of Kessler's head. He toppled forward, half out the open door.

Before Kaplan could react, his rear door was pulled open. A stunning shock engulfed Kaplan's body. His whole body went into a violent series of spasms. He fell back across the seat, body arching in reaction to the paralyzing agony that swept over him. He was barely aware of the hands reaching in to pull him out of the car. Or of the sharp jab of a needle into his neck. The powerful sedative worked quickly and Kaplan lost all conscious thought and feeling…

WHEN THE VEHICLE failed to arrive as expected, an alert was initiated. Although fitted with a tracking device, no sign of the Air Force car could be found. Electronic searches detected nothing; the tracking device was not working. Search vehicles were sent out from the Zero Command Center. They followed each route, in reverse, but found no sign of the vehicle until almost two hours after it had disappeared.

Just after 9:40 a.m., a member of the public spotted the abandoned car and contacted the local police. It was in a stand of trees off the single-lane rural road that made up one of the routes. Once the Air Force designation on the vehicle was seen, the AF was informed and the car checked out. It was quickly identified as the missing vehicle that had been transporting Saul Kaplan.

Air Force Sergeant Steven Kessler's body lay half out of his driver's seat, the door open. He had been shot in the head. A single bullet, later identified as a 9 mm, had been fired into the back of his skull.

The rear door of the car was open, as well. Saul Kaplan was missing. As was the briefcase that he always carried with him.

AGENT CLAIRE VALENS had been on the security team assigned to the Zero Project at the time there had been an attempt to sabotage it in its early existence. She had seen her partner, Jackson Byrd, killed in front of her eyes during that incident. She had been actively involved in Zero security ever since, over the years moving up the promotion ladder and now heading the Zero security team that worked alongside the Air Force at Zero Command. She knew Saul Kaplan well, having forged a good working relationship with the man, and on hearing he had vanished she put herself on standby. Valens, along with her partner, Larry Brandon, drove out from the Zero Command Center and headed for the location.

Valens was already getting a feeling of déjà vu. Since the first attempt at disrupting Zero, the sensation of something similar happening had stayed in Valens's memory. It had fueled her desire to make certain the project was never compromised again. Up until now her fears had been nothing more than shadows—but the possibility of Saul Kaplan having been kidnapped was starting to raise those shadows. Valens found the resurgence of memories unsettling.

Agent Brandon drove fast but safely. He was a couple of years younger than Valens, in his early thirties. He was a good partner and Valens counted herself lucky to have him siding her. He knew all there was to know about the original incident and understood how it drove Valens to maintain tight security around the Zero Command Center. The last thing he would ever do was to remind her of what had happened before. He didn't need to, because he was aware how Valens reminded herself on a regular basis.

"I can't believe this is happening again," Valens said.

"Is it the same?"

"Saul is missing. Work it out, Larry. The car didn't crash. It was stopped. Steve Kessler took a bullet in the head and Saul Kaplan is missing."

"So, who?"

"The original conspirators were all dealt with," Valens said. "At home the threat vanished but…"

"The Chinese?"

"I don't believe they've forgotten about Zero. The Chinese are good at playing the long game. Watching and waiting. They'll know that Zero performs as it was designed to. And as long as it does, it presents them with a perceived threat. Let's face it—what country wouldn't like a piece of hardware like Zero? It would be a hell of a prize."

"It's not like they can just walk in and take over," Brandon said. "Zero is an orbiting platform in space."

"Saul Kaplan is *not* in space. And taking him would be something the Chinese could go for. And maybe even a hit against Zero Command. Cripple the nerve center. Do that and if they can gain control of Zero…" Valens shook her head. "Larry, do I sound like some gibbering conspiracy nut? Because that's what I'm feeling like. Right now I'm having a nightmare in broad daylight."

"After what happened last time, I couldn't blame you."

Brandon swung the car off the narrow road onto the side strip and pulled in beside a local police cruiser. The area was busy with cruisers and Air Force vehicles. Crime scene tape was strung out from tree to tree, and a collection of police and military personnel milled around.

"Great," Brandon said. "The circus is in full swing."

Valens had her ID out as she climbed from the car, clipping it to her belt.

"Agent Valens."

Valens saw a broad-shouldered man approaching. He was average height, in his mid-forties, his receding hair peppered with gray. He was a local cop named Jerry Zeigler. He and Valens had met before. He wasn't deliberately obstructive but harbored a slightly abrasive attitude toward the agencies that stepped in and took over, pushing the local PD aside. He didn't take too kindly when it happened, so Valens tried to maintain a professional presence whenever she met Zeigler.

"Detective," she said, offering her hand, which Zeigler took.

Zeigler glanced at Brandon. "You brought your backup, I see."

Valens smiled. "Agent Brandon is my partner. And, yes, he has my back."

A thin smile curled Zeigler's lips. "I'll refrain from making any inappropriate comments on that," he said.

"What can you tell us?" Valens said. "Seeing as you've been here a while."

"Only because the original call was made to us. But there's not much more than you can see. One of your vehicles. Uniformed Air Force man shot dead. I was informed by your people there was a passenger. He's missing. A preliminary search hasn't turned up anything, so I guess the passenger has been removed from the area."

Valens checked out the place. A spot off the road where trees and foliage helped to mask the site. A smooth operation could have been mounted and completed quickly on the quiet stretch before anyone was aware.

"They chose a good spot. Away from the main highway. Pretty quiet. Whoever it was, they were well prepared. All nicely worked out. Must have worked fast."

Brandon had gone to talk to the investigative team near the Crown Victoria. Valens saw him check inside the car before he returned to where she was standing.

"It's Steve Kessler," he said. "Bullet to the back of his head. No sign of any struggle in the back."

"Passenger some kind of VIP?" Zeigler asked.

"Yes," Valens answered.

"That it?"

"I'm not at liberty to give out that information. Sorry."

"Oh, I know," Zeigler said. "Classified, huh?"

"If I was able, I'd tell you, Detective Zeigler…"

"It's Jerry."

"If I was able, I'd tell you, *Jerry*…"

Zeigler glanced at Brandon. "Is she always this hard-nosed?"

"Actually, you've caught her on a good day," Brandon said. "No fingers missing, are there?"

"I can believe she bites if provoked."

Valens's cell rang. She moved away to answer it, knowing it was Zero Command by the caller ID on the screen.

"From all the bodies here," Zeigler said, "I figure you people have a lot to deal with."

"Nothing gets by you, Detective Zeigler," Brandon said.

Zeigler grinned. "So smart, so young, so full of bullshit. Nothing you can tell me. Yeah, I know."

Valens rejoined them.

"If anything comes up that I can tell you," she said,

"I will pass it on, Jerry. Right now I have a missing VIP and it's my job to get him back. You have problems with that, you can talk to Colonel Corrigan at the base. Best I can do."

Zeigler felt the frustration rising as he eyed Valens. She didn't lose a beat and the cop knew she wouldn't give anything away even if they stood there all day.

Goddamn it, he thought, all this need-to-know crap is killing me.

He let out the breath he'd been holding and managed a strained smile.

"Okay, Agent Valens, you win. Just remember I'm not one of the bad guys. Just doing—trying to do my job." He turned and made his way to where his police cruiser sat waiting.

"I DON'T ENJOY freezing the local cops out," Valens said. "Zeigler has it right. He just wants to do what he's paid for. And all we do is put up a solid wall and stall him."

"Your call? Anything important I should know about?"

"That was Colonel Corrigan on the phone. It appears we have a specialist team joining us back at base," Valens said.

She noted Brandon's frown. "What specialists?"

"An undercover group—and that's all you need to know—from the covert agency involved when the original Zero problem occurred. Larry, we need all the help we can get on this. I don't have any problem accepting that."

"If you say so. You are the boss."

"Yes, I am," Valens said. "So no sulking over this."

"*Moi*? Sulk? And here I thought you knew me better than that, Agent Valens."

"I know you hate bullshit as much as I do. I prefer having stuff out in the open but we have to follow the ground rules. So let's wind it up and get back to base. I don't think we'll be any use here any longer. Let the investigative team do their thing. Something tells me they're not going to find anything."

"Yeah. Hey, these covert operators don't all wear tights and masks and fly around in invisible planes, by any chance?"

"Sometimes I wish we had some of those guys," Valens said. "Might make our job a damn sight easier."

"I wouldn't look good in tights," Brandon retorted. "You, on the other hand…"

"Do not go there, Larry."

Walking ahead, Brandon grinned like a schoolboy.

BACK IN THE CAR, Brandon took the wheel while Valens made a call to their department chief. Brandon was not deliberately listening but couldn't help picking up the reference she made to a Jui Kai. All Brandon knew about the young Chinese woman was that she was on a long-term undercover assignment in China. Valens took occasional messages from their chief but said little to him about it. Brandon, understanding she was not prepared to discuss the matter, didn't question her.

Claire Valens was a determined woman with strong opinions about her work, and she held unshakable feelings, most notably the one that resurfaced every so often; Valens was convinced, as she had been for a long time, that the Chinese had not forgotten about Zero. It was as close to a conspiracy theory as any belief Valens held. It seemed to be there in the background, a vaporous image that Valens could not—perhaps would not—shake off. And the fact Jui Kai was working the China beat backed up Valens's suspicions. Her assignment at Zero Command occupied her day-to-day business and this out-of-left-field move and the disappearance of Saul Kaplan would have been a blow to her pride. It would only strengthen her resolve to stay with her theory.

Familiarity with the situation may have been partly to blame, even though Valens would take it badly. The protocols in place had been working well. Kaplan was delivered to the AF base and returned home each evening—unless some urgent matter arose with Zero. It had become the norm. Perhaps too much so. The delivery of Kaplan to the base, a routine that had been smooth and undisturbed, had become an accepted ritual. The route changed daily, allowing for some flexibility, and operated with clockwork efficiency. Valens was charged with on-base security, the Air Force with the actual fetching and carrying of the man who was responsible for the oversight of the Zero Platform's daily routines.

Over the preceding months, the ongoing routine never varied. Kaplan in. Work done. Kaplan home. A hard routine. It was as set as the ticking of a clock. Checks were made on timing and routes. The Air Force maintained a tight schedule for the daily trip—which was the reason Kaplan's absence was picked up so soon after the event.

Even so, Kaplan was gone.

Where, no one knew.

The why was a little easier to work out.

The man carried knowledge of the operation and the know-how about Zero.

The platform was up and running, monitored day and night.

Kaplan's imaginative dream had become a working reality, giving America a unique piece of hardware.

Everyone at Zero Command would know with all certainty why Kaplan had been taken.

A deliberate attempt at gaining a hold over Zero's creator and possibly an outright and hostile try for the platform itself.

That seemed to have been the easy part.

The hard part—getting him back alive and well— was something else.

WHOEVER WAS BEHIND the kidnapping had upfront knowledge. The AF vehicle had been fitted with a tracking device that had gone off-line. And Kaplan himself had an implanted signal tracker that was supposed to show his whereabouts. It was not transmitting, either. The snatch had been well planned. The disabling of the trackers only highlighted how well organized the kidnappers had been.

Claire Valens took note of these items. It concerned her that somewhere, someone had gained such knowledge and used it against Zero.

She was unable to stop wondering what came next.

Valens felt her thoughts turning toward Major Doug Buchanan, the man who controlled Zero's 24/7 functions through his command position. Buchanan would not be happy when he learned about Kaplan's kidnapping. Buchanan had an abiding faith in the man. There was more than the simple dependency that Buchanan had with Kaplan. He had become so tied in with Zero's creator the bond was as strong as Buchanan's with his biocouch. Maybe even stronger.

Buchanan, for all his characteristic strength, depended on Saul Kaplan as a son with a father. It had become far more than their working relationship. Buchanan owed his continuing existence to Kaplan's genius, to the superior intellect that had devised and overseen the electronic wonder of the Zero Platform. It had been Buchanan's salvation, drawing him back from a certain, painful death and allowing him the opportunity to carry on doing what he loved—working for his country. Offering back something for the debt he would never be able to pay completely.

Doug Buchanan knew and accepted that he was as much a part of Zero now as one of the circuit boards. An integral part of the complex machine Kaplan had envisaged and seen through to completion, Buchanan knew his life was with Zero. The ravaging cancer that had started him on the countdown to the end of his life was held at bay by the bioimplants that fed his body on a continuous basis, holding the cancerous cells at bay and maintaining his existence.

Buchanan had only asked Kaplan once how it worked. Kaplan's explanation had lost him within the first couple of minutes and Buchanan had asked him to stop. Buchanan decided the only thing he needed to know was that the process worked. As long as he remained on his biocouch, linked to the system via the implants in his body, he would survive. The question as to how long never came up. To have been given even a short extension to his life was enough. The fact that it allowed him to function in his capacity as an Air Force officer, defending his country, was reward enough.

The multiple functions of Zero, as a defensive as well as an offensive weapon, presented Buchanan with day-to-day operational involvement. His routines were mapped out for him by the electronic machine that surrounded and sustained him. Buchanan monitored and collated information, passed it back to Zero Command and took his orders from the base.

Learning that his mentor had been spirited away would not be welcome news to Buchanan. He would utilize Zero's functions to search for him, and Doug Buchanan's unflagging spirit would not back away from that task.

If there was a chance to locate Kaplan, Valens thought, Buchanan would do his best to find it.

CHAPTER TWO

China

Colonel Xia Chan had the ghost of a smile of satisfaction on his face as he replaced the telephone receiver on its cradle. Such shows of pleasure were unexpected. He was a solemn man, entirely dedicated to his position and responsibilities, so the officials gathered in his presence were surprised at the emotion. Chan sat back in his seat, facing the group of men around the conference table. His hands were placed on the smooth surface, fingers tapping gently. He studied the group until he was satisfied he had their full attention.

"It has begun," he announced. "The successful apprehension of the American Saul Kaplan has taken place. Even as I speak, he is being moved on the first stage of the journey that will remove him from the country."

A thin-faced, balding major asked, "Are congratulations in order, Colonel?"

"A little premature, Ling. Let us wait until the man has been removed from American soil. It's not wise to presume too much."

Ling nodded. "Perhaps you are right, Colonel."

"Even so, we should be allowed a degree of satisfaction. As operations go, this first phase appears to have been executed with precision and timing."

"That was thought when the first strike against the Zero operation was mounted."

The speaker was seated halfway along the table. A thick-set figure with a shaved head set on a squat neck, Yang Zhou was wearing civilian clothing. As always, he looked as though he had just stepped out of a tailor's store; Zhou made no concessions to the austere dress code of the Chinese system. No one ever thought about challenging him over that. The man was head of a security section and had complete autonomy over what he said and did. He was on this occasion assigned to be Colonel Chan's personal bodyguard, ordered to accompany him wherever he went and to protect him. The order had come from the highest authority, and even Zhou was required to accept.

"Zhou, we are talking about something that happened a number of years ago," Chan said. "I have read the reports that were written about the affair. General Tung Shan paid the price because his operation was ill-conceived and he failed to anticipate the opposition. He made his strike on American soil and was in unknown territory. There was no backing for him. No means to call in assistance when things began to go wrong."

"He was reckless," Zhou argued. "He placed his people in jeopardy and they were abandoned."

"If I remember correctly, didn't a couple of Shan's team desert and stay in America?" Major Ling returned.

Chan nodded. "It has not been forgotten. Shao Yeng and Yin Tang. To date we have not been able to locate them. But the search continues. When they defected, they were in possession of a great deal of money that had been allocated to the mission. That will have enabled them to move around and stay concealed." He raised his hands. "As we are all aware, if you have money in America it is possible to buy anything. Including anonymity."

"We are still active in searching for those traitors. We *will* find them," Zhou declared.

"I do not doubt that," Chan said. "Would it were in my own lifetime."

Zhou stiffened, face taut with anger, but there was little he could say. His operatives had failed and were still failing to locate the two men.

The door at the far end of the room opened and a wheeled trolley was pushed inside. It held pots of tea and coffee. Cups were filled on request before the group around the table was left alone again.

There were seven other uniformed attendees sitting around the table. Each had an open folder in front of him.

Placing his cup on the table, Chan said, "I understand there are questions to be asked. Shall we begin?"

"As I have only recently been assigned to your group, Colonel Chan, my knowledge of this project is not complete. May I ask for clarification?"

The speaker was a young military officer. His uniform was in pristine condition, hair neat and precise. Eagerness shone in his eyes. His name was Kung Lang. Chan had heard good things about the man's progress through the ranks.

"For the benefit of Major Lang, and any others not fully aware of this operation, I will take you through it this one time," Chan said. "Make notes, because if you miss anything it will not be repeated. I have no time to keep going over the facts."

Chan spent the next twenty minutes cataloging the Zero operation from its inception to the less-than-satisfactory conclusion of the original Chinese strike against it. He held nothing back, giving all the names and locations.

"We became entangled with a separate operation mounted by disaffected Americans who were attempting a coup d'état. That and our presence became known and, as you all are aware, our operation was defeated. We were forced to abandon, but we did not forget.

"The Zero prize is still something we covet. It is still, as then, something we would like to get our hands on. In your files you will have read and realized the potential threat it poses. Our Pacific Rim friends, who were anxious for us to gain control of the platform at the time, have not backed down from their desires. Apart from the weapons technology, the ability for Zero to see and hear so much could prove embarrassing. If that ability fell into our control, everything would be reversed."

"Surely the Americans would resist any attempt to take control from their hands," one of the listeners said.

"Of course they would. Which is why we need help from this man Kaplan. He understands Zero like no one else. In reality he *is* Zero. The man carries everything there is to know about his creation. He has refused from day one to reveal certain details about Zero's human-machine interface. He cleverly kept the details of his creation in his head, allowing only as much as was necessary to make the process possible. Saul Kaplan is an extremely clever man. Holding back on certain aspects of the design and interface technology has placed him in a unique position."

"If he dies?" someone asked. "Surely he must have considered that possibility."

"Even I do not have insight into that. It will be something we will attempt to find out once Kaplan is safely in our hands."

Kung Lang leaned forward. "There must exist a contingency plan for the sudden death of this man," he said. "I find it difficult to conceive there is nothing held in reserve."

"You may be correct, Lang, and it will be one of the matters under consideration when Kaplan is being questioned. I must myself admit to having reservations over that very aspect of this affair. Rest assured that I will be pursuing that extremely thoroughly."

The session went on for another hour and by the end of it Chan was convinced his team was up to date on every aspect of Zero known to them.

When he returned to his office, leaving them briefly to discuss the meeting between themselves, his mind was full of unanswered questions that only Saul Kaplan could answer. Chan was anticipating the confrontation of minds when he finally came face-to-face with the man. As confident as he was of his own abilities, he hoped he would match up to the American. Kaplan was no simpleton—the man who had devised and orchestrated the building of the Zero Platform had nothing to prove to anyone. The sheer brilliance coming from inside his head told Chan he would be facing a man capable of a technological marvel. Kaplan's genius had conceived and produced something that had never been done before. Not just the floating platform—

but the convergence of man and machine on a new, unheard-of level.

If he did nothing else with his life, Chan was determined to gain that knowledge so he could present Zero to his beloved country. If China could get its hands on Zero, the balance of many things would change—away from the United States and toward his country.

It was, Chan knew, a dream worth pursuing.

Having Zero in China's control would be a major coup, for him as well as for his nation. If he, Chan, could present Zero to his leaders, he would be able to stand tall in the hierarchy. From such heights he would command not only respect but power. And power was something Chan desired. It was a need he had long harbored. He had little need for monetary gain. That was only a fleeting thing. But long-term power was something else. To achieve strength in a position of influence stirred deep feelings inside him. A basic, intoxicating feeling that demanded fulfillment.

If he could achieve total control over the American creation, it would offer him everything he wanted. His name would be forever remembered in China's history. He, Xia Chan, would be known as the man who took the Zero Project away from the Americans and offered it to *his* people.

That was a victory worth aiming for.

And it was to that end Xia Chan looked.

ONE OF CHAN'S OFFICERS called him on the office phone.

"Arrangements are complete. You will be able to leave within the next hour."

Xia Chan allowed himself a brief smile. He acknowledged the call and put down the phone. He leaned back in his padded chair, going over the details of the forth-coming trip in his mind. Finally he picked up the phone and spoke to one of his aides.

"Call the airstrip and tell my pilot to be ready when I arrive. He can be advised of our destination now so he can key in his route. Tell him I need to leave as soon as possible. I will need to speak to the group again before I leave. Tell them the meeting will continue shortly. Then come into my office."

The aide was a thin, prematurely balding young officer. He always appeared nervous in Chan's presence.

"You know what to do?"

"Yes, Colonel."

"No mistakes. No one is to leave with any written notes. We keep everything in-house. If you find anything it must be burned. You understand?"

"Yes, Colonel. It will be done."

When the aide had gone, Chan retired to his private quarters, where he changed from his uniform and dressed in a smart suit, shirt and tie. He stepped into soft-soled black shoes, already polished to a high shine. He checked the expensive attaché case sitting on the floor. It contained his passport and documentation and a fully charged sat phone. There was money and credit cards—not that he expected to need them, but it was always a wise move to have such things handy.

He left his office and made his way to the conference room where his team was waiting. He stood at the head of the table as they all turned to face him.

"As I told you earlier, the man Kaplan is now in our hands and I am leaving shortly to fly to the rendezvous where the American will be held while he is interrogated. Yang Zhou will accompany me. While we are away, I want the facility made ready. Check everything and then check it again. I want all systems up and ready when I return." Chan stared from face to face. "I hope this is fully understood. No excuses. The facility must be ready when I return with Kaplan."

The discomfort around the table was noticeable. That pleased Chan. He needed the team fully focused. No wavering.

"We will not let you down," Major Ling said.

"I am pleased to hear that, Ling. In your case I hope nothing goes wrong, because I am leaving you in charge. All of you will report to Major Ling. Is that understood? While I am away he is responsible. He acts for me and his orders will be followed."

Major Ling remained silent, aware of the responsibility and just as aware of what would happen if he failed.

"I must be excused to collect my things, Colonel," Yang Zhou said.

"Very well. In my office in twenty minutes." As Zhou left, Chan returned to face his team. "We must make this work. If we wish to take control of Zero, our efforts must be doubled. You will remain at your stations day and night. Ling, you will arrange for food and drink to be delivered to you. Bedding is to be provided. I give you the authority to use my name. If anyone raises objections, simply refer them to me. Understood?"

"Yes, Colonel."

Chan took Ling aside. "This is your opportunity to make your mark," he said. "Do not fail yourself or me. There is much riding on this project. If we succeed, we bring a great deal of glory to China. Important eyes are on us, Ling. You understand?"

"Yes, Colonel."

"All the electronic equipment must be fully readied. When I return with Kaplan, I am confident he will be ready to comply. His input will be vital and must be matched by the setup. Make sure all is prepared."

Ling nodded.

Chan left the conference room and returned to his office to find Zhou already there.

"The car is waiting for us," Zhou said.

They went outside where the official car was idling. An aide stepped forward to open the rear door. "Your luggage is in the trunk, Colonel," he said.

As soon as they were seated, the car pulled away and drove out of the grounds, picking up the near-deserted road. Neither man spoke. They both had their thoughts to deal with, and small talk was not a skill either had learned.

The drive to the isolated military airfield took just over a half hour. Sitting on the runway was a sleek Gulfstream G650. Powered by twin Rolls-Royce BR725 turbofan engines, the executive jet had a cruising speed of around 560 mph, with a ceiling of 51,000 feet. It would cruise 7000 nautical miles before needing refueling. Chan had exclusive use of this luxurious aircraft and had used it many times. The Gulfstream had civilian markings and a logo for a company that existed only on paper, based in Hong Kong. The crew wore smart nonmilitary uniforms and the young woman who welcomed them aboard was fresh-faced and attractive. She guided them to their seats as their driver brought the luggage on board.

The woman's name was Jui Kai.

Chan knew her very well. On an extremely intimate level. His involvement with her had been ongoing for some months. Her natural beauty and her entrancing personality charmed him. He enjoyed her company immensely.

"It is good to see you again, Colonel. It has been some time," the young woman said, playing the game for the plane's crew. "I hope you enjoy the flight."

"I am certain I will, my dear."

Zhou studied the Gulfstream's well-appointed interior with a jaundiced eye. "A very expensive toy," he stated.

"But necessary," Chan said.

"If you believe so," Zhou said.

Jui Kai moved away to the rear of the jet, where the galley was located.

Zhou mumbled something about it being a long flight as he pushed his way to a seat.

"Look on this as an adventure," Chan said. "We may be witnesses to China's greatest success in the field of espionage."

"Just because we have this *gweilo* does not mean we yet have his secrets," Zhou said.

"Foreign devil? Ever the pessimist, Yang Zhou."

"I prefer to call myself a realist. Nothing is won until the race is over."

"Very good," Chan said. "But I have a good feeling about this, Zhou. I don't deny we have much work ahead of us. From what I have learned about this man Kaplan, he may be difficult to break. Which in itself offers a challenge."

Jui Kai appeared again from the galley.

"May I offer you both a drink? Colonel? Mr. Zhou?"

"A glass of very decadent American whiskey would be pleasant," Chan said, smiling.

"Mr. Zhou?"

Zhou managed a sharp nod. "The same," he said. "With ice."

"Ice?" Chan said. "What a disrespectful way to treat good whiskey."

Zhou slumped into his seat and stared out the side window.

The Gulfstream began to move as the pilot increased power. It held position at the end of the runway, the engines building until there was sufficient power to speed it along the tarmac and into a fast rise.

Minutes later they were at cruising altitude.

Jui Kai brought the drinks, handing them to Chan and Zhou. "Please call me if you require anything further."

Chan nodded. He smiled at the young woman. An expression of familiarity. Extreme familiarity. He sometimes found it difficult to control his feelings in her presence.

"When do we eat?" Zhou asked. He was so concerned with his stomach he failed to notice the looks exchanged between Chan and Kai.

"Whenever you wish, sir," she said.

Chan relaxed into the soft, cream-colored leather seat, savoring the mellow whiskey. He could still hear Zhou grumbling to himself.

It was, he realized, definitely going to be a long flight—around fifteen hours with a stop for refueling. All that time with Yang Zhou sitting across from him. As much as Chan recognized the man as an expert in his work, he was not so impressed with Zhou's social skills.

From what he knew of the man, it was obvious Zhou had little in the way of a social life. He gave himself to the job, denying pleasure and spending much of his off-duty time in his office. A strange and reclusive life, Chan decided, but one Zhou chose.

Chan tried to push the negative thoughts out of his mind, concentrating on the task ahead.

He was looking forward to meeting Dr. Luc Melier again. It had been some time since he had been involved with the man. Melier, Chinese-French, was an excellent choice to work on Kaplan. He resided in France and refused to travel very far to carry out his work, which was why Chan was coming to meet him.

Melier's reputation as a skilled manipulator was without equal. Chan had seen him on other occasions, working to break through stubborn minds. He did it with comparative ease, very seldom having to resort to anything close to violence—not that it was ruled out entirely because there were times when the minimal amount of force could tilt the balance.

That would be where Zhou came into his own. The man had no kind of conscience when it came to using brutal methods. It was quite an education watching the man at work; the only thing that troubled Chan was how Zhou obviously took great pleasure inflicting hurt on others. Yet there was a place for Zhou, and Chan never interfered when it came time to employ the man's talents.

An hour into the flight, Zhou fell asleep. He had already eaten, downed a couple more whiskies and had even stopped grumbling. Chan hoped the man might sleep for the rest of the flight. He doubted that would happen.

He took tea when Kai offered it, not yet ready for food himself, allowing a pleasured smile when her slim, warm hand brushed his as she passed him his drink. When she left, he slid a file from his attaché case and spent some time going through work-related documents. There was, he thought, always something that needed his attention. Not that he minded. Xia Chan was dedicated to his profession, the demands of his position keeping him fully occupied. At present it was the Zero Project that demanded his time. Though it was a consuming matter, Chan did not regret a second. It was the single most important thing in his life at the moment. Sanctioned by the supreme authority in the country and placed in Chan's hands, he understood that nothing of such importance would come his way again and he was aware of the honor that had been bestowed upon him.

Failure was something he refused to even consider.

It would not happen.

He would breathe his last before he would concede victory.

THEY MADE THEIR one stop for refueling and then continued with the flight. Chan was able to steal a little time with Kai as Zhou settled back in his reclined seat, covered in a pair of blankets. In the well-appointed galley, she came into his arms and they allowed themselves some personal time. For Chan it was a welcome distraction from the demands of his office and Kai gave him much to think about. She was as skilled as she was beautiful, and Chan found himself briefly allowing his demanding mission to be pushed aside.

THE LONG FLIGHT ended in late afternoon. The Gulfstream took a lengthy sweep as it lined up on the single runway of the private airfield and made a fast approach, with barely a jolt as it touched down. It slowed and cruised to the parking area, coming to a gentle stop adjacent to the small airport building.

Chan had rested, worked and was in a pleasurable mood.

"Colonel, it may be cold when you disembark," Kai said. "I have your overcoat here."

"Thank you, my dear." Chan stood and allowed her to assist him in putting on the long coat. "The flight has been made bearable by your presence once again, Jui. I am so pleased you are here."

"Of course, Colonel. The aircraft will be serviced and refueled for your convenience."

Chan touched her shoulder, a pleasant thought filling his head. "Perhaps you would join me for a meal when I have some free time. Come and see where we are working. The house is a delight. I am sure you would enjoy seeing it."

"That would be my pleasure, Colonel Chan."

"Then I will send my driver for you."

"I look forward to that and seeing you once more."

They said no more while there was the chance of being overheard.

Having spent the flight sleeping and sipping whiskey, Yang Zhou roused himself from his reclined seat to gaze through the window. He stared out at the ranks of snowcapped mountain peaks rising above the green forests of fir and pine. Above the high crags the sky was crystal-clear and blue.

Chan smiled at the man's discomfort. He took his attaché case and made for the now open exit. As he stepped onto the tarmac he breathed in the fresh, cold air. It felt good. Zhou, still fastening his own coat, was muttering under his breath, not at all happy. As they moved away from the Gulfstream, Kai, who had followed them out, said quietly, "I will look forward to your call, Colonel."

Chan smiled at her. "It will come," he said. "I promise you that, my dear."

He paused and patted his companion on the shoulder. "Zhou, welcome to Switzerland," he said.

CHAPTER THREE

Hal Brognola, head of the covert operations based at Stony Man Farm, walked beside the President of the United States. They were at Camp David, where the President was taking a brief respite from the demands of the job. But even while he tried to wind down, he still maintained a hands-on attitude. The Commander in Chief never truly stepped away from his responsibilities, which was why he had requested Brognola's presence to discuss a matter that was on his mind.

The tranquil atmosphere of the presidential retreat surrounded the pair as they strolled through the grounds. Unobtrusive Secret Service men followed them at a discreet distance. Brognola and the President were wearing thick topcoats against the chill of the wintery weather. The odd snowflake drifted between them. There was a promise of more in the air.

"You've probably worked out why I asked you to join me, Hal."

"Kaplan going missing? We already got the word from Doug Buchanan. He picked up on Kaplan's tracker going off-line and the failure of the device fitted to the Air Force vehicle. Agent Valens briefed us, as well. So we know about Kaplan going missing, which brings Zero into the picture."

"Am I ever going to catch you Stony Man people out?" the President said.

"I hope not. If you ever do, Mr. President, that will be the day I resign."

"Don't even think about it, Hal." The President paused to stare around him at the tranquil scene. "I sit in my office at the White House, door closed, hoping to catch a minute. Never works. But coming here is a different ball game. Just walking through these trees, surrounded by silence…it gives me space to sort out what's buzzing around in my head."

"And right now that's Saul Kaplan," Brognola concluded.

"We have to find him, Hal. Get him back alive and well." The President hesitated before he said, "The bottom line would be to say if he can't be retrieved then his life might have to be forfeit. I hate having to even think about that, Hal, but the knowledge Kaplan has must not be allowed to remain in enemy hands."

"I understand that, Mr. President. Stony Man is already on this," Brognola said.

He knew that even as he was speaking to the President the cyber team at the Farm was working flat-out as it searched for information on the whereabouts of Zero's creator and guiding light. Stony Man had been involved with the Zero Project from its early days, with Mack Bolan stepping up to investigate when Doug Buchanan had gone AWOL. The resolution of that incident had been getting Buchanan back into the program and finally installed on Zero. If there was anything to find, where Kaplan was concerned, Aaron Kurtzman's team would unearth it. They had the best equipment available, along with the ability to hack into databases and systems that were supposed to be hacker-resistant. The state-of-the-art technology was only as good as the people using it, and the Stony Man cyber team had no equals. If it was out there, Kurtzman's team would find it, interpret it and strip out the data they needed.

"Zero has become a valuable listening post for us," the President said. "I don't have to tell you how valuable. When we complete the development of the laser-particle beam weapons systems, Zero is going to become even better than it already is."

"Are we still having operational problems with the laser-particle beam systems?"

"Zero has conventional missiles and Slingshot capability," the President said. "The added refinement of the other weapons is proving to be difficult. Development is ongoing. We will get there, Hal, but right now those weapons are still in the theoretical stage. There are complex problems we are still trying to overcome. Major Buchanan is working with Zero Command in the development alongside Kaplan, which is another reason why we mustn't allow a foreign power to have their chance to get that kind of information out of him."

"I can understand that, sir. Even without them, Zero is still a hell of an achievement. No other country has anything to match it."

"Not at this moment in time. Which is exactly why somewhere like China would like to get their hands on it. Hal, we cannot allow this to happen. Zero is our high card. It gives us one hell of an advantage in the defense game. I won't let it be taken from us. We fight this, Hal, with everything we have. Stony Man. Your teams. I'll give you whatever you need in backup all the way down the line. No question here. We keep Zero because if someone like China gets its hands on it, we'll all be in trouble. My God, Hal, can you imagine what would happen if we lost Zero to Beijing?"

"Unfortunately, I can, sir. Which makes this latest move against Saul Kaplan something we need to fully address. Stony Man will put everything we have on this."

"I don't care what toes you step on or who you upset. If there are territorial borders you need to cross, I'll stand by you."

The President's mood and his willingness to stand by his people made Brognola aware of the implications if Zero was compromised.

"What about…?" the President started to ask.

He was asking about Mack Bolan.

The Executioner.

"The guy is off somewhere on a mission he initiated himself. He's gone black. We've had no contact with him for over a week. We have no idea where he is right now. And we don't have the luxury of waiting for him to make contact."

"I only mentioned him because he was so deeply involved the first time around. No slight on the other teams, Hal, since I know they'll offer us the best way out of this."

"You can depend on that, sir. This will be our priority from right now."

"Keep me informed, Hal. I want to be kept apprised every step of the way," the President said. "Which brings me to ask, do you need anything?" The Man paused. "Hal, anything."

Brognola's phone began to ring. When he took it

out, he saw that the screen was showing a call from Stony Man.

"Like I said, Mr. President, we're on this as of right now. Excuse me, sir, I need to take this."

The President watched as Brognola took the call. The expression on the big Fed's face told America's leader he wasn't being delivered good news.

"I need to get back to Stony Man, Mr. President. This is hotting up already."

"Then get out of here, Hal, and good luck."

Minutes later Brognola was leaving Camp David. Jack Grimaldi, who had been entertained by Camp staff while their bosses liaised, powered the chopper into the bright, cold sky. Stony Man's ace pilot set course for the Farm.

CHAPTER FOUR

Stony Man Farm

David McCarter followed his team into the War Room and took his seat next to Barbara Price. The Phoenix Force commander was clutching a chilled bottle of Classic Coke; he still refused to drink the other flavors currently available, claiming they were technically not the real thing. The Briton stuck to his preferences and would not consider changing; that applied to the Player's cigarettes he occasionally enjoyed and his beloved 9 mm Browning Hi-Power pistol.

He glanced at the manila folder Price, the Farm's mission controller, had placed in front of him. He idly scrolled through the pages without comment as the War Room filled up with the Able Team and Hal Brognola, who had arrived at the Farm only minutes ago. Aaron Kurtzman, clutching a steaming mug of his deadly coffee brew, rolled up to the table in his wheelchair.

Five men comprised Phoenix Force, all experienced warriors who carried a long list of credentials that enabled them to face any odds put in their way. McCarter, who had inherited the mantle of leader from the late Yakov Katzenelenbogen, led his team by example.

With a legendary background that included the SAS, McCarter was an accomplished combat veteran and a noted brawler. He could handle aircraft as well as wheeled vehicles and was proficient with most any kind of weapon he could get his hands on. The man had an infectious sense of humor that often got him looked at sideways, but there was not a better man to have at your side in a firefight. He had a reputation for taking chances and ignoring the rules, but McCarter had long ago decided that in the middle of an armed conflict, where the saving of his skin and that of his partners was involved, anything went. He was ultimately proved right.

Some would label him reckless, but the Briton saw breaking the rules mattered if it led to ultimate victory. His manner got him into trouble on more than one occasion, but that did not worry him in the slightest. McCarter had a tough hide, and verbal barbs bounced off him, though after becoming leader of Phoenix Force he had made an effort to temper his impetuous nature.

His team trusted his instincts, and it was a given they would follow him to the gates of Hell to face the Devil if asked. The connection was often close to the truth. The violent savages they had to face were often close to being the mortal equivalent of Satan. McCarter was more than satisfied with the people who backed him.

Calvin James, a tall, lean black man, was the team's resident medic. James was good-looking, wore a thin moustache and had an easy way with the ladies. As well as being handy when it came to saving lives, James was also a ferocious fighter. Coming from the south side of Chicago had given James a taste of the tough life. He had enlisted in the US Navy at seventeen, and his natural skills and dedication had brought him to the attention of the SEALs. After his service, he had become a cop in San Francisco and it was while on SWAT duty that he had been approached and recruited into Phoenix Force. He might have been a little unsure at the outset, but he now admitted it was the best thing he had ever done.

An expert demolitions man and sniper, Canadian Gary Manning had been a time-served RCMP operative and had spent time with GSG-9, which had given him detailed insight in global terrorist organizations—something he still kept up to date on. He had been a security consultant for an American company and had come to the notice of Brognola's Special Operations Group. Manning, a powerfully built man with superb reflexes and a no-nonsense attitude, took to the closeness of Phoenix Force quickly. He was a fast thinker and maintained a tolerant attitude toward McCarter's brashness, even though they engaged in deliberate banter at times. Over the years both men had come to respect each other.

To Rafael Encizo, a Cuban, Phoenix Force had become his family after losing most of his natural one. His experiences back in his home country, including his incarceration in a Cuban political prison from which he eventually escaped, had left Encizo with little to fall back on and a problem with trust. That was before he became a member of the team and found lasting friendship with his adopted country, having taken on citizenship, and with the men of Phoenix Force. The powerfully built commando had excellent reflexes and was a noted martial arts expert.

For Thomas Jackson Hawkins, Phoenix Force had turned out to be the best move of his life. The youngest member of the group, T.J. was also its newest recruit. Born in Georgia, he was raised in the Lone Star State and staunchly considered himself as Texan as the Alamo. After graduating high school, Hawkins joined the Army. After successfully completing Basic, he volunteered for Airborne and was later trained by the Rangers and detailed to the 75th Ranger Regiment. Years later, he moved on to Delta Force.

Following the divisive resolution of Operation Restore Hope, where Hawkins and twelve others of his Delta Force unit successfully secured a Somali village from a small-time warlord, he resigned his commission. News of his actions during that assignment had reached the ears of Hal Brognola, and he offered Hawkins a position with the SOG. "Hawk" to his friends, his genius with electronic communications and airborne ops made him a vital member of the SOG team.

The talents and skills each man brought to the table made Phoenix Force a formidable combination. Their successful missions were mute testimony to their dedication. They went into each new situation with one single purpose—to give their best under extreme circumstances and to never back down from any challenge. Putting their lives on the line did nothing to deter Phoenix Force in any instance. They saw that situations often developed because no other agency would step in, and with the anonymity of Stony Man and the ultimate backing of the President, Phoenix Force stepped into the breach and did what they could to redress the balances. Their reward was the satisfaction of a task brought to a successful conclusion with, hopefully, the closure they desired.

Phoenix Force's five were complemented by Able Team, who dealt mainly with domestic threats, though they occasionally took on assignments abroad. Three men from widely divergent backgrounds had blended together to form a resilient and tough team that worked on the same premise as Phoenix Force.

Carl "Ironman" Lyons was a blond ex-cop who led the trio. He was one of the hardest men around, his bull-at-a-gate attitude often resulting in utter carnage. He did not like bad men and treated them all with equal contempt. His credo could be summed up as "kill them all and let God sort them out."

During Mack Bolan's early career, Lyons had been one of the cops assigned to hunt him down, and though their paths had crossed, seemingly on opposite sides, the berserker that was Lyons came to not only understand the Executioner but also to change sides and back him. That backing went as far as Lyons's becoming a member of the SOG and ultimately the head honcho of Able Team.

Lyons was fully competent with any and all kinds of weapons. He kept himself geared up to understand the latest developments and spent many hours at the Stony Man shooting range, familiarizing himself with the latest weaponry under the tutelage of John "Cowboy" Kissinger, the resident armorer. Kissinger had the skills and the expertise to advise on any kind of ordnance and would give his time willingly, because he understood what the combat teams had to face out in the field. Spending time with Kissinger and increasing his skill with weapons was one of the ways Lyons relaxed.

Lyons's partners, also survivors of Bolan's original war, were Hermann "Gadgets" Schwarz and Rosario "Politician" Blancanales. Each had particular skills and each was equally proficient when it came to out-and-out combat. While Blancanales had the gift of persuasion, Schwarz was the man for inventiveness with gadgets of every kind. He loved nothing better than working with electronic components, always searching for adaptations and improvements of existing hardware.

Blancanales and Schwarz also had an insatiable appetite for constantly ribbing their sometimes touchy leader. It had become an integral function of their makeup. It was part devilment and part need to release tension in stressful situations. That aside, they understood Lyons and were able to put up with his often curt responses to their verbal pronouncements. They were both older than Lyons, but they had no problem keeping in step with the former LAPD detective.

Also at the table was Hal Brognola, the Stony Man chief, his Justice Department role giving him cover for his covert running of the SOG, something he achieved with a skill even he often couldn't understand. As far as he was concerned, it was his job and he did it the best way he knew how.

And then there was Barbara Price, the mission controller. Her wide-ranging responsibilities included mission briefings such as this one; she also had the day-to-day logistical matters to handle, and in the opinion of the Stony Man teams there was no one better. The honey-blonde, strikingly attractive former NSA agent, who felt at home in blue jeans, simple shirts and Western boots, had a magic touch when it came to organizing missions, whether she was simply buying air tickets or engaging in more involved dealings with the US Air Force when unnoticed insertions into risky areas were called for. She made sure the teams had what they wanted, where they wanted and when. If it was humanly possible Barbara Price would go that one step beyond to make sure her guys were delivered safely and, if needed, picked up under the same auspices. When they were in the field, she worried about them constantly and was always there at the end of a phone call with much-needed backup. Given the opportunity, she would have armed herself and gone to their aid if they asked.

Across from Price sat Aaron "the Bear" Kurtzman, the ruling hand of the cyber team. Confined to a wheelchair after a bullet severed his spine during an abortive attack on the Stony Man facility years back, Kurtzman was the driving force behind the team that provided logistical information for the Farm's teams. His skills behind a keyboard, allied with those of his cyber people, meant that no digital stone was ever left unturned.

Kurtzman and his team—Akira Tokaido, Huntington Wethers and Carmen Delahunt—openly stole, siphoned and worked magic to obtain their data. Brognola had one rule: do what you have to, just don't get caught, and don't tell me, if you can get away with it—the last always accompanied by a knowing smile. Kurtzman's cyber team did just that and stayed well out of reach of every agency in the country and abroad.

The Computer Room that was Kurtzman's lair was equipped with high-power computers and lightning-fast internet connections. The walls were filled with large plasma monitor screens, and the cyber crew used their wireless appliances to push data back and forth with ease as they probed and dug for the information they needed. They had a direct connection with Zero and could deliver and exchange information with Doug Buchanan whenever needed.

The President's covert group, from the combat teams

to the on-the-job blacksuits and maintenance personnel, worked in obscurity. They asked for and received no recognition or praise. When it came to job satisfaction, Hal Brognola and his clandestine outfit found it in bringing a mission home to success.

Once everyone was settled, Brognola nodded at Kurtzman and the Stony Man cyber chief used a touch pad to power up one of the large plasma screens fixed to the wall.

"No need to ask if you are all familiar with Saul Kaplan," Brognola began as the Zero creator's photo appeared on the wall screen.

"The man behind the Zero Project," Rafael Encizo attested. "Smart guy. Nice guy, as well. You don't often get that combination."

"I am sitting across from you," McCarter quipped, grinning at his own wit.

Brognola interjected, "Kaplan's missing. All the signs point to an abduction. When the Air Force car he was traveling in was found, the driver was dead—shot in the back of the head—and Kaplan was gone."

"Any suspects?" Manning said.

"If I compiled a list we'd be here all day," Brognola said. "Zero, as much as we want to keep it low-key, has created interested parties."

"There haven't been any demands," Price noted. "Nada, from anyone."

"I don't anticipate that happening," Brognola said. "Saul Kaplan is not known outside his working environment except by a select few, so I don't believe he's been taken by someone liable to want to ransom him. This isn't about someone who wants a shedload of cash for the return of Saul Kaplan."

"On the other hand, a foreign power might want him for a particular purpose," Price said.

"Like coercing him to spill what he knows about Zero?" Hawkins asked. "I mean that's his thing. Having knowledge about the setup."

"That's how we see it," Brognola said. "And our chief suspect—coming from Agent Claire Valens—is the same one who was involved last time."

"China," McCarter said. "Well, we all know they were the main perps last time around. They attacked the Zero base and burned it to the ground. Doug Buchanan escaped by a fluke before they found him. And we all know how it went from there."

"You figure they're still in the game?" Blancanales queried.

"They have a degree of knowledge about Zero," Encizo said. "And they still have alliances in the Pacific Rim. As long as the US has presence and influence in that area, there are going to be interested parties who want an advantage over us."

"According to long-term analysis," Brognola said, "the overall consensus points to China and the Pacific Rim nations. Anything that would give them a hold over the US, force us to withdraw, weaken our defenses, is going to be looked at. China, with control of Zero, would dominate the area. Hell, they would be able to threaten half the world."

He slid a printed sheet from his file and placed it on the table. "This is the current text from a US asset in China. Been in place a couple of years. Her name is Jui Kai. She's been able to send back a number of reports on sensitive ops being worked by the Chinese under this guy." An image came up on the wall screen.

"This is Colonel Xia Chan. Chinese military, in charge of a special projects division. And recent data points to him having been appointed as top man in a group looking at Zero."

Kurtzman said, "We're still building identification data. More we get, the more we will release to you. This has all come to us out of the blue."

The image of a woman next appeared on the screen. It showed an attractive and seemingly wise individual and the text next to the image simply added to her qualifications.

"Jui Kai. US covert agent," Kurtzman told them. "Long-term undercover in China. As Hal said, she has been in the country a couple of years using a well-established cover role. She has got herself close to Chan."

"Hope she's as sharp as she looks," McCarter said. "Not an assignment I'd fancy."

"Not you," James said. "Let's face it, David, you just don't have the legs for one of those Chinese slit-sided dresses."

"Don't knock it until you've tried it."

Price held up a hand. "Not something I'd like to imagine."

Carl Lyons flicked the data sheet. "It says here Kai has worked herself onto the flight team providing trips for important Chinese officials."

"It seems she caught the roving eye of our Colonel Chan, who has a thing for young women, and was assigned to his flight roster once she established a relationship with him. Whenever Chan takes a trip, Kai is on his flight. It seems he insists she is assigned. His influence is strong enough to get him what he wants.

Kai's feedback tells us Chan is highly thought of by the Chinese top brass."

"How did she manage to work that position?" Blancanales said.

Price cleared her throat. "I believe that's something we don't need to go into too deeply."

Blancanales glanced across at her. *"Really?"*

"Pol, I'm sure I don't need to go into sharp details. Suffice it to say that Miss Kai really has Colonel Chan's attention."

"She's one brave lady," Hawkins said. "From that picture, our Colonel Chan looks a pretty mean hombre."

"Past history does show Chan has a suspect past with females," Price said.

Brognola continued. "Phoenix Force will take a run out to Zero Command and make contact with Agent Valens. Pick up whatever you can from there. Intel is thin on the ground at the moment, but we have to make a start somewhere. Able Team can take a lead from the background data Aaron and his team have started to pull in from traffic cams in the area following the kidnap. We might get a lead from those according to what comes up. I wish we had more to go on, but for now that's all she wrote. So let's do it, people."

The teams began to disperse, heading out to claim paperwork and travel gear. Stony Man transport would provide them with vehicles, and if any long-distance needs arose Price would, as usual, organize that.

Finally alone, Brognola sat back and considered what might lie ahead. The Zero Project was important. It offered America a degree of protection no other nation had, so he was not surprised that whoever was behind Kaplan's kidnap had taken the step. If Kaplan could be persuaded, in whatever form, to spill what he knew about Zero, then trouble could be just on the horizon.

If the US lost Zero, it would lose a powerful security asset.

One that could not be replaced so easily.

Even the thought caused Brognola to shake his head in frustration.

Now it was down to the Stony Man teams to step up and be counted. If anyone could resolve what had happened, it was his collection of experts. He knew they would not let him down.

CHAPTER FIVE

"Joshua, have you heard from Saul Kaplan?" Claire Valens said.

Joshua Riba sensed the concern in her voice even over the phone. The Apache private investigator knew her well enough to sense a problem.

Riba's initial connection with the Zero Project had come about when Doug Buchanan had survived the attack on the New Mexico facility that housed the fledgling operation. Partway through his treatment to turn him into the human component of Zero, Buchanan had managed to survive the hit. Sick and in pain from the implants in his body, he had been found by Riba's uncle, who had run him down when Buchanan had suddenly stepped into the path of his truck.

Taken back to the Apache settlement, Buchanan had been looked after. Riba had become involved after Buchanan had taken off. His detective skills had brought him into contact with the people looking for Buchanan and Kaplan, and he had tracked the group to Albany, New York, where he had met Mack Bolan. After an explosive confrontation, the two had decided to team up and become fully involved in the Zero conspiracy.

"If you have to ask, then I guess something has happened."

"Saul was taken from the Air Force car on his way to the Zero base. Taken by force, as far as we can figure out."

"When did this happen?"

"Only a few hours ago."

"Any signs he might have been hurt?"

"None we've found yet, but his Air Force driver took a bullet to the back of the head."

"So Saul has been kidnapped."

"Looks that way."

"Nothing beforehand? Threats? Hints something might be going to happen?"

"You know the Zero operation, Joshua, from when you were involved before. It's still being kept low-key. As covert as we can keep it. Which doesn't always work out."

"No suspects, then?"

"Suspicions, but no proof."

"That the official take or just yours?"

Valens smiled. "No fooling you, is there."

"It's my heritage. Anything we can work on? That old man is special. He needs finding."

"That sounds suspiciously like you want to help."

"We were connected last time round, Agent Valens. Kind of makes us blood brothers."

"We did make a good team."

"What about Pinda Lickoyi who lives in Big Sky and sees all?" Riba said in a mock-solemn monotone.

"We checked with Zero. Told Buchanan. He's no wiser than we are at the moment. He's run all the checks he can via the Zero setup. No trace. He'll keep looking and listening."

"Listening?"

"Saul had an implant. A small receiver that gives out

a traceable signal so his whereabouts can be tracked. Designed and built it himself. Had it surgically inserted at the back of his left shoulder. Idea is that it emits a permanent signal."

"But it isn't doing that?"

"No. The signal has gone silent. And so has the tracker fitted to the Air Force car."

"What does that tell you?"

"That maybe we have an inside mole working for the kidnappers—someone capable of disabling the car tracker. That the kidnappers knew about the tracking device on the vehicle and put it out of action."

"So you have something to work on. Also means you have a weakness in your security shield."

"Don't remind me."

"What about the implant device?"

"I don't see that being public knowledge. It was inserted just below the surface of Kaplan's skin soon after Zero was launched. Like I said, it was Saul's own idea."

"Not easy to get at?"

"It would have to be cut out."

"Anything else affect it?"

"If they had the equipment the signal could be interrupted. That suggests whoever took Saul would have had to have known about it. Joshua, as of right now, we are running in the dark here. Reaching out."

"Okay, but if these kidnappers have something they can disable your tracking devices with, then they have to be more than a bunch of perps out looking for ransom. Last time, we came up against renegade government individuals—and a bunch of Chinese trying to get their hands on Zero."

"Don't think that hasn't crossed my mind. All the

files on the previous attempt are being reviewed and individuals looked at."

"The ones still alive, you mean?"

Valens understood the reminder. People had died before the Zero affair had been concluded. She also recalled that some of the Chinese operatives had escaped. But they had run off with a considerable amount of Chinese cash and lost themselves somewhere in America.

She had to go through everything, no matter how vague or how dead-ending it might turn out to be. She had to look into all aspects of the matter.

"Is Cooper involved this time?" Riba said.

"His name hasn't been mentioned so far. Could be he's working on something else. But the people he works with have their teams involved."

"You want me to do some snooping around?"

"Off-the-reservation kind of snooping?" Valens said.

"Sharp as ever, Agent Valens, but just as you say. I'll deal myself in. I'm closer to Saul's lodge than you people are. I do remember where it is, too."

"Joshua, stay in touch. If I can give you any backup I will. Use my name if you need to. Let me know if you find anything. But for now, keep it between us."

Valens sent the data to Riba's cell.

"Okay, got it," Riba said. "Hey, you watch your back, Agent Valens. The way this has gone down, we've got some serious people out there."

"I will, and for the record, it's Claire. Drop the 'Agent Valens,' okay? I think you've earned that."

"Okay. You can call me Josh. I hate the full-on Joshua. Makes me sound old and serious."

"You're a funny guy, Josh."

"Got to redress the Hollywood version of solemn,

hatchet-faced Indians. And don't start me on the 'Native American' deal. Listen, I'll be in touch soon as I have anything."

CHAPTER SIX

Phoenix Force made contact with the Zero base a short time later. The credentials they carried got them inside the Zero Command Center. The isolated base, created solely for the operation of the Zero Project, was purpose-built. It stood in a wooded tract of land in rural Virginia and had a complement of around thirty, which comprised the Zero operating team and a rotating security force of Air Force personnel. A small number of highly vetted civilian personnel also worked on the base.

Even with their official Stony Man–provided IDs, McCarter's team was well aware it was on site under sufferance. That made no difference whatsoever to the Stony Man squad; they had a job to do and territorial marking wasn't about to stop them.

Colonel Rance Corrigan, the base commander, came out to meet them. In his late forties, Corrigan was a bluff, iron-gray-haired man who matched David McCarter in height and general build. His uniform fit him perfectly and was so neat it looked as if he'd had it dry-cleaned overnight while he was still wearing it. The perception the man might just be a poster boy for the Air Force faded quickly for McCarter. He could see behind the outward vision and recognize a true military character; Corrigan would match every word he spoke with dedication to his position in the Air Force of the United States.

"Colonel, we're not the enemy," McCarter said. "Right now finding Saul Kaplan is the only thing that concerns me. Run up the chain of command all you want. When you reach the highest level—and I mean the highest—you can make your feelings known. In the meantime we'll go right ahead and see if we can figure out what happened. It's why we're in your face."

"You're a Brit," Corrigan said, not disrespectfully. It was simply a statement of fact.

"Yes, Colonel. Hope you won't hold that against me."

Corrigan's shoulder went back a fraction. "I've known a few RAF guys." His expression didn't change. "They can hold their own in a fight, and they respect the chain of command. So just explain what a Brit is doing in this outfit."

"I work for the same government you do. Doing what I'm ordered," McCarter said. "Whatever it takes. The same goes for my men."

Corrigan scanned the rest of Phoenix Force. He saw a tight group who looked as if they would take no shit from anyone.

"We need to talk in my office," he said. "I'll have your equipment secured." Corrigan called over a waiting sergeant. "Blaney, see to it."

Corrigan turned and led the way to the main admin building, Phoenix Force falling in behind him. He took them through to his office, past a main area that held desks, computers and half a dozen Air Force personnel. He paused at one of the desks.

"Sergeant Ryker, call Agent Valens and have her

report to my office immediately. And arrange coffee for us all."

"Could you add one Classic Coke to that order, Sergeant, please?" McCarter said.

The colonel's office was sizable, the main window looking out across the base. On an outsize, neatly arranged desk, there was a large-screen computer angled in one corner. A number of office chairs were ranged in front of the desk. It appeared that Colonel Corrigan favored regular meetings with his staff. Considering what went on at the base, McCarter realized it was not surprising; the Zero initiative was, to say the least, unusual, and its existence ranged well beyond what the Air Force would normally handle.

"Sit down, gentlemen," Corrigan said. He took his own high-backed swivel chair and composed himself before he spoke. "I assume you've been brought up to speed on Zero and the current incident?"

"We had a briefing before we shipped out," McCarter said. "I'm hoping you can add to what we know. Which is still coming in as we speak."

Before Corrigan could say any more, there was a knock on the office door. Corrigan told the visitor to enter. The door opened and the Phoenix Force operatives were treated to Agent Claire Valens in the flesh. They had seen photographs of her at Stony Man, but without a doubt, they didn't do her justice.

In the photos, Valens had worn her dark hair long; now she favored a shorter style that accentuated her open, strong-featured face and generous mouth. The eyes that surveyed Phoenix Force were sharp and showed the intelligence that lurked behind them. Her supple, toned figure was clad in a white shirt under the regulation black pantsuit. The jacket was open, exposing the Glock pistol holstered at her waist. The young woman was beautifully efficient. An interesting combination.

A man, Valens's partner, McCarter presumed, followed her through the door.

She nodded to everyone in the office and crossed to take one of the chairs closest to Corrigan's side of the desk. The man chose a seat set back where he could see everyone.

"Agent Valens," McCarter said. "Good to meet you at last."

"And you, Jack Coyle." She smiled.

McCarter made quick introductions of his partners, using their cover names. "This is Roy Landis." He nodded at James and then at Manning, Hawkins and Encizo in turn. "Samuel Allen, Daniel Rankin and Fredo Constantine."

"This is Larry Brandon, my partner." Valens sent a nod toward the back of the room. "It appears you already know who I am," she said.

"You come highly recommended," Manning said. "We've seen the file on your earlier dealings with Zero and Saul Kaplan. Impressive, Agent Valens."

"Not such a glowing file this time around." Valens held up the manila file she was carrying.

"Agent Valens feels this incident is down to her," Corrigan told them.

"Happened on my watch—I won't deny that," Valens said. "Saul is missing and one of Colonel Corrigan's men is dead."

"Has there been anything to warrant higher security recently?" Encizo asked. "Activity to make you suspicious?"

"Nothing. Everything was running normally. Saul was collected from his home and driven to the base each day. Returned home each evening, unless there was a need for him to remain here. He has assigned quarters on the base. Often stayed here due to some involved operation he was running. Saul is constantly upgrading Zero. He is determined to improve the way it functions."

"And this has been running for...?" James queried.

"The current arrangements have been in place for well over two years."

"During that time," McCarter asked, "have there been any security concerns?"

"None. Ever since the initial incident, Zero has been kept low-key," Valens advised. "No one has ever been suspected of planning anything. We try to keep our business and our presence under the radar as much as we can." She cleared her throat. "Obviously not as under the radar as we thought."

"What about Jui Kai?" McCarter said. "The information she has sent through about Colonel Chan?"

Valens hesitated for a few seconds. "You know about her involvement with Chan?"

"We've been brought up to speed about her. Look, Agent Valens, our intel comes from a secure source. Us becoming involved is no good if we're not kept in the loop one hundred percent.

"We know Kai is an asset planted in China. That she has established one hell of a cover. We also understand she's been maneuvered into a close relationship with Chan and his group. Seems they have a vested interest in Zero."

McCarter leaned back in his seat. "Let's get the cards on the table, here. I told Colonel Corrigan we are here to help. Not pointing fingers and labeling people. I can understand your reluctance to pull us all the way in—this mess has caught everyone on the hoof. So let's start from scratch. We each tell what we know and try to get a grip on it."

Corrigan said, "Agent Valens may have been a little slow in telling all, but in her defense I have to say that she has a restrictive brief on certain matters. One of those being able to reveal information about Jui Kai. Understand, gentlemen, Kai is operating *within* China. An extremely difficult assignment and one we have, so far, kept under wraps. It is difficult for her to send us information, and the little we have has simply let us in on the fact that the Chinese have been looking at Zero again."

"The fact that they made the move to kidnap Saul," Valens interjected, "was not expected at this stage. From what we had learned, the Chinese were simply looking at developing their own platform. This sudden advancement even caught Jui Kai off guard. It's a big step, from a committee having weekly meetings, to putting into action an actual body snatch in broad daylight on American soil. Kai is sending us anything she can learn about the incident."

"All right," McCarter said. "Let's go back to the kidnapping. Any thoughts on that from your point of view?"

"This is an Air Force base," Corrigan said. "We have no more than a few civilian attendees, highly skilled personnel from the people who supply our computing equipment. They have been vetted and re-vetted. Approved by Washington. We're also pretty far away from any civilian enclaves." He hesitated. "I hope you're not suggesting any military involvement in Kaplan's disappearance."

"Colonel, sir, with all due respect," Hawkins said, "we have to look at all options. After all, someone did manage to shut down the tracking unit on the car. And Kaplan's implant signal went down, too."

Corrigan didn't like the suggestion, but he was not blinkered so much he couldn't acknowledge the possibility.

"As of now, I can't give you an answer. We are looking into it."

Sergeant Ryker appeared carrying a loaded tray. He placed it on Corrigan's desk before he retreated.

"Help yourselves, people," Corrigan said.

They all helped themselves to coffee; McCarter his chilled bottle of Classic Coke.

The Phoenix Force leader glanced across at Valens. "Where have we got to?"

"Early for much to have happened," she told him honestly. "I've checked with Joshua Riba. He hasn't heard anything but he's volunteered to help. He's closer, so he's going to check out Kaplan's lodge in Wyoming. I don't hold out much hope, but it's worth a look."

"Riba? Agent Valens, who is this Riba? Just how many more friends do you have up your sleeve?" Corrigan raised the mug of coffee he was holding and took a long swallow. "I just said this base was secret. The way things are going, I'm not so certain about that any longer."

"If it hadn't been for Riba's involvement at the beginning," McCarter said, "Doug Buchanan wouldn't be alive today."

"This is all very interesting," Corrigan said. "But how is it going to help us find Kaplan?"

"It might simply prove a blank. We just need to look at all angles, even if only to scratch them off the list," Encizo explained.

"Did you find anything at the abduction site?" McCarter said.

"No," Larry Brandon said. "Apart from a few tire tracks."

"My people are checking those," Valens said. "If we get lucky they might be able to identify them, but I'm not holding my breath."

McCarter drained his Coke and pushed to his feet.

"Do we get a guided tour, Colonel?" he said. "Give us some background on what this is all about. At least a chance to say hello to Major Buchanan?"

Corrigan sighed as he stood. "I suppose you do need to understand the background. And your clearance does cover Zero."

He led them from his office and through the complex to the Zero Command Center.

The center was a generous room full of electronics that none of them could fully understand. Over the banks of equipment the main wall was lined with large-screen monitors.

Corrigan nodded to the technician on duty and the man tapped in the coordinates that alerted Zero of an incoming call. The large plasma screen directly in front of Corrigan came online and he found himself facing Doug Buchanan.

"Colonel," Buchanan said.

The image was a head-to-waist shot of the major. He had his biocouch in a sitting position. Behind him Phoenix Force could see the circular layout of the Zero operations facility: scan monitors and control consoles and an occasional flashing panel. The overall impression was of controlled efficiency.

"Any further intel?" Corrigan said.

Buchanan's head moved in a negative response. "Nothing, sir. We've had probes working since the initial report. We can't find anything."

We.

Not I.

Not me.

We.

The collective term for the partnership between man and machine.

From the day Zero had come online and Buchanan had made his first report from the platform, he had used the epithet "we" when referring to Zero. His assimilation into the system through the bioimplants keeping him alive had worked with far greater success than anyone, Saul Kaplan included, had expected. Doug Buchanan's melding with the implants designed to keep his cancer at bay and offer the major a chance to continue as a viable Air Force member had proved out. With Zero online, the orbiting platform had become a vital part of America's defense system, and Kaplan's cherished dream had become a reality.

"Our scans will continue."

The voice coming through the speakers was Zero's. The modulated tones, with a slight mechanical edge, emanated from the platform's integrated synthesizer system.

Saul Kaplan had developed and installed the system just under six months ago. It was one way to get a manual response from Zero when there was a need for communication and also served as a direct link for Buchanan, enabling him to have verbal interaction with Zero's responses. There had been another, less obvious reason for the interaction—being able to converse with Zero gave Buchanan a companion to talk to. Kaplan had seen that as an important function for Buchanan's solitary existence. He had programmed Zero with a wide range of interactive knowledge that included a number of languages and as much encyclopedic data he could put in. The process was ongoing, allowing Zero to self-improve and to develop a coherent personality. It made for interesting social intercourse for Buchanan and the Zero team.

Kaplan had seen this interaction as a necessary advance on the Zero program. It had needed to happen if the platform was to extend its existence beyond the present. Kaplan was looking to the future. Science did not stand still. It would stagnate if it did, and Saul Kaplan refused to allow that to occur.

"Major, we have visitors with us," Corrigan said. "The team assisting in the investigation."

A second plasma screen showed Phoenix Force and Claire Valens.

"These people are from the same group Cooper is with," Valens said.

"Cooper pulled me out of a hole way back. Hell of a guy."

"You said it," McCarter agreed.

Buchanan said, "I hope you're having more luck than we are at the moment."

"Information is still skinny on the ground," McCarter told him. "We know Kaplan is missing. We have a feeling the Chinese are involved…but that's about all, Major Buchanan."

"It's Doug. Let's drop the rank, huh? Colonel, no offence, sir."

Corrigan managed a faint grimace that might have been labeled a smile.

"My fancy bag of tricks isn't working its magic today," Buchanan said. "I had Saul on track from the time he left home, but his signal cut out at around the time he was snatched."

"You think the kidnappers knew about his implant?" Encizo asked. "Disabled it?"

"A possibility," Buchanan allowed. "It was our main chance to keep him online. Of course there might have been a malfunction. I'm still trying to reengage his signal."

"The implant may come online again," Zero said. *"Unless it has been removed and destroyed."*

"Always looks on the bright side. We're initiating a wider scan," Buchanan said. "Using all our surveillance."

He tapped keys and his biocouch began to traverse the interior on the monorail that circled the equipment banks. An alternate-view screen showed his progression around the facility. View ports set around the platform allowed him to see the exterior behind the curved instrument consoles. Buchanan could make a complete three-sixty run around the cupola, allowing freedom of access to each and every function. There were duplicate control panels around the circular access, so he was never far from a control point. The same applied to the plasma screens he used for communication and exterior viewing. The whole of Zero's working area had been designed by Kaplan to cater to someone who was restricted to the biocouch.

Buchanan never felt restricted. He had come to accept the couch as part of himself now. He was dependent on the couch to keep his bodily function controlled and fed through the implant system, and early, but brief, concerns had been wiped away when Buchanan realized his body was responding to the medical stimulants and banishing the pain and discomfort he had been plagued with as his cancer grew. It could have been said Buchanan's life had been encapsulated within Zero to the degree he was severely denied any kind of normal life. Buchanan saw it from his personal view— Kaplan's creation had freed him from the debilitating illness and had gifted him something newer. Better. A unique perspective on life and a chance to be of service to the Air Force and humanity, which meant a great deal to Doug Buchanan.

"We have a good view from here," Buchanan said. He paused the biocouch and pointed to the image beyond the port. It was a full view of Earth, the blues and greens evident; continents could be clearly distinguished. It was an impressive display. Buchanan held the image for a while. His face on the monitor showed the expression in his eyes: a recall of what life had been when he had stood on his own two legs and had been able to walk the real world.

"Doug, listen to me," Valens said, breaking the moment. She could understand his reluctance to move on. Doug Buchanan could view the scene from his lofty perch, but he would never be able to set foot on home ground ever again. "We won't give up on Saul. My word."

"I know," Buchanan said. His gaze remained on the earthly vista and Valens picked up on his mood. "We'll talk again later," he said quietly, tapping his console and closing the connection.

"He sometimes has a melancholy fallback," Corrigan said. "When he does, we've found it best to let him phase it out. Have to say I can't blame him under the circumstances."

"Must be difficult for him to see a view like that," Manning said.

It was obvious to Valens the man had also seen the look on Buchanan's face. "I know how I'd feel," she said.

"Man, I don't know if I could take it," James admitted. "That's one brave guy."

"Major Buchanan is an exceptional officer," Corrigan said.

"He's more than that," Hawkins said. "Talk about above and beyond…"

Manning asked, "He ever get relieved? I know he can't get up and walk away but…"

"There's a time when he needs treatment through his biocouch," Corrigan said. "We have a link where someone here in Zero Command can assume remote control for the time he needs to stand down. Not the same, because we don't have the integration Buchanan has with Zero. Since Doug was assimilated he's developed an affinity with the platform. With Zero. That's something that can't be manufactured. No one standing in down here can match how he operates."

"What about a second string?" McCarter queried.

"Someone else who could be based on Zero...if something happened to Buchanan."

"That's something Kaplan has been working on over the past months," the colonel said. "He's aware more than most that Major—*Doug*—is mortal. The bioimplants are working at keeping the cancer at bay, but if the worst-case scenario happens there would be a need for a replacement. That is being initiated right now. Still a way off. Finding a match for Doug is proving difficult. Sorry if I sound cold-blooded. It always comes out that way no matter how it's phrased."

"We know what you mean, Colonel," Valens said. "Since Zero came online we've become a close family. There's no other way to put it. Our lives are so intertwined now. There's more than a working relationship that exists."

"A good combination," Corrigan said.

"And part of that is lost now that Kaplan's been kidnapped," Valens said. "We have to get him back. No question about it."

"Saul Kaplan is the life-force behind Zero. He's constantly adding to and fine-tuning things," Corrigan said. "The man never stops. Just when you think he's added all he can, he comes up with a new theory. A fresh attachment. If I come across as sounding selfish, I still have to say we'll be taking a step back if we lose him."

"Then we had better make sure we don't," McCarter said. "It's not going to be easy, but we'll find him."

"Agent Valens." McCarter turned to her. "How about you run us out to take a look at the site?" He had sensed the slight tension in Corrigan's presence and decided it might be easier on them all if they got Valens off base, even if it was only for a little while.

"Any problem, Colonel?" Valens said.

Corrigan shook his head. "If you think it might help."

"We have nothing to lose," James pointed out. "And we need to start somewhere."

"We'll do it this way," McCarter advised. "Constantine and Rankin, you stay here and liaise with Brandon. Go through anything you can see. That okay with you, Agent Valens?"

"Fine. Larry, you can use my office."

"If that's what you want," Brandon said.

Valens smiled. "That's what I want. Okay? Good. Shall we do this, gentlemen?" She led the way to the motor pool.

VALENS WAS DRIVING the black SUV. It was a large-edition model, with enough room to accommodate them all. McCarter was in the passenger seat beside Valens. She glanced at him.

"Nicely handled, getting us out of there," she said. "Thanks for that."

"We appear to be a pain in the arse as far as the colonel is concerned," the Briton said lightly. "I guess he's got enough to be worried about without a bunch of cowboys invading his range."

"I think he sees us as raining on his parade," Manning said.

Valens said, "He's touchy because his command lost Kaplan. Can't expect anything else." She gave a weak smile. "I know how he's feeling."

"Right now soothing his tender bloody brow isn't my concern," McCarter said.

"Well, look at it from his viewpoint," Valens said. "This whole setup is his responsibility. His top man has gone missing. He isn't going to take that lightly. Not Colonel Corrigan."

"I'll lie awake tonight thinking about that," James said dryly.

"What's your gut telling you about all this, Agent Valens?" Manning asked.

"Hey, let go of the 'Agent' angle. It's Claire—or Valens, if you do feel official."

"So what does your gut tell you, Claire?"

"Off the wall? My money is on a feeling I have that the Chinese are involved. Tying it in with the information we received from Jui Kai, it's all starting to fit."

"That's pretty direct," Manning said. "I'm guessing you don't have any concrete proof?"

"General Tung Shan was the man in charge of the original Zero strike. He ran the operation and when it fell apart he was dismissed. From gathered intelligence at the time, it meant he would most likely have been executed and replaced. Failure in the People's Republic is not something to be dealt with lightly."

"I'm seeing something coming here," James said.

"Kai has sent us updated data," Valens said.

"How up-to-date is 'updated'?" McCarter asked.

"Last contact we had was a day ago. Kai has been concentrating on our identified player."

"Colonel Xia Chan," McCarter said.

Valens nodded. "Really been doing your homework."

"We like to keep up," Manning replied.

"Kai has confirmed Chan as the man promoted to engage in the task of bringing a major military prize into Chinese hands. Chan is a rising star. Real go-getter. Zero would be the project to push him up the ladder."

"After all this time?" McCarter said. "I can see where your line of thinking goes—"

"The Chinese went after Zero before because they saw it as a threat, especially in the Pacific Rim," Valens said, cutting him off. "They have allies in that theater. Removing Zero would have maintained the status quo. When we canceled their attempt, China lost face. That would have hurt. They withdrew active interest at the time, but I don't believe for one second they forgot about Zero."

"Put it on the back burner," Manning suggested. "Went into slumber mode."

"Exactly. The old Sleeping Dragon scenario," Valens said. "Something China is very good at. Patience in all things. The long game. Gathering data. Waiting for the next opportunity."

"You make them sound a little paranoid," James said.

"Read up on it," Valens said. "The debate is still going on but there's a consensus that wars could be waged from space in the not-too-distant future. If that's so, the nation with the technology is going to be able to call the shots."

"As with Zero," James said. "It gives us the advantage at the moment."

"Which is why the Chinese may still have an interest. And with Kaplan's sudden disappearance, it starts to make sense."

"Are they thinking if they have Kaplan they can make him work for them?" Manning said.

"They won't have taken him just so he can visit the Peking Opera," McCarter returned.

"They may have Kaplan," James challenged, "but it's a long leap from that to having a platform of their own."

"Maybe the idea is to coerce Kaplan into providing them with the information that might allow them to break into the system and gain control," Manning said.

"No argument from me," Valens said. "It would certainly be a faster way to get what they want. But just the thought of it happening is enough to make me nervous."

"Next question…" McCarter said, moving on. "I can't see the kidnappers staying in this country. They'll want to get him clear of the US. That could be happening right now. If they get Kaplan out of the country, they have a whole world to hide him in. And we have a larger playing field to search."

"The minute we realized he was missing there was a clampdown on exit points. Sea. Air," Valens said. "And I know what you are going to say. There are no guarantees we'll pick them up. If they work at it they'll find a way to get him out of America. Let's not forget private airstrips and failing to declare exactly who is on board and where a particular aircraft might be going."

"Same could be applied to seagoing vessels," James said.

"Let's not give up yet," McCarter said.

Valens gave him a hard stare. "Didn't Cooper tell you I never give up?"

"From the report he put in, he has you down as stubborn. Driven. Totally focused."

Valens couldn't help smiling. "He knows me too well."

"Take them as compliments hard won, love," McCarter said. "Cooper doesn't use words like those loosely. If he said them he meant every word."

"Next time you talk to him, tell him I said thanks."

"Will Agent Kai be able to keep us advised?" James said.

"Her last message said Chan's about to make a trip out of the country. It's been kept low-key until now," Valens said. "But don't worry. Jui Kai is very resourceful and she is very close to Chan. *Very close.* She's been with him on a number of official flights. The man racks up a lot of miles, apparently. She got herself assigned, through his influence, as one of the crew who flies his jet around. She's the in-flight attendant. Chan likes her. Expects her on all his flights. And that gives Kai an in as to where they'll be going."

"So where is the colonel jetting off to next?" Manning said.

"All Kai knows is it's going to be a long flight. No destination yet but as soon as she knows she'll pass it along. We just have to wait until she has an opportunity to call. Sometimes getting even a short text is difficult for her. She has to choose her times. Be careful when she sends."

"Who wants to bet this is a rendezvous with an incoming Saul Kaplan?" McCarter said. "My lucky guess of the day."

"Be nice if we knew where that meeting was going to be," Manning said. "We could be there to say hello."

"Wouldn't it just be nice," McCarter said. "But something tells me it isn't going to be as easy as that."

Calvin James raised his hands. "Tell me the last time it ever was?"

"You want the quiet life?" McCarter said. "If you do, mate, you're in the wrong line of work."

CHAPTER SEVEN

"Do we have anything?" Hal Brognola asked, almost a hint of desperation in his voice. "And I mean *anything*."

"We're running on an empty tank," Kurtzman said. "Hate to admit it, but we don't have squat."

"This is crazy," Brognola muttered. "All this damn equipment and we can't find anything to help."

"If it's not out there, we can't pick it up," Kurtzman said.

"Guys, I think I might have something," said Akira Tokaido, the youngest member of Kurtzman's cyber team. The cyber genius was of Japanese descent. He preferred denim and kept his long black hair in a Samurai topknot. He constantly listened to rock music via earphones. What he lacked in years he made up for by being an instinctive and dedicated operative who always managed to impress.

He tapped his keyboard and sent the data to Kurtzman's monitor.

"What are we looking at?" Brognola asked.

"Needs cleaning up," Tokaido noted, "but I think this may be the car that picked up Saul Kaplan."

"How the hell did you work that out?"

"Traffic cams in the area show the Air Force car passing along this secondary road, then out of sight because there are no more cameras on that stretch."

Tokaido used an on-screen pointer to show the car. "Check the bottom left of the screen. I superimposed the signal from Kaplan's implanted tracker—picked it up from the AF monitoring unit. He was in that car we just saw passing. The tracker stopped functioning a couple minutes later. Add on a couple more minutes, and *this* vehicle appears on the traffic cam. It came from the opposite direction, and it is the only vehicle on that stretch of road for the next twenty minutes. Picked up model and make. Even got the rear plate and the number."

"You think this might be the snatch car?" Brognola said.

Kurtzman had been studying the monitor. He increased the size of the image.

"Looks like two guys in the front, three in the back. Pretty fuzzy, so this is all supposition. But I go with Akira. Time frame fits for pushing Kaplan's car off the road and making a quick switch. If this was a planned snatch, it would be carried out fast. No hesitation. They had their mark and they went for it. Bundled Kaplan into their vehicle and took off."

Kurtzman leaned back in his seat and fixed his gaze on Brognola.

The big Fed checked the images again as Tokaido replayed them. "Have you managed to track the car?"

"Yes," Tokaido said.

He hit his keyboard and showed a montage of the suspect vehicle picked up by various traffic cams. After a few miles it turned onto a wide parking lot adjacent to a truck stop. The truck stop had its own security cameras and the monitor showed the vehicle swing around and vanish from sight behind lined-up rigs and road trailers.

"Great," Brognola snapped.

"Not over yet," Tokaido said.

The view of the truck stop continued for a long few minutes before the suspect car came back into sight. It rolled across the lot and stopped while passing traffic forced it to wait before it swung right and drove away.

Brognola sighed. "So they stopped for a few minutes to use the toilet. Maybe pick up takeout coffee."

Kurtzman chuckled. "He doesn't see it."

"See what?"

Tokaido zoomed in on the image of the car waiting to merge into traffic. This time the image was clearer. Even Brognola was able to see the picture now.

Where there had been five men in the car when it arrived, there were only four when it departed. Only two passengers in the rear instead of three.

"They lost one passenger," Brognola said. "Son of a bitch."

"Question is where did he go?" Kurtzman said. "Could have been transferred to one of those rigs. A waiting van. Another car. Then they played the waiting game."

"How old are those images?" Brognola queried.

"Late yesterday. Few hours after the kidnapping," Kurtzman answered. "Transfer vehicle could have waited until dark before it left. We don't know because we have no idea which one it was."

"When the car stopped I was able to get good images of two of the passengers," Tokaido said. "I'm running facial recognition programs right now."

Brognola couldn't hold back a grin. "You got any other goodies you're holding back?"

Tokaido shook his head. "That's it."

"Good work, Akira," Brognola said. "Damn good work."

Kurtzman caught Tokaido's eye and gave him an approving nod.

"If we get any identification, send Able Team to check the perps out," Brognola told the cyber chief. "If they did take Kaplan, they might be able to point the finger to where he's been taken."

"We'll do our best," Kurtzman said as the big Fed left the room.

Tokaido's perseverance paid off. His patient analysis of the images, which he pushed through FBI and National Facial Recognition databases, gave him what he needed. He got two images, with names, addresses and vehicle ownership. The main perpetrator came up as the registered owner of the suspect vehicle and the data sheet offered his address and known associates. The guy had a police record for violence, various misdemeanors and a predilection for anything that would gain him money.

Once he had the information in a recognizable form, Tokaido sent it to Carl Lyons's cell phone and then left it to the professionals.

CHAPTER EIGHT

"It's the car," Blancanales confirmed. "Plate matches the details Akira sent."

"House fits, too," Schwarz said. "Description we received on the address for the car owner."

Lyons said, "Keep rolling. Take us clear."

Blancanales drove on until they passed a heavy stand of trees and thick bushes. He eased the SUV to a stop and Able Team piled out. They kept their handguns concealed under their jackets in case any civilians saw them and raised the alarm. Not that there seemed to be much in the way of neighbors. The area was less than salubrious.

"Check your com sets," Lyons ordered.

The three Able Team operatives were each equipped with a communication set. The compact units, complete with ear buds, would allow them to maintain contact even when separated. Satisfied they could keep in touch, they took a circuitous route until they were near the house.

"You two take the rear," Lyons directed. "I'll go in by the front door. Let me know when you're in position."

Blancanales gave Schwarz a wide-eyed glance. He knew as well as his partner that their commander was liable to go in once the mood took him. Lyons had that reckless streak that denied him the patience needed to wait around. They slid quickly to the side of the house and moved toward the rear corner, crouching low as they passed windows.

Carl Lyons took a deep breath as he fisted the big revolver. The Colt Python in .357 Magnum was an impressive piece of hardware; it had been Lyons's preferred weapon for some time and he had no intention of changing it. With the Colt Python and his Atchisson shotgun, Lyons would face any opposition. In addition to the Colt being a powerful handgun, Lyons was an excellent shot. It was a combination that presented any enemy with a formidable foe.

The Able Team commander flattened against the stucco wall and watched as his partners slipped out of sight.

BLANCANALES AND SCHWARZ took their time. There was a lot of scattered debris where they were walking. It seemed the people in the house simply dumped their trash rather than having it hauled away. Empty beer cans, bottles and fast-food containers were strewed along the side of the house. It meant the Able Team pair had to walk carefully lest they make too much noise...

AS HE WAITED pressed against the wall, to one side of the front door, Lyons felt his impatience growing. It was part of his makeup that sometimes forced him to act impulsively. He had the skills to back up his eager-beaver ways, but his partners were not always amused when he went ahead without waiting for them. Despite their opinions, they knew that Lyons would never change his ways, so they made the best of it.

Lyons pressed his thumb against the Python's hammer, ready to launch his entrance, when he heard the double click over his com set that informed him Blancanales and Schwarz were in position.

He didn't wait any longer.

Pushing away from the wall, Lyons launched a powerful boot at the door, just below the lock. The mechanism shattered under the kick. The lower panel splintered as the door swung wide, allowing Lyons to see into the entranceway. He stepped inside, eyes scanning ahead of him.

A stocky figure in jeans and a striped shirt came barreling out of a door partway along the passage. His shaved head caught the light from a low-wattage bulb overhead. The guy was wielding a stubby double-barreled shotgun, the barrels cut down to a few inches.

The moment he stepped into view, he jerked the shotgun in Lyons's direction, lips peeling back from yellowed teeth as he started to yell a warning when he saw the big revolver Lyons was carrying.

"Goddamn cops—"

Lyons angled the Python, his arm already extended, and triggered a single .357-caliber slug into the guy's chest. The range was short and the velocity powerful enough to push the slug into and through the chest. It splintered ribs, punctured the guy's heart and emerged through his spine. The guy folded on the spot, his finger going into a spasm that pulled the shotgun's trigger. The barrel expended its load, the blast fanning Lyons's left cheek and gouging a number of shallow cuts.

Lyons sucked in a breath against the burn but didn't miss a step as he walked by the dead guy…

"SOUNDS AS IF the boss man has moved in," Schwarz said as he and Blancanales closed in on the back door.

"I am *so* surprised he went ahead so fast," Blancanales said.

His dry comment brought a smile to his partner's lips.

The rear door crashed open and a figure burst into view. Blancanales and Schwarz both recognized him as one of the men identified as having been in the car from the image Tokaido had captured. He was clutching an autopistol that he showed no inclination to use when he laid eyes on the Able Team pair. His forward motion brought him to them in seconds, and he was unable to pull himself to a halt. That worked in Schwarz's favor as he threw up his right arm in a rigid clothesline sweep. The solid impact caught the guy at the right spot, the force slamming him off his feet and dumping him flat on his back. His handgun slipped from his fingers as he struggled to breathe through his badly bruised throat.

Schwarz holstered his Beretta, kicked the dropped gun aside and fished out a pair of plastic ties. He flipped the gasping thug onto his stomach, wrenched his hands behind him and slipped the plastic loops into place, pulling tight. He repeated the procedure with a second tie around the guy's ankles.

"Pretty slick, partner," Blancanales said. "You've been practicing again."

"I get bored watching TV."

Schwarz shrugged, took out his pistol and followed Blancanales in through the back door, their weapons tracking ahead of them as they stepped into a rough furnished room.

They met a pair of men almost head-on. There was a moment of confused hesitation until the Able Team pair broke the stalemate.

Schwarz saw one of the men go for the autopistol jammed down the front of his jeans. The weapon's front sight snagged on the waistband of the guy's pants. Schwarz had no such holdup and snapped his Beretta 92 into position, triggering a double tap that punched holes in the guy's shirt. He fell back with a soft grunt, hitting the floor with a thump.

As Schwarz fired, Blancanales took on the second man, aware that he had his weapon in hand and was already targeting. Blancanales dropped to a crouch a fraction of a second before the guy opened fire, triggering wildly. The three shots he fired went over Blancanales's head and chunked into the wall behind him.

"You had your shot," Blancanales said, and he returned fire, the 9 mm pistol delivering a pair of slugs that hammered into the target's right shoulder. The impact shattered bone and mashed flesh, the force half turning the guy as he started to go down; one flattened slug blew out a ragged hole as it emerged. The guy screamed long and loud as he slumped to his knees, clutching both hands to his bloody shoulder.

It was over as quickly as that, as most shooting confrontations were—a swift exchange of shots with harsh results.

Schwarz moved forward and kicked weapons away as Blancanales moved to the door.

"Clear," Lyons announced, his voice loud in the silence that followed the gunfire as he appeared in the passage leading to the back room.

"One out front of the house. Dead," he growled. "What have we got here?"

"Two down. One dead, one wounded. Another hog-tied and alive out back," Schwarz said.

Lyons cast an eye over the downed men and lowered his weapon.

"I suppose we'd better call this in," he said. "Get medical help."

Blancanales glanced at Schwarz and grinned. "Aw, he's all heart."

"Shows through like a fuzzy glow," Schwarz said.

"Just make the call," Lyons grumbled. "Where's this live one?"

Blancanales jerked a thumb over his shoulder. "Outside."

Lyons followed him while Schwarz made the call on his sat phone.

The thug Schwarz had tied up lay on the ground, glaring at the Able Team pair. He was still sucking air noisily through his badly bruised throat.

"I ain't telling you assholes squat," he said. His voice was raspy and he had to keep clearing his throat.

"Kind of sets the tone," Blancanales said. "Cooperation is what I like."

Lyons stood close, his Python still in his hand, the large bulk of the weapon making its own statement.

"What happened to my buddies?" the guy panted.

"Two dead. The other one not in good condition healthwise," Lyons said. "How do you want to end up?"

"That sounds as if you're offering me a choice."

"Catches on fast, doesn't he?" Blancanales said.

"You can't just shoot me."

Lyons eased back the Python's hammer so it made a solid sound.

"Right about now, scumbag, I can do just about anything I want."

The man stared at him. The expression on Lyons's face showed he was not fooling around. Carl Lyons had a way of projecting his menacing air without saying a word. His very presence gave him away.

"You can't prove we did anything," the guy said.

"Videos of you in the getaway car with the victim say different," Blancanales said. "And we have your license plate on detail, as well. Plus we tracked you to that truck stop where you handed your captive over."

"When we check the guns these guys have, what do you bet we match one to the murder weapon?" Lyons said.

"To the guy who shot the Air Force driver?" Blancanales asked.

"Yeah."

"And somebody goes down for the rest of his natural."

"Sounds fair. Maybe we should let the Air Force take this guy in," Lyons said. "They'll have a vested interest in him."

"Sounds good to me."

The captive shook his head. "You ain't doing that."

"You think? I can vouch it won't be a smooth ride," Blancanales said.

"Or we could still just shoot this piece of crap here and now," Lyons said. "Save everyone a lot of hassle. Make it a clean sweep."

"Son of a bitch, you can't do that—"

"You don't want to test him on that," Blancanales said.

"I got rights."

"So did that guy you executed."

"It was…" the man started to say then fell silent.

"Part of the contract?" Blancanales suggested. "Kidnap Kaplan and don't leave any witnesses?"

"That was Mackie did the shooting," the guy rasped. "So he's either dead or wounded."

"You're still in the frame," Blancanales said. "You took part. Blame is shared."

"Shit, all I did was drive the car."

"Always one trying to dump responsibility," Schwarz said as he joined his partners.

"What did you do to Kaplan?" Blancanales asked. "Is he hurt?"

"All we did was Taser him. Then he was given a needle to keep him quiet."

"Where did you deliver him?" Lyons said.

"This count as being helpful?" the man choked out. "If I tell you?"

"Maybe," Blancanales said. "We can say you were cooperative."

"Cops are on their way," Schwarz said. "Ambulance, as well."

"Make it fast, before you're taken into custody," Lyons warned. "Clock's ticking on any offers."

"We handed the guy over…"

"We already worked that out," Blancanales said. "Who to?"

"Bunch of guys at the truck stop."

The same information Stony Man had pulled from the cameras and relayed to Able Team.

"You got names?"

The guy shook his head. "No names. But, hey, you sure this will help me?"

Lyons began to raise the Python.

"Okay, okay... All I can really tell you is that they were all Chinese."

CHAPTER NINE

"Hey, you want to take over while I have a break?" Akira Tokaido said, swiveling his chair to face Hunt Wethers.

"It getting too much for you?" Wethers said.

"That's right," Tokaido said. "I don't have the stamina of you *older* guys."

"I heard him say that," Carmen Delahunt said from her station. "I'm surprised you haven't fallen facedown on your keyboard. You're pushing too hard."

"Can't let go of this. Too much riding on it."

"Then go and catch your breath," Delahunt told him. "Take a walk. Get some air."

"Send the files over," Wethers said, still smiling. "Where have you got to?"

"Monitoring chatter from that merc group dealing with the Chinese guy in Hong Kong."

Tokaido sent the open files across and Wethers began a slow read-through.

"Send me a look-in," Delahunt said. "Let's see if we can crack this while our cyber whiz takes a breather."

"If Aaron comes back, tell him I won't be away too long."

"Akira, get out of here," Wethers said.

"I think there might be something on Harry Rosen. Civilian contractor at Zero Command. Something's a little off with his secondary bank accounts. There're a number of big deposits coming in over the past few months. Certainly they weren't from his job. So I ran background checks and traced the deposits to a source in Hong Kong."

"We're on it," Delahunt said. "So go and take a break. Now you're just being a pest."

Tokaido shook his head, knowing he was being gently ribbed, as he made his way out of the room. His eyes were tired from prolonged hours staring at the monitor. Even with his youth and reserves, there came a time when concentration started to lapse and, despite the need to get answers, even the most dedicated person slipped over the edge. Tokaido headed for the surface and the chance to get out into the open air. Allow himself to relax and recharge his batteries. He knew he was leaving his research in the most capable hands around.

HUNTINGTON WETHERS MOTIONED for Aaron Kurtzman's attention.

"We think we may have hit our break," Wethers said. "We've followed through on what Akira had pulled up." He brought an image up on his monitor, scrolling down to show Kurtzman the details.

"Our suspect, Harry Rosen, is a computer tech with accreditation that allows him to work at Zero Command on units supplied by the company he's legitimately employed by. Problem is Rosen is hoarding money he didn't earn through his work. Seems he has a couple of alternate bank accounts he doesn't declare. Akira ran them down and came up with deposits from a source coming off the back of a company called Multi State

Freight and Storage. MSF is owned and controlled by Dan Swoford.

"Now, as far as we can tell, MSF is more or less simply a dummy corporation handling large chucks of cash. The interesting thing is that MSF is listed by a parent company based in Hong Kong. The way they weave all this stuff together is fascinating. All credit to Akira for figuring it out."

"I guess this is all leading to the payoff?" Kurtzman said.

"Talking about payoffs, over a four-month period there have been regular deposits into Rosen's hidden accounts. In total…over half a million dollars."

"I don't suppose he won the lottery or was left the money by a late relative?" Kurtzman said.

"Rosen must be a pretty cool character to work this under the noses of the Air Force," Delahunt said.

"Won't be the first time it's happened," Kurtzman conceded. "Stay the course and bluff it out. If Rosen suddenly started to break his routines, it's a sure way to put himself under suspicion."

"Or attract the attention of Akira Tokaido."

"Something like that," Kurtzman said.

"There's a tie-in between the guys who snatched Kaplan and Swoford. Looks like they've done backdoor deals with him before," Wethers added. "Now we have a way in. The more we dig the more we seem to be uncovering. Swoford. Our kidnap crew. Now Rosen. All tied together with a faint but direct line that goes to the Chinese and this Colonel Chan."

"China using these guys to push their illegal payments for deals they mastermind?" Delahunt suggested.

"We need to tie all this up and see if we can figure

what else these bastards are planning," Kurtzman said. "I'm going to contact Agent Valens. We have to pull Rosen in before he can do any more damage. Stay on this and see if there's anything else brewing."

CHAPTER TEN

Saul Kaplan woke slowly, drifting in and out of awareness. He felt sick, his body sluggish, muscles aching, reactions dulled by whatever had been pumped into his body. He was not a young man, so recovery took its time and was accompanied by the overwhelming sensation of disorientation. Kaplan understood it was going to take a while before his faculties returned to normal, so he made no overt moves. He simply remained where he was, allowing his senses to readjust.

He hated not being in control of himself. It went against his principles and he fought against that whenever it occurred. Just as he had rebelled when his overall control of the Zero Project had been hijacked by the Air Force. He had walked away, but after long consideration had stepped back in and allied himself to the experiment. It had paid off and after the recovery of the project following an attempt to take control by hostile forces, Kaplan had devoted himself to making sure Zero became active and successful. Even now, in his less than cohesive condition, Kaplan was sure that once more Zero was under attack.

He wasn't aware how much time passed, but gradually his senses began to readjust themselves. Sound and sight and smell. He became aware he was slouched on a soft couch, his body slumped against leather. Sound reached his ears: a mix of voices and general noises of movement and activity. He picked up the smell of coffee. When he made a slight move he realized he was not restrained in any way. His hands and feet were not bound, and he accepted that was because there was little he could do to effect an escape. Simply raising an arm required an effort on his part, and at that moment he would not even have been able to stand on his legs, which felt leaden.

A dark figure crossed his line of vision—dark because his eyesight was still weak, blurred. Kaplan blinked furiously in an attempt to clear his vision.

"The sensation will pass, Dr. Kaplan. The blurred vision is one of the effects of the powerful tranquilizer doses you have been given. You may also experience some muscle aches. That will be from the Taser charge we used to initially subdue you."

The voice—calm, almost soothing—sounded as if it came from a distance. Kaplan sensed there was a slight accent, but in his current state he couldn't pin it down.

"I am not a doctor," he said. His voice was hoarse, his mouth dry. "My name is Saul Kaplan, nothing else. No title… I never liked titles…"

"*Mr.* Kaplan, then. As you wish."

"Why am I here? Who are you?"

"Questions that will all be answered in due time. First you need relax and allow your body to recover sufficiently."

The man spoke to someone in the room, and shortly a glass was held to Kaplan's lips. He tasted cold water and drank, his lips still not quite under control so that some of the liquid dribbled from his mouth. He did swallow enough to ease his dry throat.

"Control will return, Mr. Kaplan, given time. I advise you not to struggle. That will only serve to prolong the effects."

"Don't tell me you are concerned about my condition."

"But of course. We require you to be in good health. Otherwise everything we have done would be a waste."

"And we can't have that, can we?"

"I detect an abrasive attitude, Mr. Kaplan."

"Forgive me. I suppose I should be grateful for being kidnapped and held against my will."

"I must admit if I was in your position I would harbor similar thoughts. However, you may as well accept your position. Anger, though expected, is not going to set you free."

"I learned many years ago that anger is a negative endeavor. So I abandoned the emotion."

"But you must experience some kind of feelings at the present time."

Kaplan gave a weary smile. At least he hoped it was a smile because he wasn't yet fully in control of his expressions. "Right now I am thinking about that man you murdered. Not anger, but sadness that because of me a human being had to die."

"Forgive my indifference. It was a necessary act. We could not afford to leave a witness who might provide the Air Force with information about us. And do not put the blame on yourself. There was no way you could have prevented it."

The effort of speaking had wearied Kaplan. He felt darkness closing in and had no strength to fight it.

"Allow yourself to sleep. It will help. Later, when you are feeling more yourself, we will talk. Oh, be aware you are not alone. You are being watched, so any attempt to remove yourself from this room would be futile. My dear Mr. Kaplan, accept that you are my prisoner and you will remain so for the foreseeable future."

Kaplan understood his position. There was nothing he could do at the present time, so he allowed sleep to take him again and drifted off.

HE CAME OUT of it much later—hours later, he was told—and despite some remaining lethargy he did feel distinctly better. The room he was in, which turned out to be a well-appointed lounge that was comfortably furnished, was now lamp-lit and contained Kaplan and two men.

One sat some distance away from him, an automatic pistol resting in his lap.

The other man, who Kaplan guessed was the one who had spoken to him earlier, stood watching him as he roused from his sleep.

Both men were Chinese, and for some reason Kaplan was not surprised. Now he understood the mystery of the man's accent.

"I trust you feel better," the man said. "The effects should be well on their way to dissipating by now."

The man was medium height, solid without being overweight. He wore a neat gray suit and a dark shirt with a crimson tie. The shoes he wore were black leather and highly polished. His black hair, brushed straight back, was collar-length and well cut. He had a well-defined, near-handsome face, and he was smiling at Kaplan.

He doesn't look like a murdering kidnapper, Kaplan

thought. He corrected himself because he had no idea what such a man should look like.

"My name is Nan Cheng. I do have a title, but will dispense with it during our relationship, so we are equal in that respect, Mr. Kaplan."

Kaplan cleared his dry throat. "Let's dispense with the formality. It serves little purpose. I'll call you Cheng and you can simply call me Kaplan."

"As you wish." Cheng's tone was still polite but Kaplan sensed there was another side to the man he did not want to visit.

Kaplan examined the lounge. At least they weren't keeping him in some dirty back room. He began to sense that despite being Cheng's captive he was not in any immediate danger of being harmed.

When he strained his ears he picked up subdued sounds coming from beyond the room. When his mind sorted the sounds he realized it was passing traffic. Voices. A faint and tinny sound of music.

A street?

Was he hearing street noises? Was this place in the city? A town?

Not that any of those things were going to be of help to him.

"So, Kaplan," his captor said, "I would hazard a guess you would welcome a refreshing drink. Coffee? Tea? Something stronger?"

"Coffee. Black. Strong."

Cheng gestured at the man in the chair. "Bolo, coffee for our guest. I will have my usual tea."

The man stood immediately and left the room. He left the door open.

"Bolo has extremely good hearing. He is also very fast."

"You don't miss a trick."

"You are an extreme valuable person," Cheng said. "I cannot allow anything to happen to you."

"Okay, Cheng, enough of the cozy chitchat. Isn't it time you told me what it is you want with me? Though I can most probably guess."

Nan Cheng took a seat in the deep, leather armchair facing Kaplan. He patted the soft leather arms.

"Very comfortable," he said. "So, *why* have I kidnapped you, Kaplan?"

"Zero. The American orbiting platform piloted by Major Douglas Buchanan. Facts you are obviously aware of. The Chinese government would like to gain control for its own ends. Control it, or destroy it. I created Zero. I have knowledge of how it functions and you, as a representative of the People's Republic, want that knowledge."

"Very astute, Kaplan."

"A simple enough deduction. China tried once before, if you recall," Kaplan said. "It failed then, so what makes you believe you can succeed this time?"

"As you said, Kaplan, this time we have you. The creator of Zero. The one man who has all the knowledge about it. The earlier attempt by General Tung Shan was mounted clumsily. He tried too hard, believing he could outwit your people by force and violence. He and his group were beaten and the general paid for his errors with his life."

"A lesson to be learned," Kaplan noted.

Cheng raised his hands. "True. And we have learned," he said. "This time we will bring the creator of Zero to a safe place where we will have the security and the time to *persuade* you to give us what we want."

"Are you so desperate to learn Zero's secrets? Is it so much of a potential threat?"

"Let us say there is new thinking within China," Cheng said. "You must understand, Kaplan, that my country cannot allow itself to fall behind in areas of technology. Times change and so does policy. We are both intelligent men and we are aware of the ongoing struggle for dominance. America desires to remain the most powerful nation in the world. Which is why Zero exists.

"There is more to its makeup than a powerful eye on the world for sophisticated mapping and weather forecasting. Zero is, in reality, a formidable weapons platform. We know it carries missiles. From the position Zero offers your Air Force, the United States could launch devastating attacks on any target it chooses. Am I correct?"

Kaplan made no comment.

"At least you don't deny the facts. We can play all the games you like. At the end of the day, you have something we want—why be coy about it?" Cheng pointed a finger at Kaplan. "Zero's secrets are inside your head. We need the means to unlock them."

"Good luck with that," Kaplan said. "You believe one man can store all the information about something as complicated as Zero? It doesn't work like that, Cheng."

"You are not the mild peasant you pretend to be. In your head you carry the encryption codes that ultimately control Zero. Plus much more. They are what we need and, Kaplan, my friend, you are going to give them to us. As well as much of the design for the platform."

"No. I won't. Coercion will not make me talk."

"Time will tell, Kaplan. Keep this in mind. We are prepared for what you would term 'the long haul.' We are not worried about a few weeks. Even a few months. We have great patience and you will find we are extremely persistent people. So we may be in each other's company for a long time, Saul Kaplan."

Bolo beckoned Cheng. They stood together, speaking quietly, until Bolo left the room and Cheng returned to his seat in front of Kaplan.

"Bolo tells me our transport will be here shortly. Then it will be time to leave. We have a long journey ahead of us, so prepare yourself for that."

Bolo reappeared, pushing a wheeled trolley that held the tea and coffee Cheng had asked for. He placed the trolley so Cheng could reach it, and returned to his seat across the room, taking with him a mug of something hot.

Cheng poured for them both and passed a cup to Kaplan. When they were served, Cheng sat back, delicately sipping his tea and watching Kaplan closely.

"Despite our political differences, I am truly in awe of what you have done, Kaplan. The Zero Platform is a wonderful creation. And the assimilation of Major Buchanan into the machine? Truly ahead of its time."

"Perhaps if you had asked nicely we might have given you the information, rather than you trying to steal it."

Cheng laughed. It was a pleasant sound of genuine amusement.

"Somehow I do not think so. America wishes to keep Zero as its own. And I can understand that. The platform is unique. America will not want to share it."

"So China must take it?" Kaplan chided.

"We cannot allow your country to dominate space. To put it bluntly, Kaplan, we must have *our* Zero, albeit by proxy, and I make no excuses for that."

Kaplan emptied his cup and leaned forward to refill it.

"You understand people will be looking for me."

"That doesn't exactly surprise me. We have embarrassed them by taking you. The Air Force will search high and low. And the police. It is to be expected. They will not find you. Be aware that the tracking device fitted to your car was disabled before it left the base."

"You have someone working for you there?"

"Of course. You do not think we did all this by good fortune? We had help—paid help. Our way to success."

"You sound confident."

"Soon we will be gone from this place and out of the country."

"To where?"

"Good try. Let me say our destination will not be where you might expect."

"A mystery tour?"

"In a manner of speaking, Kaplan."

Saul Kaplan studied Cheng's expressionless face— bland, calm, giving nothing away. The word *inscrutable* came into Kaplan's thoughts. The man was not going to give anything away. Kaplan decided there would not be any profit in pushing his line of questioning. Cheng would tell him when he was ready and not before. He drank his coffee and relaxed as much as he was able.

With their conversation lapsing, Cheng made his excuses and rose from his chair. He spoke briefly to Bolo before he left the room.

Left alone to consider the situation, Kaplan allowed a train of thought to grow. He was thinking about the small tracking unit implanted in his shoulder. It was something Kaplan had devised and had implanted early in the Zero development as a safeguard for himself. Not generally broadcast outside the upper chain of command, he was confident no one except a small group knew about it. Tested on a regular basis, the unit had always worked as expected. If it was transmitting its signal, it should have been registering back at the base. If that was the case, the AF should have been able to pinpoint his position by now.

So where were they?

Why hadn't there been a rescue attempt?

Kaplan reached over his shoulder, fingers probing the slight bump in his flesh that told him the implant was still in place. So why hadn't the Zero Command picked up the signal?

Was he already too far away?

He knew the unit had an extremely powerful range. He had built the thing himself and knew its capabilities.

So why had it not worked?

Had it malfunctioned? Been damaged in some way?

Kaplan didn't have answers for his own questions.

That worried him. He liked to be in control of his own destiny. Right now that seemed to be way off.

All right, Saul, work this out piece by piece if you can. They waylaid your car, shot Steven and… He recalled a paralyzing sensation as something was thrust against his body…a searing jolt that threw him into spasms, left him sprawling across the rear seat, barely aware of rough hands dragging him from the car… A sharp jab as something was thrust into his neck and then a hazy sensation before he lapsed into unconsciousness… Nothing, then, until he woke here, with the man called Nan Cheng…

Kaplan's thoughts went back to the something that had incapacitated him in the car. The jolt that had stunned him—and it came to him in that moment. The shock. Damn it, an electric shock. A Taser. They had hit him with a Taser. The electric surge had engulfed his body. Stunned him…with enough voltage to have knocked out the signal from his implant. That had to have been what happened. Cutting through the signal and leaving him without his tracking device. The realization dismayed Kaplan. His link to Zero Command was wiped out.

The only question—would the signal come back, or was he even more isolated than he had imagined? He had no way of knowing whether the interruption was permanent, the cell damaged irreparably. Could it reset itself and start sending out the pulse again?

That was all Kaplan knew. Everything else was out of his hands. Until—or if—the situation changed, he was going to have to deal with whatever came his way. It was not what he would have chosen. Choice didn't come into it at the moment.

He was in the hands of the Chinese, and what they wanted did not promise him a comfortable future.

He found himself wondering where they would take him. The way Cheng had spoken suggested somewhere other than China. At least, that was what Kaplan had surmised. He could be mistaken. Kaplan admitted he was still not fully recovered from the drugs that had been administered, so perhaps he had heard incorrectly.

Kaplan decided there was no use taxing his brain. He would no doubt find out soon enough. It wasn't the destination that concerned him as much as what might be waiting for him at the other end. As Cheng had said, the Chinese wanted Zero. Its secrets. He began to realize they would go to any lengths to gain that information, and as determined as he was not to give his secrets away, he knew he might not succeed. He would resist for as long as he could, but if they employed extreme methods to strip away his resistance, there was no guarantee he would not give in.

He comforted himself with the knowledge that he would be missed by now. That would have galvanized Zero Command to start looking for him. And they would not give up. If there were any clues as to his disappearance, they would be followed.

Kaplan thought about Claire Valens. The young woman possessed a stubborn nature, which would not allow her to rest as long as he was missing. If the chance existed, she would find him one way or another.

CHAPTER ELEVEN

The news McCarter had received earlier had come from Stony Man: the feedback from Able Team had pointed to a Chinese connection. As he relayed the basic information to Claire Valens, he saw the flash of vindication in her eyes.

"If you think it will make you feel better, love, go ahead and say I told you so," McCarter said.

Claire Valens only smiled briefly at the Briton. Being proved right in this instance gave her no sense of victory. She felt only dissatisfaction. Disappointment that the security protocols in place had not prevented Kaplan's kidnapping. She was the one charged with keeping things safe at the base and watching out for Saul Kaplan's safety. She had let him down, let herself down. Things had been going so well at Zero Command and now everything had blown up in their faces—*her* face, to be correct.

"Damn," she said. "We got complacent. Too sure of ourselves. It was all going smoothly…"

"Hey, Claire, kicking yourself isn't going to do any good," McCarter said. "Only way out of this is to find Kaplan and bring him home. We're here to help. Not point the finger. Things go wrong. It's the way of the world."

"And so there we have the motto for the day," James

said. "'Things go wrong. It's the way of the world.' Just hearing it makes me all warm inside."

Despite her mood, Valens couldn't hold back a smile.

McCarter took out his sat phone and connected with Stony Man again.

Brognola answered the call. He listened while McCarter told him what they needed.

"We're already on it," the big Fed said. "Bear has the team checking out every Chinese connection they can think of. Maybe we'll get lucky and someone will come up with a name or a location."

"If we assume the Chinese do have Kaplan, they're going to want him out of the US," McCarter said. "Somewhere they can work on him in peace and quiet. Last thing they'll want is to keep him where they could encourage interference."

"That could mean taking him directly to China—or some other isolated place. If that happens," the big Fed grumbled, "our chances of getting to him are thinner than I'd like to guess at."

"Maybe they figured on that," McCarter said.

"Meaning?"

"Meaning they may take him somewhere other than China. The information from Jui Kai suggests our Colonel Chan is making a trip *out* of the country."

"Thanks for coming up with that suggestion," Brognola said. "I'll check with Bear to see how they're getting on and get back to you if there's anything to tell."

BROGNOLA PUT THE phone down. He leaned back in his chair and found himself staring up at the ceiling. It was out of frustration more than anything. Gazing at the ceiling tiles didn't change a thing.

"Well, hell, that isn't going to tell me the secrets of the universe," he muttered.

A gentle cough caught his attention. Barbara Price was standing in the open doorway to his Farm office, a bemused smile on her lips.

"Don't ask," he said.

"I was on my way to the Annex. You want to join me?"

"Going there myself." Brognola pushed to his feet. "Right now I feel like taking a long drive into the countryside and just playing hooky."

As they headed down the corridor Price noted, "But you won't."

"You know me too well, Miss Price."

They took the electric rail car that whisked them to the below-ground facility that housed, among other things, the Farm's blacksuits' communication center and the War Room. And, of course, the Computer Room where Kurtzman and his computer geniuses worked their cyber magic.

"What are your thoughts about the Zero problem?" Price asked.

Brognola glanced at her. "Right now, not happy ones."

The low, almost inaudible hum of the electronic equipment inside the Computer Room enveloped the pair as they stepped inside.

Each member of Kurtzman's team was busy at their workstation. Each station was complemented with a full state-of-the-art computer setup and an ultra-high-speed internet connection—all linked to a central hub that facilitated information-sharing.

Price looked at a number of the large wall monitors displaying real-time assessments of global hotspots thanks to the Farm's exclusive-use satellite. Another dedicated monitor scrolled data from a national TV news channel. She knew the cyber team was keeping 24/7 tabs on world events, searching for anything that might trigger a lead for any of the incidents the Farm's teams were pursuing.

Huntington Wethers, a distinguished black man who resembled a college professor rather than a member of the Stony Man cyber team, glanced up at Brognola and Price. A former UCLA cybernetics professor, Wethers had been recruited by Aaron Kurtzman for his expertise in computer science.

"We might have that link you've been looking for," he told the big Fed.

"The words I love to hear," Brognola said.

Wethers's fingers moved across his keyboard and one of the wall monitors was immediately filled with images.

"Colonel Xia Chan," Wethers said. "Best picture we have of him. Caught when he was attending military exercises in Hunan province about four months ago. Info says Chan has been building a tight little group around himself. Some special project he's involved with."

Wethers brought up other images, detailing each man as he appeared.

"There's a face only a mother could love," Price said.

"Yang Zhou," Wethers announced. "Security head for Chan. He's a hard man according to our asset. One of his assignments has been trying to run down the two

Chinese who defected at the end of the original Zero affair. If you recall, they ran off with a large amount of Chinese money."

"Probably way off the grid by now," Brognola conceded.

"Information is that Zhou hasn't had much luck finding these men," Wethers continued. "Coming up to date, we also have this." He brought up a recent image of another Chinese individual. "Kam Ho. Resides here in the US. All legitimate as far as documentation goes. He's into real estate. Has his own company. According to bank statements, he's well-off. Now, his background is a little vague, but he's been checked out by security agencies and they can't fault him. Not sure where the money originally came from to set him up. It just shows up. He has a great deal."

"Real estate must be paying off," Price said.

"Not that well."

"So why is he of interest?" Brognola asked.

"Because he was tagged talking to this man." Wethers brought another image on-screen. "About two months ago Kam Ho was spotted in conversation with Nan Cheng, who happens to be one of Xia Chan's subordinates. Ho met Nan Cheng at an open house gathering for a new housing project outside Washington. It appears our friend Ho was one of a number of Realtors invited to the gathering—him being a well-known businessman."

"A clever way to meet someone, under the pretext of discussing house selling," Brognola said.

"Maybe Colonel Chan wants a vacation home by the sea," Price said facetiously.

"Or maybe they were discussing somewhere they

could keep an unexpected houseguest under wraps."
Brognola shrugged. "Just a thought."

"Can you get into Ho's property list?" Price asked.
"To see if there's—"

"Already running that down," Carmen Delahunt
called out from her station. "We're checking all sales
and rentals after the date Ho and Cheng had their little
bonding session."

The vivacious redhead, former FBI, was the third
member of Kurtzman's team. Smart as she was attractive, Delahunt was an intuitive and dedicated individual,
her previous life as an agent leaving her with skills she
had enhanced under Kurtzman's tutelage. She had insight that often surprised her cyber companions.

"What does your intuition tell you?" Brognola said.

"I'll put my money on a lease," Delahunt admitted.
"Short-term. Once the operation is over, Ho can clear
the house and put it back on the market. Make sure
there're no indicators left behind. On the surface it all
looks aboveboard."

"We all agreed on that?" Kurtzman said, returning
from topping up his acid-scarring brew of thick, black
coffee. He rolled his wheelchair up to his station, swinging it around to face the room. "For now," he said, "we
concentrate on tracking down property Ho has handled.
Split between the four of us, it shouldn't take long."

"Makes sense," Brognola said, turning to leave the
room. "Keep me in the loop. I need to talk to the teams."

"Man's concerned," Kurtzman noted after Brognola
had left.

"He probably feels frustrated," Price said.

"Join the club," Kurtzman conceded. "If we have the
Chinese involved in Kaplan's abduction, which is look-

ing more likely by the minute, it's a given the whole thing concerns Zero."

"I'd hoped they had backed out after the last time," Delahunt said.

"The Chinese have long memories," Wethers argued. "And they are long on going for what they want. Zero caught their attention big-time. It's been on the cards that they might deal themselves in for a second try."

"Using Saul Kaplan as their way in," Delahunt said.

"Okay, people," Kurtzman said, "let's keep looking. There has to be something in cyber space that we can use."

CHAPTER TWELVE

While Bolo held Kaplan in a powerful grip, Cheng administered more drugs. They didn't take effect immediately, so Kaplan was able to watch with interest when Cheng came back into the room about thirty minutes later and stood beside Bolo, quietly speaking with the man. Bolo nodded, stood and crossed over to where Kaplan sat.

"Up," he said, gesturing with his large hands.

Kaplan noticed the calloused edges of his palms, suggestive of someone trained in one of the martial arts. The buildup was the result of many hours of repetitious practice strikes against resistant surfaces. Kaplan didn't have in-depth knowledge of the how and why, but it was enough seeing those hands to advise him not to antagonize the man.

When he responded slowly, Bolo took hold of Kaplan's arm and ushered him through the house and out a rear door to where a large SUV stood in a cluttered yard. It had tinted windows. Bolo placed a hand on Kaplan's shoulder and directed him to the vehicle, opening one of the rear doors and pushing Kaplan inside.

The big Chinese followed Kaplan in, slamming the door as they settled on the seat. There was already a driver behind the wheel. Cheng himself climbed in beside the driver and gave him instructions in Chinese.

The SUV moved smoothly away from the house, along a narrow alley that ended where the vehicle turned left and cruised along a busy street. The image through the tinted glass was restricted, but Kaplan was able to make out what were plainly Chinese stores; he could see colored signs, waving banners and even hear the ever-present shrill of music. He recalled the sounds he had heard earlier.

Chinatown?

But where?

There was no telling how far he had been moved while he'd been unconscious, or to where. Another mystery to add to the confusion crowding his thoughts.

Kaplan was also left wondering about where he was being taken now. He supposed that question would be answered in time.

They had only been driving a short while when the administered drugs began to fully take effect. Kaplan would have slipped off the rear seat if Bolo had not pushed him upright. The interior of the vehicle began to blur. Kaplan felt nauseous and then became aware of the leaden feel to his limbs. His vision wavered as the drugs hit him full-on, and he slipped away into a drifting world, his senses closing down once again…

CHAPTER THIRTEEN

Able Team arrived back at Stony Man just as Erika Dukas was about to deliver the transcribed data to the War Room via sat link. In her late twenties, Dukas had a natural affinity with languages and was currently fully skilled in more than seven, including Cantonese and Mandarin. She was also learning Russian and Greek. It was an ability inherited from her father, a language professor, and the support of her mother, Helena, had encouraged her. Dukas had been with the NSA when Price had first recommended her to Hal Brognola. The Farm had since relied on her linguistic abilities on a number of occasions.

Able Team joined the others around the table. Brognola and Price were there, as well as Kurtzman. Price had activated the video–conference call link so that Phoenix Force could also participate from Valens's office at Zero Command.

Brognola opened the session. "Agent Valens is sitting in with our team," he said for everyone's benefit. "She has past experience with Zero, as most of you know, and is heading the base security team."

"At the moment I'm eating humble pie," Valens said. "An extremely large one. Saul Kaplan was under my watch and I make no excuses over what happened."

"I think this caught all of us on the back foot,"

Brognola said. "What we need to do is to get a handle on it and move forward.

"Now that we're all together, in a manner of speaking, we'll recap the gathered intel so everyone has the same. If you've heard some of this already, bear with us and take it in again."

He addressed Dukas. "Go ahead, Erika."

"The data we downloaded from the two cells was in Cantonese. It was not in any kind of code. I've extracted a page of cell phone numbers and these are being checked out as we speak. There were also a few names to go with the numbers and here we struck a couple of lucky breaks. I'm sure these should not have been on the phones but they're to our advantage.

"Our earlier identification of Chan tells us he has a reputation as a powerful man and is held in high regard by Beijing. From what we've been able to extract from our probes, he's the successor to General Tung, the guy who led the original attempt to hijack Zero. Zhou is security, reputedly a nasty piece of work. Hard as they come and not someone you would enjoy being in a locked room with.

"We have a few more names being checked out through sources," Dukas continued. "Oddly enough the name of Kam Ho, our Realtor, cropped up a few times on text messages."

"Any locations for us to work on?" Valens said.

"Okay," Kurtzman interjected. "We have some leads coming up. And not least of all is where Kaplan was being held…"

"Hold on a minute," McCarter said over the conference line. "Did I hear you say *was* being held?"

"Yes. We believe he's been moved."

"From where—to where?"

The big screen on the War Room wall flashed up a satellite image. Kurtzman used a laser pointer to indicate positions, which were also visible to McCarter and the others via their video link.

"This has come via Zero," he said. "Doug Buchanan managed to pick up a faint trace from Kaplan's embedded tracker—not the best signal and it had been offline for some time. Akira came up with a possible reason for that. When Kaplan was snatched, it is possible that a strong electrical charge from something like a Taser was used to subdue him. The charge could have interfered with the tracking device, which is why we couldn't pick up the signal after the abduction. Buchanan monitored the source and kept trying to reestablish contact. He finally did get an intermittent signal and was able to follow Kaplan's movements until the tracker went out of range."

"We know Kaplan designed and built the tracking device himself, so it's considered top of the line," Brognola said. "Even so, it has a pre-determined range. As soon as it goes over the limit the signal is lost."

"So we're not much better off," Manning muttered.

"That's not strictly true," Kurtzman said. "Before the signal faded Buchanan followed it to here." He paused the pointer on a location. "This is a private airfield located outside the city. Buchanan lost the signal but Zero was able to lock on an aircraft that took off within minutes of Kaplan's signal showing up. It faded just after that."

"They took him on a plane?" Hawkins said.

McCarter studied the image. "Was Buchanan able to track it?"

"Once Zero hits a target there's no wriggle room. It can follow it anywhere," Kurtzman said.

"And where did it follow this plane to?" Encizo asked.

"Across the Atlantic." Kurtzman's pointer moved again. "It landed here. In Switzerland."

"Then we've got him," James said.

McCarter looked across at Price. She gave him her best I'm-way-ahead-of-you smile.

"Colonel Chan left China a while ago. He flew in a Gulfstream jet and our asset has confirmed his destination," Price advised the group. "It appears Chan is going to Switzerland."

"And not for the skiing, I'm sure," Valens said via the link.

"The last contact we had with Jui Kai indicates Chan has his security man, Yang Zhou, with him. He has a reputation for being well capable of using violent methods of persuasion on anyone he gets his hands on."

"Physically harming Kaplan wouldn't be in Chan's best interests," Blancanales noted. "They need him to be able to function if they want to extract information."

Over the conference link, James said, "Data forced out of someone isn't always to be trusted. If Kaplan gave false information, it wouldn't give Chan what he needs to take control of Zero."

"Which is where this man's name cropped up," Kurtzman said. "Dr. Luc Melier. He resides in France. Home is in Paris. Guy had a Chinese father, French mother. He's known—we pulled this from other agency files. This guy is suspected of having worked with the Chinese before, but it's never been absolutely proven. And he's been used by other agencies in the past. Admittedly the man seems to have a charmed existence. He remains untouched. I won't go into why, because it could prove embarrassing in certain known quarters."

"You're saying he might have worked for agencies close to home?" James asked.

"I think we all understand what it means," Brognola said. "This guy hawks his expertise around, and these days he'll always find a client. From what we know he has no problems working his business."

"What we do know for certain," Kurtzman said, "is that he is a skilled chemical interrogator. His persuasion techniques come from a needle."

Kurtzman flashed another image up on the wall screen. "Melier," he said. The man's head-and-shoulder shot had obviously been taken from a long distance: a surveillance photo on a street. "Taken in Paris, near Meiler's apartment building. He lives in the city when he's not on one of his assignments. Likes his lifestyle."

Melier was a lean-faced man with his hair brushed well back from his forehead. He looked relaxed. Comfortable. One hand could be seen in the photo, with a cigarette held between long, slender fingers.

"Here's one for the files. We ran a trace on Melier's credit cards. Checked his movements recently and picked up information he took a flight to Switzerland," Kurtzman said. "Guy is on the move."

"Why am I not surprised at that?" McCarter said. "Do we assume the good doctor is making a house call?"

"It all seems to be coming together," Brognola said. "Chan on his way to Switzerland. Now our errant medical man is going to the same location. Got to mean something."

"If we have all this correct," McCarter noted, "it isn't going to be a vacation for Kaplan when Melier gets his grubby paws on him."

"Nearer to home…we found this." Kurtzman carried on. "Two weeks ago our Realtor rented out a location in Washington. It's an apartment in Chinatown. Our check into the background shows Kam Ho rented it through Star holdings, which we know is a cover for the Chinese."

"Worth having a look at," Lyons said. "Could be a stopgap to hold Kaplan before moving him on."

"If that's so," Brognola said, "it might not leave us with much time."

"We need to move now," Lyons said. "Time to saddle up and go."

"Coordinates are downloading," Kurtzman said.

"Send them to our guy in the sky," Brognola directed. "Zero might be able to take a peek at the place while Phoenix is on the way. Agent Valens, you liaise with Able on this."

"A set of wheels will be at the rear exit in ten minutes," Price told Lyons as he led his team out of the room. "Valens will meet you near the location. Good luck, guys."

CHAPTER FOURTEEN

Fully equipped, Able Team piled into the waiting SUV, Blancanales taking the wheel. He was rolling around the main building as Lyons tapped in the coordinates from his phone and watched the route come to life on the vehicle's GPS.

"Should take us about an hour," Blancanales said. He punched up the speed as the SUV rolled past the main gate and onto the road.

Ten minutes later Lyons's phone rang. It was Price.

"Open your laptop," she directed.

Schwarz took the equipment out of his backpack and powered it up, tapping in the connection to Stony Man. He followed Price's instructions and a projected view from Zero filled the screen.

"We're focusing in on the location now," Buchanan said over the link. "This is in real time."

"Close view coming on in five seconds," Zero added.

The view over the city zoomed in on a specific building in the Chinatown area. The image, through Zero's powerful cameras, was sharp and detailed. The shot moved in to hover over the location.

"That's your building," Buchanan said. "From the data we were given, you should be looking at ground floor—the three windows we're focusing on."

The display changed to three-dimensional, the an-

gled frontage giving Schwarz an unobstructed view of
the suspect apartment.

"Hey, can you show us inside the room?" Schwarz
said.

"Nice try," Buchanan said. "We haven't perfected
that yet."

Zero said, *"Not as yet. Give us time."*

Schwarz grinned. "I believe you."

"Let's hope our targets are still at home," Lyons
grumbled.

By the time Able Team reached the location, Valens and
Brandon were parked along the street some way down
from the address, waiting patiently. Blancanales spotted an empty space and pulled in. Able Team climbed
out and walked back to join them. Lyons was easily
able to recognize Valens from the file photo shown to
them at Stony Man.

Lyons introduced his team, using their cover names.

"Your picture does not do you credit," Blancanales
said smoothly.

"I like you, Agent Comer," Valens said.

"It's working already," Schwarz said. "Mr. Charm
is out of his box."

Lyons sighed but said nothing.

"What about me?" Brandon quipped lightly.

"You'll be fine when you grow up," Blancanales said.

"Enough," Lyons said. "I can feel my stomach starting to churn."

From where they stood, they could look back along
the street and examine the building frontage.

"Pretty innocuous place," Valens said. "They could

come and go pretty easily here. Busy area, lots going on. Who's going to take any notice?"

Schwarz said, "More than likely took Kaplan inside through a back entrance."

"Then just waited until they got their orders to move him."

"Okay," Lyons said. "Let's go see if all this guessing pans out."

"How do you want to do this?" Valens asked.

"You pair go round the rear," Lyons said to Blancanales and Schwarz. "I'll take the front with Valens and Brandon."

Blancanales and Schwarz immediately moved along the sidewalk to the end of the building and vanished from sight.

"Shouldn't I have a cover name, as well?" Valens said.

Lyons stared at her and then realized she was joking.

"Good looking *and* funny," he muttered. "You'll fit in with the others just fine."

They made their way across the street and Lyons led the way inside the building.

"Ever get the feeling you're in the right place, but not necessarily at the right time?" Lyons said.

Valens drew her Glock. "Explain that to me later."

Lyons had his Python in his fist as they neared the door. He paused and leaned forward as he picked up sound from the other side of the apartment door. Someone moving around the interior. Voices were added to the mix; Lyons could hear Chinese and English being spoken.

"Go in low and fast. You break left. I'll move right. Brandon, you watch our backs."

"You got it," Brandon said.

Valens simply nodded, positioning herself for a fast entry.

Lyons felt his sat phone vibrate three times. It was the ready signal from his partners.

"It's that time again," he said.

Lyons reached for the door handle, turned it gently. He felt the latch slip free—indicating the door was not locked. Beside him Valens took a steady, deep breath. The Able Team leader pushed the door open and followed its inward swing.

The large, open-plan room showed basic furniture and decor. On the wall opposite Lyons were two doors and an archway that led into a kitchen-dining area.

A pair of Chinese, dressed in work clothes, were busy cleaning the main room with dusters and spray polish. Lyons wasn't interested in them. His attention was grabbed by four men around the table in the dining area. Three were Chinese, one Caucasian. The added attraction was in the weapons the four had on the table: autopistols and SMGs.

As Lyons and Valens swung left and right, the men at the table, alerted by their sudden appearance, went for the weapons.

One, faster than his partners, snatched up an SMG and brought it into play, jerking back the trigger. A spray of 9 mm slugs went over Lyons's head and plowed into the wall behind him.

Lyons stayed low as he lined up his Python, but Valens was faster. Still moving, she snapped up the Glock and triggered a triple burst that took off the Chinese guy's jaw and spun him around, leaving a mist of blood in his wake. It was accurate, well-placed shooting that found its target and put the man down.

Lyons gripped his Python in both hands and faced down the second man. He was no slouch with his own pistol, and his first shot slammed into the guy's chest, followed by a second shot that ripped into his throat and sent him back across the table, the pistol he had snatched up flying from his loose fingers.

At the far end of the kitchen area the door leading to the outside crashed open and Schwarz and Blancanales came through, weapons up and firing. The room crackled with gunfire, shots flying and finding their marks. The Able Team duo were sound shots, way ahead of their opponents. The would-be shooters tumbled, bodies taking multiple shots. Discarded weapons fell to the floor, followed by their owners.

The pair of cleaners stood in a silent pose, staring at the bodies.

"You speak English?" Valens said.

She stood facing the pair.

"I do," one said.

Valens showed her shield.

"You understand that?" she asked. The Chinese nodded. "Then go and sit over there on that couch and do not move." The severity of her tone worked and the cleaners went over to the big couch and sat. Valens stood in front of them. "Are you armed?"

The English speaker shook his head. "Only have cloth and wax spray."

"Remain still. Do anything stupid and you might be shot."

"Cleaning crew," Brandon said as he stepped up beside his partner. "Making sure their visitor didn't leave any fingerprints behind."

"Covering themselves," Valens said. "They don't miss a trick."

"It's nice to be tidy," Blancanales said as he went from body to body, checking for vitals. But the four would-be shooters were all dead.

Schwarz joined him and they checked each man for ID and cell phones.

Lyons turned to Valens. "That was a fast move," he said. "I owe you one."

Valens shrugged. "They train us well."

"He never thanks us when we save his ass," Schwarz said.

"That's true," Blancanales said.

"Couple of phones," Valens sighed when the two had finished their search. "No IDs and not much else. These guys travel light."

Schwarz examined the phones. "Couple in Chinese."

"We need to send the content home," Lyons said. "Dukas will run the downloads and translate. If there's anything of use, she'll let us know." Lyons gave Schwarz the nod to contact the Farm.

Schwarz had a detailed conversation with Kurtzman, explaining what they'd found and what they needed. In a matter of minutes he was able to transmit the data from the dead men's phones to the cyber team at Stony Man.

As each cell was drained of its information, Lyons found himself once again impressed by the skill of Kurtzman's cyber team. He saw the results they achieved, took the help they offered. It made no difference how many times he was privy to their technical skill—Lyons understood very little of the way they did it. He could operate a computer on a basic level, yet some of the things Kurtzman's people achieved were beyond him.

Before they left, Lyons took pictures of the dead men and sent them through to the Farm.

CHAPTER FIFTEEN

"Okay, we have it all," Kurtzman said. "Looks like it's mostly in Chinese, with a few pages of what appear to be phone numbers in English. I'll send it to Erika. She'll translate and get back to us. Heads up as soon as we have anything."

He transferred the files over a secure connection. One of the high-tech printers was already sliding out printed sheets. By the time the downloads had been collated, there were more than twenty-five pages covered in Chinese characters. Among them were what looked like telephone numbers in English characters.

The pictures Lyons had sent along were being run through databases for facial recognition. Results came through quicker than expected.

The Caucasian from the apartment turned out to be Eddie Kessell. He had priors. Known associates were flagged and two were from Able Team's earlier shootout at the house of the kidnappers. The main piece of information tied the men to a Jake Moretti, an ex-military man who had turned his hand to setting up a private security unit. His clients were a step away from being upright citizens and the least surprising connection was to Nan Cheng.

"It might be useful if we sent the details about Moretti's crew through to Valens's Detective Zeigler,"

Brognola said when Kurtzman told him. "I'm sure the police should be able to pull it all together. Let them handle the evidence."

ABLE TEAM RETURNED to Stony Man and joined the others around the table in the War Room. Brognola and Price were there, as well as Kurtzman. Price had activated the link so that Phoenix Force could listen in and comment. Phoenix Force was seated in Valens's office, where she and Brandon had just made their way back.

Brognola was just wrapping up the call, saying, "That's another reason to get you people on a plane and across to Switzerland. Barb will set you up as soon as we finish speaking."

"We can leave here right away," McCarter said.

As soon as the call was ended, Brognola turned to Able Team.

"Aaron has updates for you. So don't get too comfortable. You'll be heading out shortly."

Blancanales leaned back in his chair. "Ain't life grand?"

"The various phones, downloaded images and data have let us do some matching up," Kurtzman said.

He passed his hand over the touch pad on the conference table and set up the sequence.

"From Chan down, we have Nan Cheng, aide to the colonel. Connected to Chan is Yang Zhou. This guy is a hard case. He has form as a strong-arm enforcer. Chan has previous history with Dr. Luc Melier." Kurtzman couldn't repress a smile. "It's amazing what comes to the surface when you start raking the bottom of the pile. Have to thank various agencies for their assistance, albeit unknown. CIA, NSA, even the FBI. French and

British secret services. It's like some days I could just sit at home and let them hand me what I need.

"Internet trawling and bank accounts give up a lot of data. Who pays who. Cell phone records. We lucked out here and got a slew of calls from Jake Moretti. He runs the outfit the hired guns Able tangled with come from. I think we can safely say Moretti is the US side of Chan's business. Hired to supply guys and guns to do the Chinese group's down-and-dirty business. He made contact with Chan just after Able took down his guys. Only got a tail end but it looks like you spoiled his contract with Chan. He had to man up and admit he'd screwed the pooch to his paymaster. We didn't tap into anything Chan said, but I don't imagine he'd be all that happy."

"Give them the last call," Brognola said.

"This was from Moretti. Way it sounds, he was talking an upcoming mission these guys were supposed to be involved in. Hunt picked up a trace on the call and found it came from a location upstate. An old farm site that's stood empty for a few years. When we dug a little deeper, guess who the Realtor was?"

"Kam Ho?" Blancanales ventured.

"None other. Chan's Realtor buddy rented it out a few weeks ago. Before that, there hadn't been a query for months." Kurtzman swiped the documentation on screen. "All looks sound. Only, when you follow the trail back it doesn't go anywhere."

"Dummy deal?"

"All signed and sealed to keep everyone happy, but I'd be surprised if the new tenants have a cow to milk or a chicken to lay eggs."

"What the hell does Chan want with a derelict farm?" Schwarz said.

"Stands on its own on an open tract of land," Blancanales observed. "Lets people do what they want without being overlooked."

"While they plan something," Lyons said.

"Plan what?" Brognola said.

"That's for them to know and us to find out," Lyons said.

"Jack is waiting outside to fly you to the location," Brognola said. "Wheels up in thirty."

"Let's go talk to Cowboy," Lyons said, referring to John Kissinger, the Farm's weaponsmith. "And load up for Bear."

"I hate it when he talks all gung-ho," Blancanales said as they left the War Room and headed for the Farm's armory.

"Pol, he always talks like that. That guy must have gung-ho dreams. Or nightmares," Schwarz added with a smirk.

Blancanales slapped his partner on the shoulder. "Nightmares for anyone else. Just dreams for Carl."

It wasn't long before Kissinger had the team fully outfitted.

Lyons carried his Colt Python .357 Magnum and a razor-sharp lock knife in a leather sheath on his belt. For Blancanales and Schwarz, it was a 9 mm Beretta 92FS model. The autopistol came with 15-round mags. They each had a sheathed Cold Steel Tanto knife clamped to their belt.

As they prepped to leave, they finalized their gear inspection. They were all clad in blacksuits and each man had a thin harness over the ballistic armor he wore.

The harness carried extra magazines for their weapons. The duffels they carried held larger weapons.

Lyons had his Atchisson Assault shotgun—the AA-12. The combat weapon handled a combination of 12-gauge shells, delivering them from either an 8-load magazine or a 20/32-round drum. Gas operated with little recoil, it was a powerful piece of hardware that was easy to operate yet delivered a deadly rate of fire. A single pull of the trigger fired one shot, while holding back turned it into a full-auto burner.

Blancanales and Schwarz went for the more conventional 9 mm SMGs. This time around they were both equipped with Uzis. A veteran of many wars and agency uses, the Israeli subgun was still a reliable and accurate weapon in the right hands.

CHAPTER SIXTEEN

When Able Team walked out of the Annex, they saw Jack Grimaldi waiting in the pilot seat of *Dragon Slayer*, Stony Man's helicopter. He waited as they loaded their gear and settled in, taking off with a minimum of sound.

The powerful mat-black aircraft, equipped with an array of sophisticated equipment and fearsome ordnance, had been designed and built for the Farm with a great deal of input from Grimaldi himself.

State-of-the-art barely covered *Dragon Slayer*'s capabilities, one of which was an effective silent-mode system that reduced engine noise to a whisper. A feature that allowed Grimaldi to get his teams in close, often before anyone was the wiser.

By the time Able Team had double-checked their weapons, the ace pilot had put down less than a quarter mile from where they needed to be.

With the chopper on the ground, Grimaldi shut down. He flicked a switch that rendered the cockpit and side windows to a blackout condition. They could see out, but no one would be distracted by movement inside the helicopter.

"You sure you don't want me to come along to hold your hands?" Grimaldi teased.

"Gee, Dad, there has to be a first time we do this on our own," Blancanales said.

"Check your com sets?" Grimaldi said, grinning.

Each Able Team member wore a lightweight communications setup that allowed them contact with each other and Grimaldi. They went through quick checks.

"If you get the call," Lyons said, "you come in fast. And you can shoot everyone who isn't me, Pol or Gadgets."

"I hope I can remember those instructions," Grimaldi said. "Bit technical for a mere chopper jockey. Now get out of here."

The side hatch opened with a soft hiss of hydraulics. Able Team slipped out and moved off, the hatch closing behind them. They moved through trees and grass as they approached their objective.

The day was cool, the air heavy with the scent of fir and brush, the light casting a brightness so startlingly clear it was not difficult to see their way. On the higher ground the air was clear and fresh, a contrast to the less pure stuff they breathed down in the city.

Able Team trekked to the target area, using the plentiful timber for cover.

"I could get to like this country life," Blancanales said into his throat mike.

"Too quiet for me," Schwarz said.

"Nowhere could ever be quiet with you two around," Lyons growled.

"Remarks like that can hurt," Schwarz said.

Lyons raised a clenched fist and they all stopped, crouching.

"Two o'clock," Lyons warned. "By that single tree."

"I see him," Blancanales said.

The guy was armed with a subgun.

"For sure he isn't out hunting varmints with that thing," Schwarz said.

Lyons passed his Atchisson to Blancanales and slid his lock knife from its sheath. There was no need for him to issue orders or to explain what he was about to do.

While Schwarz kept his eyes on the lounging sentry, Blancanales followed Lyons as the Able Team leader made a circuitous route to where the man stood. Likely supposed to be watching the surrounding area, the guy had his back to them and was facing the low silhouette of the farmhouse.

Big as he was, Lyons moved smooth and silent, staying low until he was directly behind the sentry, who was totally unaware of his presence.

Blancanales saw the Able Team commander rise. One of his big hands reached around to grasp the guy's hair and yank his head back, tautening the flesh of his throat to offer the open lock knife a clear area to cut.

Lyons's right hand brought the ultra-sharp blade across the guy's throat, cutting deep to sever flesh and sinew, slicing from left to right. Blancanales couldn't see from his position but knew a rush of blood would burst from the deep gash and spill down the sentry's front in a warm flood.

Lyons kept his hold on the guy's hair as he jerked, his body shuddering in a resistant response to what was happening. His body weakened quickly and Lyons allowed him to sink to his knees and then fall face-forward on ground already spattered with his blood.

Lyons turned and snapped his hand to bring Schwarz and Blancanales to him quickly.

"Let's hope the rest of these guys are as slack as

this one," Lyons said as Blancanales handed him his shotgun.

"We're catching them at the right time," Blancanales said. "Early morning. Low response time."

"Unless they're all non-sleepers," Schwarz said.

"Let's do this," Lyons grumbled.

They came in close and paused to survey the area with a red-painted old barn between them and the house. They were able to see a couple of SUVs parked up near the front of the house. As the trio paused to take stock, the relatively peaceful scene was suddenly changed as the chatter of an SMG broke the silence. Slugs hit the wall of the barn they were passing, tearing ragged holes in the weathered timber.

"That's an extreme welcome," Blancanales said. "Somebody is nervous."

"Maybe it's the guns *we're* holding," Schwarz quipped.

"Could be."

"Luckily he's a guy who *can* only hit a barn door," Schwarz said.

"Not the damn door I'm bothered about," Blancanales muttered.

Lyons had spotted the shooter's position. "South corner of the house."

"I see him," Blancanales said.

"And another one," Schwarz said as a figure broke cover and ran for the protection of a rusting John Deere tractor. "That house could be full of them," he added.

The man behind the tractor opened up, sending a long burst that ripped more wood from the barn wall. Wood chips dusted the air.

"Sooner or later," Blancanales said, "they are going to get too close."

"Only if we let them," Lyons said. He checked the shotgun. "Give me some cover."

Knowing better than to even question what he was about to do, Schwarz and Blancanales raised their SMGs and laid down hard fire on the two shooters. The second they opened fire, Lyons moved out from cover and ran in the direction of the tractor; when it was needed, Carl Lyons could move fast, and that was what he did now. As he closed in on the covered shooter, the guy angled his weapon around but was blocked by the metal frame of the machine.

It was what Lyons had been hoping for. With seconds to go, he took a rolling dive, hitting on his left shoulder and letting his forward momentum take him in close to the front of the tractor. He pushed the Atchisson in front, raising the muzzle, as the shooter leaned forward and triggered a burst.

Slugs hacked at the metal surrounding Lyons and slammed into the ground, kicking up dirt. He felt something tug at his sleeve, and that was as close as Lyons wanted it to be. His finger squeezed the shotgun's trigger and the Atchisson boomed. The concentrated burst caught the shooter in the torso, enough of the shot getting through to open him up. The guy stepped back, the front of his jacket shredded and starting to glisten with blood. He gave a startled yell as the pain registered.

Lyons had pushed to his feet by this time, stepping around the tractor and coming face-to-face with the shooter, who still had the ability to lift his weapon. There was no hesitation in Lyons's actions as he triggered his shotgun again. Up close, the concentrated blast took the guy's face off, leaving a shattered and bloody mask behind.

Seeing his partner go down made the shooter behind the house corner hesitate for a few seconds. Schwarz and Blancanales took the moment to push forward, splitting up as they powered in the direction of the house. By the time the shooter realized what was happening, the Able Team partners had gained the advantage and opened up, firing at the shooter's position. Their combined autofire chewed at the timber frame, splitting the corner post and peppering the shooter with 9 mm slugs and a hail of shredded wood. The guy twisted away from cover, body riddled and torn, and walked into a burst from Blancanales's subgun. He dropped to the ground, body shivering in a final spasm.

"Cover the rear," Lyons said as he appeared, waving a hand at Schwarz.

Schwarz nodded and ran along the side wall toward the rear of the house.

With Blancanales at his heels, Lyons hit the front porch steps, booting the front door open and moving aside so Blancanales could rake the interior hall with a burst. As the salvo ended, Lyons went in through the door, his SMG tracking ahead.

SCHWARZ REACHED THE house's rear corner. He picked up the approaching thud of boots from inside the back door. The Able Team member saw the rear door crash open and an armed figure burst out onto the porch. The guy spotted Schwarz as he emerged and brought his SMG up from waist level, face contorting in a twist of anger. Schwarz dropped to a low profile as he centered his already raised weapon. He fired a second later, the stream of 9 mm slugs hitting the guy above his waist. The man slipped sideways, hitting the door frame as he crumpled to his knees, letting go of his weapon as he clutched his middle.

A burst of autofire from behind the guy sent slugs over Schwarz's head. He made out the shadowy form of a second shooter moving forward. As the guy, unable to halt his forward progress, stepped into the light, Schwarz fired again, angling his trajectory over the head of the man on his knees. The burst slammed into the target's throat and face, tearing at flesh and bone alike. The wounded shooter fell back over the exit, and Schwarz had to step across his body as he moved into the kitchen.

It was as if he had warped back into the previous century; the kitchen comprised ancient wood fittings and a heavy wood-burning stove. The family-size table and wooden chairs that sat in the center of the larger room was cluttered with the remains of half-eaten meals and empty beer cans. There was an abused Kenmore cooking stove and a Philco refrigerator with a scratched door. For a moment Schwarz felt as if he had stepped onto the set of *The Waltons*.

His fragment of retro imagery was shattered when he heard gunfire from the front of the house. He crossed the kitchen, passed through a doorway and emerged into a large family room.

He heard a window shatter. Harsh voices were raised in anger.

Schwarz caught a glimpse of moving figures heading his way along the passage to one side of the room. A sudden crash of sound that could only have come from Lyons's Atchisson led to the solid thump of a body falling.

Schwarz picked up a wild shout—someone aware of

his precarious position but still defiant. The crackle of autofire cut the cry short.

Ahead of him he saw a door slam shut as someone took cover...

LYONS AND BLANCANALES met resistance as they moved farther into the house.

Armed resistance, as a trio of shooters pushed through an open doorway, each trying to be the first to face their attackers. It was not a smart move because it left them uncoordinated, struggling to bring their weapons on target while attempting to find a clear spot to stand.

Lyons felt like shaking his head at the clumsy tangle of bodies as the three tried to pull themselves clear. His survival instinct took over and he swept up his shotgun and fired. The main impact of the shot caught one guy side-on and opened him up in a burst of ravaged flesh. If he had not had his arm raised, the blast would have severed his arm. As it was, he suffered heavy trauma, his torn flesh exposing the splintered remains of his ribs. His body jerked under the force of the charge.

Almost in the same second Blancanales triggered his Uzi, laying down a volley at the other extreme. The scything burst ripped into the guy's chest and through. He suffered damage to heart and lungs, his spine clipped by passing slugs. His legs gave way and he fell back, his finger freezing on the trigger.

The surviving shooter, blood-spattered and still hyped up by the moment, shrugged his stricken buddies aside, his own subgun seeking a target. It was obvious he still harbored thoughts of taking down Lyons and Blancanales.

It turned out to be a bad idea and one the guy would never get to rectify.

In the microsecond it took for him to make his choice, Carl Lyons moved the muzzle of the Atchisson and pulled the trigger. The angle was close enough for maximum effect and literally took the would-be shooter's head off his shoulders, leaving in its wake a blood-spurting, ripped stump. The headless body remained standing for a few seconds before gravity and a lack of brain commands made it fall...

THE THUD OF boots from the upper floor reached Able Team.

"I'll take it," Blancanales said and broke away to head for the uncarpeted flight of stairs.

He was halfway up the stairs when a pair of armed guys tumbled into view, racking their weapons as they appeared. Blancanales dropped to one knee, tilting up the muzzle of his Uzi, and burned off a long stream of 9 mm slugs, sweeping the weapon between the two men. Blancanales was a sure shot and his blast ripped into the pair with fatal results. The two men dropped onto the landing, weapons spilling from their fingers.

Pushing forward again, Blancanales headed to the landing and swept his weapon back and forth, covering both sides as he stepped clear of the stairs. He picked up the beat of running feet seconds before a squat, shaved-headed guy burst into view from the left passage leading off the landing. The guy was naked to the waist and clutching a subgun he was trying to jam a magazine into as he came into view.

For all his bulk, the guy was fast on his feet and he closed the distance before Blancanales could realign his

SMG. The guy let out a wild yell, swinging his subgun at Blancanales, causing the Able Team warrior to step back. The barrel of the subgun slammed against Blancanales's left arm, above the elbow. The impact was enough to draw a gasp of pain from Blancanales. He felt the arm go partially numb and felt blood soaking into his sleeve where the blow had gashed his flesh.

Then the bulk of the guy slammed into him, pushing Blancanales across the landing. As the pair struggled to regain balance, the guy swung his subgun again, this time aiming for the Stony Man operative's head. Blancanales ducked under the blow and used the moment to hammer a clenched fist into the guy's stomach. The punch hurt and the squat attacker gasped, sucking up the pain as he dropped the subgun. He launched a sideways kick that slammed into Blancanales's thigh. He then followed up with a second kick that missed its target when Blancanales twisted away from the blow, countering with a snap kick of his own that held enough force to crunch the guy's left knee.

The sound of the kneecap shattering was audible to Blancanales, so he repeated the move, the force of the second blow buckling the knee, sending the guy down on his good knee. Continuing his physical attack, Blancanales hit the guy again. This time it was a brutal palm-edge that connected with the target's nose. It collapsed with a soft sound, blood suddenly gushing down the guy's face and naked chest. The excruciating pain briefly incapacitated the guy, allowing Blancanales enough leeway to strike again—a second blow to the throat that destroyed everything in its path.

With his nose crushed and his throat suddenly con-

stricted, the guy toppled to the floor, slowly choking
from a lack of air and the blood leaking into his lungs.

As Blancanales stepped back, sucking breath into
his lungs, he put his back to the wall so he could view
both passages off the landing in case there were further attacks.

Movement from inside the room at the end of the
landing attracted Blancanales. He heard low voices. His
angle of approach allowed him to see inside the room.

Two figures.

Both Chinese.

One of them reached for the pistol tucked under his
jacket…and then opened his mouth to shout a warning.

Blancanales fired, the crackle of his subgun drown-
ing any cry the guy might have made. The short but
deadly burst ripped into his body, coring through flesh
and tearing at vulnerable organs. The guy staggered
back, fell.

The second guy turned and took short steps that
gave him the chance to gain enough momentum to hit
the window closest to him. The weak wood frame disintegrated, glass shattered, and the guy disappeared
from sight.

Blancanales crossed to the window, scanned the exterior and saw the guy sliding off the slanting porch
roof. The dark-suited figure vanished from sight, then
reappeared, running clear of the house.

Blancanales keyed his com set.

"One guy out the side window. On foot but moving
fast. South side."

LYONS DIDN'T HESITATE. He laid the shotgun down and
pulled out his Python. He took long strides, heading

for the rear door, and moved out into the open. As he cleared the porch, head swiveling in the direction of the fleeing figure, a pistol cracked sharply, a slug slamming against the wood surround, blowing a chunk of timber clear.

Lyons ducked as splinters peppered his cheek, dropping to his left knee as he snapped up the Colt. He picked up on the shooter—a stocky figure half turned in his direction, a raised autopistol in one hand. Flame winked from the muzzle as the guy fired again, this time a double tap that sent the slugs closer than Lyons wanted.

As soon as the man fired, he twisted around and powered into a run away from the house. Lyons gripped the Python in both hands, steadying his aim, and squeezed off a single shot. He saw the runner's left shoulder jerk as the heavy slug hit. Despite the shock of the wound, the guy kept moving. Lyons took off after him, angry that his shot had not put the man down.

As Lyons moved, he caught sight of one of the upper windows gaping open. It must have been where the shooter had exited the house after waiting for his chance to get away. Scattered pieces of the window frame and broken glass littered the ground.

"Not going to happen," Lyons grumbled to himself.

If the running shooter thought he could shake off Lyons, he was in for a surprise. Carl Lyons was as fit as most men who went in for extreme sports, and better than most at long-distance running. He pounded along the side of the house, pacing himself as his body responded to the effort. Lyons's muscles stretched and flexed, his breathing quickly settling into a rhythm.

The guy cleared the corner of the building and cut

off across the open ground. Lyons realized he was heading for the ragged line of trees set back from the remote farmhouse. If the guy got in among the timber, it would be much harder to keep track of him.

"No way," Lyons growled.

He kept moving, his line of travel keeping him directly behind the guy. And Lyons was closing the distance. He called on power reserves and increased his pace. Lyons could see the spreading bloodstain marking the guy's shoulder; he was losing blood heavily and his arm hung loose at his side.

Twenty feet from the tree line the guy stopped running. He turned to face Lyons and, for the first time, the Able Team commander saw the guy was Chinese. His face was shiny with sweat and his front was soaked with blood. He said something Lyons couldn't understand. His right hand raised the auto pistol—and it was no gesture of surrender.

Lyons extended his arm, steady as he lined up the Colt and squeezed back on the trigger. The big revolver threw out a lance of flame, the barrel held firm in Lyons's powerful grip.

The .357 Magnum slug cored in through the target's chest, plowed its way past bone and tore open the beating heart in a millisecond. The Chinese stepped back, legs losing their stability. He dropped without a sound, his weapon flying from his nerveless fingers. As Lyons closed in, the guy gave a last ragged breath, a line of blood oozing from his open mouth. He gave a final spasm and then lay still.

Lyons stood over him, put away his Colt and crouched beside the guy. He had spotted a thick bulge under the man's jacket on the right side. Lyons pulled the jacket open. There was a bulky object pushed into the pocket. He jerked it free and turned it over in his hands. A thick manila envelope.

Lyons opened it and found a cell phone, a couple of data sticks and a folded number of printed sheets. They were all in Chinese. At the bottom of the envelope was a thick wad of American currency—high-denomination bills. Lyons searched the body and pulled a slim wallet from a back pocket. Satisfied there was nothing else to find, Lyons used his phone to take a shot of the man's face for the cyber team to scan.

SOMETHING MADE SCHWARZ turn to face the room across from him. He wasn't sure what had attracted him. Maybe a sixth sense. Even a faint sound that had been picked up by his finely tuned senses. It was enough to draw him to the door. Closer, he picked up a fragment of movement behind the panel.

Only one way to find out, he said to himself.

The moment he launched his kick at the door, feeling it vibrate and swing wide, Schwarz stepped to one side so that the burst of autofire from inside the room found no target and simply slammed into the opposite wall of the passage.

The moment the burst died away, Schwarz made his own move, swinging around and launching himself through the open door in a headlong dive and shoulder roll. The impetus took his feet inside the room, and even as he came to his knees he was scoping for the shooter.

The shooter was off to one side, crouching and bringing his SMG to line up on the man who had burst into the room. He was a lifetime too slow, because as he came partially upright, Schwarz acquired his target and let go with a solid stream of 9 mm Parabellum slugs that ripped into the guy, stitching him through the middle and kicking him back a number of feet. As Schwarz saw the guy going down, his peripheral vision picked up on a second shooter moving out from the shadows on the far side of the room.

The guy fired first and Schwarz felt the burn of slugs as they hit his left side. Before he gave in to the pain, Schwarz swept his SMG around and triggered a long burst that tracked across empty space before it found its target. Schwarz saw the guy fall back, a look of astonishment on his face as the tearing impact of Schwarz's slugs took effect. The burst had ripped in through soft flesh, mangling inner organs; the guy began to hemorrhage inside and felt the rising burn of pain as his body reacted. He was on the floor then, bleeding heavily and losing interest in everything around him as his body began to shut down.

Schwarz scanned the room, saw no one else and muttered a prayer of thanks. The pain from his wounds was kicking in hot and angry.

He heard Lyons's voice over his com asking if they were clear.

Blancanales acknowledged he was okay.

Schwarz said, "Room's clear in here, but I took a hit. Send for a pretty blond nurse and some bandages."

He moved to the wall and let himself slide down it, feeling an odd, comforting warmth spread across his body. He kept his subgun in his hands despite feeling somewhat helpless.

In the distance he heard the thump of feet running and voices shouting. He recognized Blancanales, but soon after felt the world close in around him. The light from the fixture hanging from the ceiling began to shrink, becoming smaller and smaller with each second, until even that went away and it all vanished.

Sight and sound.

Just the warmth left that wrapped around him…

BLANCANALES HAD RACED down the stairs and reached the room first. First he saw the two dead men, then Schwarz sprawled, unmoving, against the wall.

He took out his sat phone and connected with Grimaldi.

"Bring *Dragon Slayer* in fast. Gadgets is down. We need to get him medical assistance ASAP."

"Firing the lady up now," Grimaldi said, unflappable as always. "I'll be there in minutes. I've got some medical aid on board. Call home and get them to liaise with the closest hospital. Have them give us the coordinates and we'll fly Gadgets direct."

The moment he ended the call Blancanales dialed in for Stony Man. Barbara Price came on the line. Blancanales wasted no time on introductions. He simply told her what had happened.

"I'm checking your location and the closest medical facility to you. I'll relay to Jack."

Lyons appeared. "Place is clear," he said. "How's Gadgets?"

"I've seen him in better shape," Blancanales said. "Jack's on his way. Base is checking for the closest medical facility."

Lyons took the phone and spoke to Price.

"Have the appropriate agencies alerted—there's a store of weapons here they need to clear. We haven't had time to check the whole place so there might be more.

This looks like the staging area for a possible strike against Zero Command. Just as we thought."

"I'll advise Hal and pass the information on to Phoenix Force, just in case there's a secondary group set up. Security can be increased until this is all cleared up."

"Until Kaplan is found, nothing will be cleared up," Lyons said, catching *Dragon Slayer*'s approach through the window. He handed the phone to Blancanales. "Stay with him. I'll go bring Jack in."

Lyons made his way outside and saw the dark configuration of Stony Man's powerful combat chopper swing in to land close to the house. As soon as it was on the ground, Grimaldi powered down to an idle, keeping the rotors turning slowly. As Lyons walked to meet him, Grimaldi cleared the side hatch and climbed out. He had a med kit over his shoulder and an insulating blanket under his arm.

"Barb is checking on the closest hospital," Lyons said. "She'll alert them and send coordinates through."

"Good."

Grimaldi handed Lyons the blanket and followed him back inside the house, ignoring the bodies, his attention centered on Schwarz.

The Stony Man operatives carried their semi-conscious teammate out to *Dragon Slayer* and placed him inside on one of the rear seats that had been moved into stretcher position. With Schwarz strapped in, Lyons stepped aside.

"Pol, you go in with him," Lyons said. He pointed to the blood on Blancanales's sleeve. "Get that checked out."

"It's nothing."

"Let's get you seen to, as well," Grimaldi said. "Don't argue with the boss."

"You can call me when you know how Gadgets is," Lyons said. "Now go. I can hang around until reinforcements arrive. Give me time to look over this place."

Knowing it would be futile to argue, Blancanales climbed into the helicopter. Once he was in his seat, Grimaldi powered the hatches shut and Lyons stepped clear as the chopper powered up. He watched it lift effortlessly and swing clear. Grimaldi put the hammer down and the combat machine streaked out of sight.

A SEARCH OF the rest of the house gave up nothing, and Lyons realized what they had was the total. He checked all the bodies, removing any weapons and placing them on the kitchen table. He carried out these operations without conscious thought. He was simply clearing the scene to avoid any logistic problems later.

He had just returned from upstairs and was standing in the hall when the sound of an approaching vehicle alerted him. Lyons knew it couldn't be any of the backup vehicles yet. Not enough time had gone by. He stepped out of the house and stood in the shadow of the overhang, watching a dark blue SUV rolling in his direction. It was the same model as the black Escalade parked only a few yards away.

As the SUV swept into the yard, Lyons and the occupants came eye to eye.

And the Able Team commander found himself looking at Chinese faces. Two guys in front, one in the rear seat. The man in the rear raised his hand and pointed at Lyons, his mouth moving as he yelled something to his partners. The driver raised his hand and pointed in the direction of the dead man lying in the dirt. The

Chinese in the shotgun seat, his window already down, leaned out and started to fire.

Made, damn it, Lyons realized, hurtling to one side as the subgun crackled.

A line of slugs slammed into the dirt where Lyons had been standing. He hit the ground in a powered shoulder roll, the shotgun flying from his hands. He clawed for the holstered Python as he came out of the dive, bracing himself on one knee and leveling the big handgun. His finger pulled back on the trigger and sent a .357 Magnum slug at the SUV. He saw it punch a hole in the rear side panel as the SUV's engine roared, the heavy vehicle sliding briefly out of control as the driver pushed hard on the pedal, feeding more power to the big engine. The driver hauled on the wheel, bringing the SUV around in a sliding turn, the wide tires kicking up dirt.

The shooter leaned out farther and tracked Lyons with the subgun as the SUV began to pull away.

Ignoring the threat of the weapon, Lyons two-fisted the Colt and triggered a pair of fast shots. The handgun muzzle jerked as it expended the twin slugs. The shooter turned half-around as Lyons's shots slammed into his left shoulder. Blood squirted from the exit holes and the guy's arm lost its strength. He let go of the subgun as he slumped partway back inside the vehicle.

Back on his feet, Lyons ran forward and snatched up the dropped weapon as the SUV powered forward, heading back the way it had come. It burned rubber, bouncing over the stone edging of the frontage as the driver briefly lost control. Tires squealed as the Escalade barreled down toward the road.

Lyons ran for the parked SUV and dragged open the

driver's door. He saw the key in the ignition. Tossing the subgun onto the passenger seat, he dropped onto the driver's seat, hit the start button and felt the effortless power of the engine rise. He freed the brake, yanked the lever into Drive and stepped on the gas pedal. The surge of acceleration shoved Lyons back in his seat as he took off after the Chinese crew, leaving behind tire scores in the dirt.

The blue SUV was hurtling ahead at full speed, despite the narrow single-strip rural road. Lyons managed to haul the seat belt around him and snap it into place as he pushed his own vehicle to even higher speed.

Lyons could imagine what his partners would have been saying to him, making sarcastic comments about his reckless and life-threatening driving.

"You think?" Lyons said out loud. "Well, if I put my foot down, that sucker isn't going to lose me. What are you? Old ladies?" The sarcasm in his voice would have passed over Schwarz's and Blancanales's heads.

Ahead of him the Escalade swayed dangerously as the driver took it around a bend without reducing speed. It leaned over and for a moment it seemed on the verge of toppling. It didn't, finally regaining its forward motion on all four wheels.

Lyons didn't relent and pushed down harder on his own pedal and the SUV gained, coming to within ten feet of the first Escalade. He felt the wind gust inside as he powered down his window, leaning out with the subgun aimed at the rear of the other vehicle.

The rural road could have been in better condition. Lyons was attempting to keep the SUV on track despite the ruts and potholes. The SUV might have had large, wide-gauge tires, but even they reacted when they hit a damaged section of road.

The other driver must have become aware of Lyons's weapon. He began to swing the Escalade from side to side to make it hard for Lyons to take his shot.

Lyons's patience began to ebb. He leaned way out of the window, steering one-handed as he attempted to track the other SUV. He wanted to hit one of the rear tires.

When he fired, the short burst hit the side panel above the wheel arch, puncturing the metal but not the tire. Seeing the problem, Lyons swung the SUV to the extreme edge of the road, feeling the wheels hit the spongy grass verge. Moving out from a direct line to the rear allowed him a better view of the rear wheel. Lyons fired a second and then a third burst. He made his hit, the twin blasts tearing into the rubber, and the tire disintegrated with a hard sound.

The effect on the speeding SUV was instantaneous. It began to veer from side to side, fishtailing as the exposed rim of the wheel came into contact with the road, scraping at the ground. Lyons heard the crack of loose clay chunks hitting the front of the SUV. He eased off the gas pedal and allowed the SUV to fall back as the Escalade, still moving at high speed, swerved back and forth across the road, tearing up grass and soil from the edges of the strip.

"Crazy guy is still trying to stay ahead," Lyons said. "If he doesn't slow down he's going to—"

The words were barely out of his mouth when the Escalade lurched sideways. The driver swung the wheel in an effort to compensate but he was too late. The tilt took the SUV beyond its center of gravity and the vehicle flipped over. For a few seconds all four wheels were in the air. Then the SUV went over on its passenger side. It came back down with a heavy thump, metal screeching and glass shattering as it slid along the road. Loose debris flew free. When it came to a stop, steam was blowing from a fractured cooling system. The engine raced for a few long seconds and then cut out. The tailgate door, sprained from the impact, sprang open and deposited its cargo. Weapons and ammunition cases were dumped onto the road.

Lyons hit the SUV's brake and brought his vehicle to a crawl yards behind the crippled Escalade.

The Able Team leader was out of the vehicle while it was still moving, bringing the subgun with him. He had eyeballed the driver and saw him manhandling his door upward, pushing his way from the frame. The Chinese had a subgun in his hands. Blood streamed down his face from a deep gash to his forehead, but he still made an attempt to confront Lyons. The weapon crackled as the guy targeted the American. His aim was off as he blinked at the blood streaming into his eyes.

Lyons didn't give him a second chance. He tracked in with the subgun and triggered a burst that ripped into the man, punching bloody holes in his body from chest to throat. Lyons triggered a second, shorter burst and saw a big wedge of skull and hair fly free. The guy flopped back against the door frame, arms waving loosely as he slid back inside the vehicle.

Lyons dropped the subgun and fisted his Python, dropping to a crouch as he skirted around the Escalade. Peering through the windshield, he saw that the passenger had not survived the crash. But there was still the guy in the rear. Lyons continued to the tailgate, and through the partly open door, he could see the hunched figure of the man as he worked himself into a better position. Light slid along the metal of the handgun the guy was wielding, turning his body right and left as he searched for his opponent. Lyons caught some muttered exclamations in a language that was definitely not English.

A shot came from inside the Escalade. The slug came close to Lyons and he pulled to the right so his body was concealed by the overturned vehicle.

The Chinese guy yelled out loud, more out of frustration than bravado. He fired off a couple more shots.

Lyons leaned forward and triggered his remaining shots in through the rear of the SUV. Then he backed away again to pull a speed loader from his pouch. He ejected the empty shell casings and quickly reloaded. With six more .357 Magnum bullets in the cylinder, Lyons felt a sight more reassured.

From inside the overturned SUV, Lyons picked up subdued sounds as the surviving Chinese worked his way through from the rear seat and out to the gaping tailgate door. He pushed aside spilled goods, and Lyons saw his head and shoulders move into sight. Lyons angled his Python and covered the guy as more of his body emerged. The Chinese was still clutching his handgun. Lyons recognized it as a Beretta 92FS.

He stepped forward and slammed his foot down on the guy's gun hand, ignoring the pained protest as it was pinned to the road. Lyons jammed his Python's muzzle against the guy's skull.

"I hope you understand English, because I don't have time to conjure up Mandarin or Cantonese. Just let go of the gun and come out where I can see your hands."

The man obeyed, dropped the autopistol and crawled out of the SUV. He climbed to his feet and locked his hands behind his head. He was small and whip-lean, his black hair matted with blood from a scalp wound.

"Go to my vehicle and spread your hands on the hood. Legs apart," Lyons ordered.

He picked up the gun the guy had dropped and tucked it behind him in his own belt. Lyons kept his Python pressed against the guy as he gave him a hand search. He did it quickly and efficiently. It was a leftover from his days as a cop, something trained into him that never left. Satisfied the guy was clean, Lyons ordered him to lie facedown on the ground with his hand on the back of his head. Lyons placed a booted foot against the guy's spine to let him know he was still around.

Lyons took out his phone and called the Farm. Contacting Price, he laid out what had just happened and requested backup.

"I'd hazard a guess you might have tied up this end of the deal," the mission controller said. "I'll get help out to you."

"I'll be waiting with my surviving prisoner," Lyons said. "There's a cargo of weapons in this SUV I want to check out." There was an empty moment before Lyons said, "Too early for word from the hospital?"

"All we know is Jack got Gadgets straight to the emergency department. Nothing else yet. I will call you the minute I have anything."

"Yeah."

Lyons put the phone away. He urged the captive Chinese hardman to his feet. "So, just the two of us," he said.

He used a foot to push aside the ordnance that had spilled from the Escalade. Handguns, subguns. Filled magazines. There were also a half dozen tubular objects Lyons recognized as LAW rocket launchers. The most interesting find was a bundle of US Air Force uniforms. Pants, jackets and shirts. Even caps. Lyons stared at the stuff.

Uniforms?

That intrigued him and the only way he saw it was as cover to get people up to, or inside…then it came to him. They wanted to get to Zero Command, engineer a strike that would put the control center out of action while Chan and his crew worked on Saul Kaplan for data that would enable them to compromise the orbiting platform. The cache of weapons and clothing was being delivered to the farmhouse for distribution to the waiting team.

"Son of a bitch," Lyons swore. "You had this all worked out. Sorry, fella. Good try, but no cigar."

CHAPTER SEVENTEEN

Joshua Riba went EVA a mile from Saul Kaplan's lodge, hiding his SUV in the deep undergrowth and making his way through the forested terrain on foot, without a sound to betray his presence. This was the second time he had visited the remote habitation, and, like the first excursion, it had to do with Kaplan and Zero. Claire Valens's call had alerted Riba to Kaplan's disappearance. He had a deal of respect for Kaplan. The man had devoted himself to creating the orbiting platform and to ensuring Doug Buchanan's survival.

After talking to Valens, Riba had made his decision to check out Kaplan's lodge on a hunch. There were no guarantees he would learn anything, but to ignore the possibility would not have settled well with Riba. He made his living as a PI. One of the embedded rules in his profession was to follow any instincts, and Riba was, if nothing else, a stickler for following his hunches. When Riba took on a client and the subsequent investigation, it was his tenacious attitude that allowed him to succeed. Riba didn't like to lose. His native skills, honed by years of practice and backed by his persistent character, were the reasons he had made his chosen business a success.

His six-foot-four form, clad in black from head to foot, moved effortlessly through the timbered landscape.

He pulled out the handgun he carried and checked the loads. The Colt Peacemaker, a single-action .45-caliber revolver, was his weapon of choice; in Riba's hand it was a formidable weapon. In addition to the gun, he had a double-edged bone-handled knife in a sheath sewn inside one of his Western boots. It was more of a backup than an upfront weapon.

Riba was no throwback to the earlier era. He favored the electronic accessories available; his home office was equipped with a cutting-edge computer setup and he carried an Apple phone that had all the downloads available. That said, Riba could not be beaten when it came to tracking and picking up signs. That was part of his Apache heritage, trained into him by his grandfather back when he was a boy and living on the New Mexico reservation. He was at home in the forest. He merged with it, his very presence as one with his natural environment. Sight and sound and smell. They all allowed Riba to pass through unnoticed.

When he was near enough to observe, Riba became still. Scanning the way ahead as he concealed himself in the shadows, Riba studied the lodge. There was a high-end SUV parked close to the lodge and a single man loitering beside the vehicle. The guy was carrying a 9 mm Uzi subgun, capable of 600 rpm and with a range of approximately 200 meters. Whoever he was, the guy didn't look like a park ranger or a casual visitor.

Leaning in, Riba made out figures inside the lodge, behind the large main window.

Time to move, he decided.

He curved around the trees and emerged on one side of the parked SUV. Riba crouch-walked the length of the vehicle, coming up behind the sentry. The first thing the guy knew of a presence was when the cold muzzle of the Colt pressed into the back of his neck.

"Two ways this can go," Riba stated. "One way, I get my answers. Second way, I put a big, fat .45 lead slug in the back of your skull. I'll let you decide how you want this to play out."

Riba reached around and took the Uzi from the man's unresisting hand.

"Shouldn't wave something like this around. Could have a nasty accident with it. Now, made your choice?" The guy gave a short nod. "So tell me. What are you people doing here at my friend's home?"

"We were contracted to check the lodge. Looking for specific information that might be stored in the place."

"What information?"

"Look, Mace and Remy are the lead guys. I'm just the wheelman. I drive, they search."

"Lean against the vehicle," Riba directed. "Hands behind you."

The man did as ordered and Riba secured his wrists with one of the plastic ties he carried. He repeated the move with the ankles and made the guy lie down. Riba pulled a folded neckerchief from the inside pocket of his leather jacket and used it to gag the man.

"Damn shame to have to waste a good neckerchief."

Riba holstered the Colt, checked the Uzi, then eased to the front of the SUV where he could scan the lodge. From his previous visit he remembered a rear door that led into the kitchen. If he entered by that, it would give him a slight advantage. He ducked low and ran for the side of the lodge, staying below the windowsills and moving quickly along the timbered wall to the lodge's rear.

The kitchen door was partway open.

And it was blocked by a sprawled body, the upper torso hanging over the steps.

It was an elderly man in work clothes. Blood had drained from the wide gash in his throat, dripping down the steps to make a congealed pool on the crushed gravel below. Riba saw one limp hand, the flesh grainy and liver-spotted. He checked for a pulse and was not surprised to find nothing.

Someone who had just got in the way. Most likely a local handyman Kaplan employed to look after the place when he wasn't around.

Riba pushed away the anger threatening to rise. He needed to be in control as he moved into the lodge.

He stepped up to the door, flat against the wall. Peering through the angled glass panel, he saw through the kitchen and into the main room, where two figures were quietly ransacking the place, pulling books off shelves and checking behind hung pictures. The floor was already littered with abandoned items.

Riba pushed the door wide, carefully stepping over the body, and moved inside, padding across the smooth timber floor until he was close to the open arch leading into the main room. As he moved on by the kitchen table, he made the decision to discard the Uzi and use his handgun. He didn't need a weapon that sprayed bullets in all directions. A close-up revolver was the tool for this work. He gently laid the subgun aside but kept it close in case he needed it. Riba drew his Colt, dogging back the hammer.

"I'd guess if you haven't found anything by now there isn't anything to find," Riba said as he stood framed in the archway.

The pair froze for an instant then turned in unison, snatching for the weapons they carried.

It was a foolish move, driven by a mix of anger and desperation. For Riba it was expected; he had met this kind of reaction before. Some men were too stubborn to quit even when the odds were against them, especially professional criminals who always worked on the assumption they had the edge. It bordered on arrogance, but there was also a touch of vanity there.

Riba saw mat-black autopistols being snatched from belt holsters under their jackets, muzzles tracking in fast. He had to give them that—they had reacted without hesitation.

In the moment he assessed the opposition, Riba locked onto the one guy a fraction faster than his partner. The Colt was already on line, the big muzzle steady as he squeezed the fine trigger. The solid .45-caliber slug emerged in a spout of flame and smoke. It struck the guy in his chest, coring through to inflict heavy damage as the soft lead slug spread on impact. The guy stumbled back with a pained grunt, all thoughts of resistance dissolving as the shock numbed him.

In his peripheral vision Riba saw the second guy gripping his pistol in both hands and knew he had brief moments to avoid the shot. He was already easing back the hammer as he stepped to the side and dropped to one knee. He heard the 9 mm snap off a shot. It went over his head as Riba brought his revolver around, located his target and fired. The slug took a chunk of flesh and muscle from the guy's right shoulder. The surge of pain took over and the guy felt the power in his gun hand slip away, even as he tried to pull it back on target. Riba had dogged back the hammer again and put a second slug into the guy, the lead slug catching him in the side of his head as he turned away. It opened a ragged and bloody wound as it tore through, emerging on the other side. Blood and bone and brain matter blew out as the guy tumbled to the floor.

Riba saw the guy's pistol fly from his hands, bouncing as it hit the floor and slid across the smooth wood. He lowered his Colt, surveying the scene. Almost as an afterthought, he flipped open the loading gate and methodically worked the empty brass shell casings out of the cylinder before reaching into his jacket pocket for fresh cartridges and reloading. It was reflex action, based on a rule he always followed that made him reload after using his gun the moment he had the chance. It was a piece of advice he had learned early: never pass up the chance to reload. It was akin to the military rule of always catching sleep and always eating between actions—simple rules, but important, when a man's life depended on his being alert at all times.

A wreath of smoke hovered in the air. Riba walked forward into the room, stepping up to the bodies. He picked up the discarded pistols and placed them out of reach before he crouched to check their pockets. Neither man carried any backup weapons. He found wallets and cell phones. He examined the wallets and found driver's licenses that identified both men. They were also carrying substantial cash amounts—too much for casual needs. The cell phones gave him a list of addresses and a number both men had called a lot.

Riba made his way outside by the main door, glad to be out of the room that smelled of gun smoke and the aftermath of violent death. He took out his cell and speed dialed the number for Valens. When she answered, he gave her an update.

"You hurt?"

"No. But there are two dead guys who tried to shoot me when I caught them going through Saul's belongings. And one very alive man tied up outside." Riba paused briefly. "And I found a body out by the back door. Elderly guy. Looks like a local. Working guy. Somebody cut his throat, Valens. Damn it, they didn't need to kill him. This was a little more than I expected. These people play rough."

"Maybe your dead handyman just walked in on them, Josh. I agree, they're setting the bar really low. But it's interesting someone is ready to go through Saul's home," Valens said. "Maybe they were expecting he had Zero technical data there.

"Josh, will you wait around until help arrives? Give me time and I'll have backup come to you. You can hand him over and let them work the scene. You may have to answer some questions but I'll make sure you're not given too much hassle."

"I'll be waiting," Riba said. "Any news about Saul?"

"Afraid not, but there's certainly something in the wind, Josh. And thank you for your help."

Riba put away his cell. He went back inside and located a blanket he could cover the old man with. Then he went to collect the guy he'd left by the SUV. He took a lock knife from his pants' pocket, snapped it open and cut the tie around the guy's ankles and took off the gag.

"What in hell went on in there?"

"Your friends left a dead man on the back step," Riba said. "So when we came face-to-face, we danced around and they decided to sit the rest of their lives out."

"Jesus, you killed them both?"

"Now, things started to get rough. Your buddies weren't about to give in. They wanted me dead, too. Only that wasn't going to happen."

Riba took the guy inside through the front door. When he saw the bodies, the man tried to break away. Riba tightened his grip on the guy's arm. He led him through to the kitchen and sat him on one the chairs at the table.

Riba found the makings and set a pot of coffee on to brew. He sat facing the man across the table. "Look over there," he said, indicating the blanket-covered form.

The man glanced at the body. Looked away just as quickly.

"This is the big one," Riba said. "You're in it up to your neck. I'm guessing that old man out there caught your buddies at work."

"I never came inside."

"Something like this, you all go down."

"That guy wasn't part of the deal."

"If he could speak, I'm sure he'd agree with you. But he's still dead. A wrongful death, I think it's called." Riba said. "What do I call you?"

"Lloyd."

"That's a start."

The guy stared at Riba and then glanced through into the other room at his dead partners.

"The hell with this," he said. "I don't have to talk to you. Damned if you're even a real lawman."

"True. But right now I could shoot you and that would be an end to it all."

"Yeah?"

Riba stood, drew the Colt, cocked and fired the

.45 slug, clipping the man's left sleeve. It was close enough to burn his skin.

"What the hell? You crazy Indian…"

Riba eased back the hammer and moved the Colt's muzzle.

"Crazy? Maybe so. Keep thinking that way, Lloyd. So what were you looking for? Easy question. Even for a dumb ass like you."

"Hey, I got rights."

"Please don't start that crap with me. I get a bellyful of that from the likes of you. Every time it doesn't go your way, out comes the human rights garbage. You boys should think about that before you go out and commit crimes."

"I can ask for a lawyer."

Riba had to smile that time. "Sure you can, but, hey, I don't see any shingles hanging on tree branches out here. Figure it, Lloyd. We're a long way from home. Just you and me. So pucker up and stop doing the shuffle. Think about it—this is where the rule book gets forgotten."

Riba put the Colt away and crossed to where the coffeepot was steaming. He poured two mugs, set them on the table. Moving behind Lloyd, he cut the tie around the man's wrists.

"Go ahead," he said, picking up one of the mugs.

"First you shoot me. Now you make me coffee," Lloyd said.

"Maybe I don't like drinking on my own."

They drank in silence. Lloyd's eyes moved back and forth, and Riba knew he was assessing his chances. He let his right hand rest on the wood grips of the holstered revolver.

"Let's start with the easy questions," Riba said. "Like who hired you?"

"You really think I'm going to tell you?"

"Lloyd, all I'm doing is trying to get something to keep the people on their way here happy. If they decide you're not being cooperative...well, you know how these federal agents are. Face it, Lloyd, this is way beyond a simple burglary. It's downright murder. A capital offence. They could have you placed in one of those max-security federal lockups where you don't get visitors or see even daylight. Life sentence with no parole. Unless you can talk your way through."

Riba drank his coffee and poured himself another.

He caught a glimpse of Lloyd as he turned. The man was weighing the odds. With people like Lloyd, personal survival was paramount. He could rant and bluster, but in the end he wanted out of the mess he'd gotten himself into.

"How do I know you ain't just scamming me? Trying to scare me?"

Riba shrugged. "Lloyd, you are entitled to be scared. This is the main event. You take the full rap for it. No skin off my nose. End of the day, I go home. You don't. You got to ask yourself, Lloyd, 'am I ready for this?' It's an easy option to figure."

Lloyd stared into his coffee mug. He knew he was caught. There was no way out.

"Son of a bitch," he said. "Jesus, you talk a damn streak, Chief. I'll bet one of your ancestors was a damn horse trader."

"Well, his name was Charriba. And he was an Apache, same as me. He exchanged shots with the US Army. Ran a game with them for years, him and his bunch of wild-ass 'Pache bucks. But he didn't trade horses. He stole them from the cavalry."

"That figures."

"So you understand where I'm coming from, friend." Riba jerked a thumb in the direction of the blanket-covered body. "You boys did a bad thing there. Nice guy comes to do his work. Walks in on you guys and gets himself killed for it."

LLOYD PICKED UP his coffee and took a long swallow. He took another look around the lodge. At his dead buddies. At the body under the blanket. His mind weighed the odds. As the Indian said, he was in this on his own. His life on the edge. If the Apache took it into his mind, he could kill Lloyd and that would be an end to it.

Lloyd had been on the thin edge of life since being a teenager. It had been better than working nine to five in some ass-wipe daily job, he'd figured then. He'd started by thieving. Then he moved up to join one of the local criminal groups. Early on Lloyd had proved his worth behind the wheel of a car, so that had become his skill. He'd had some hair-raising experiences burning rubber, but he'd always gotten away. Teaming up with Mace and Remy had been good. They had known each other for years, and the three of them forged a strong alliance.

It suddenly hit Lloyd that his longtime buddies were dead. The Apache sitting across from him had wiped them out. Just like that. The thought made Lloyd feel sick. His coffee lost its appeal and he put the mug down and pushed it away. Life had changed completely. His partners were gone and he was facing jail time. Big jail time. The prospect filled him with a cold dread. He'd done a little local prison time, but this time it would be far worse. He'd heard the rumors about federal prisons and even if some of it was made up, the thought of ending up in one of them scared the hell out of Lloyd.

He saw there was no way around this.

The Apache had him dead to rights.

They would be coming for him soon. The Apache would hand him over and Lloyd would be on his way to a new life.

Some life.

CHAPTER EIGHTEEN

The limousine had only just left the airfield when Xia Chan's sat phone rang. He picked up and recognized the clipped tones of Jake Moretti. The American headed the mercenary group Chan had hired for the work in the States. From the tone of Moretti's voice, he was not about to give Chan good news.

"Go ahead, Mr. Moretti," Chan said.

One of Moretti's saving graces was the fact that he spoke Cantonese; it was something he had learned during his service time in the East.

"Things have not gone as planned, Colonel," he said. "Our teams have been compromised."

"To what degree?"

"Shot to hell. Dead men. Armaments seized by an American agency."

Chan fell silent as he digested the information. He absorbed what Moretti had said and quickly assessed what it meant in overall strategy. It was disturbing news, but not catastrophic. Hitting Zero Command would have been a helpful matter, because with the operating base damaged it would make what Chan needed to do that much easier. In truth, it had been a secondary part of the operation; a useful adjunct to the main effort, but not completely necessary.

The fact remained that gaining control of Zero came

down to extracting the correct information from Saul
Kaplan. If that did not happen, taking the main control
center off-line would not matter.

"Moretti, regroup. Calculate your situation and then
get back to me. Let us see if we can salvage something
from this mess. Call me when you have done so."

"Will do, Colonel."

Chan ended the call and leaned back in the padded
seat. Beside him Yang Zhou turned away from the window he had been staring out of.

"Something has happened?"

"Yes," Chan said.

Zhou listened to what Chan had to tell him.

"To be expected," he said. "You want my sympathy?"

"Will I get it?"

"Sympathy, no. But I am concerned."

"Your concern is noted," Chan said.

Zhou shrugged. "I was never in favor of you placing
your trust in *gweilos*."

"We needed local people. The purpose was to get
them close to Zero Command so they could inflict
damage if the occasion arose. I understand that may
be a moot point now, but a group of our people dressed
in American Air Force uniforms would not have been
helpful. And before you say more, Zhou, my operation
with regard to attacking Zero has been put on hold for
the present. We move on. We play our winning card.
Saul Kaplan is still in our hands. The main objective of
our plan. Or do you see flaws there, as well?"

"I will reserve judgment on that," Zhou said. "There
is still a long way to go before we achieve success."

"What would I do without your optimistic disposi-
tion, my dear Yang?"

Zhou gave a noncommittal grunt.

As the limousine made its way along the winding road, Chan stared at the scenery.

"Such a clean country," he said. "Don't you think so, Yang?"

"I would rather be home." He waved a dismissive hand at the Swiss scenery. "This is not *Zhongguo*. It is the land of the *gweilo*."

"Do I detect a touch of xenophobia, Yang?"

"If you do, I will not apologize. These people are not our friends, Colonel. They do not trust us, as I do not trust them. They will tolerate us as long as we pay them, but their hearts are against us."

Chan saw he would never win against Zhou. The man was an isolationist. If Zhou ran the country, he would close borders and eject every foreigner from China. He would return to the old days when China held itself aloof from the rest of the world, content with its own destiny and removed from contact with outsiders.

The man was a throwback, still dreaming of the days when the country lived by the rules of *Quotations from Chairman Mao Tse-tung*. The West had trivialized it by retitling it *The Little Red Book,* but the Chinese people had revered it. Not that they had much in the way of choice. In those years the overwhelming power from Beijing had held sway and the masses were bound to the strictures of ideology under the threat of reprisals. Over the years, with realization that the old ways were not exactly bringing about the rewards they promised, the ruling class had slackened the reins to a degree where foreign deals were struck and Chinese production was geared to making the merchandise the West wanted.

Yang Zhou remained rigidly true to tradition. The

West was his enemy. Never to be trusted. There to be taken advantage of whenever possible. In his blinkered view the West, for better or for worse, had to be overcome. If China could not create, then it would take. As with electrical goods and clothes, it could copy items and produce them in far greater quantities than the West.

A prime example was the Zero technology. All of China's efforts in the field had come to nothing. The admittedly amazing achievement by Saul Kaplan was looked on with pure envy. China needed the Zero capability and if stealing it was the only way forward, then that was how it would proceed.

Chan envied Zhou's simplistic approach, his black-and-white view of things. He just wished life could be as easy. Unfortunately that was not so. All Chan had to do was to look back at the phone call he had just received. The failure of the hard strike against Zero Command had been thwarted even before it actually got under way. He blocked off his negative thoughts. The matter, a secondary one in truth, was out of his hands now. His priority was Kaplan. He had the man en route to Switzerland and once Kaplan was safely delivered, the process of learning Zero's secrets could begin.

Chan was determined it would succeed. He had people waiting who were experts in extracting information from the most resistant minds. He did not doubt that Saul Kaplan would fight with every breath in his body to avoid giving up. The man may have been strong-willed, stubborn, but the skills of Chan's team, plus the sophisticated drugs they could employ, would break any resistance. Saul Kaplan would eventually give away the data he carried in his brain. It was inevitable.

He felt the limousine tilt as it negotiated the rising road leading to the mountain slopes. Another hour or so would bring him to the stronghold, where he would be welcomed by the team flown in from China. They had been in place for almost a week, preparing themselves and their equipment for Kaplan's eventual arrival.

The program was ready. When Kaplan arrived, still under sedation, he would be installed in the room prepared for him and allowed to recover from the drugs he had been given. He would be allowed time to return to a healthy condition, would be given the opportunity to rest before any procedures were initiated. It was essential Kaplan was in good health before Chan's specialist took over. If he was under par before the sessions began, results would be uneven, perhaps well below what was anticipated. So Kaplan would be allowed time to recover.

Chan found himself smiling. Kaplan would realize that there was no rush. He would not be put under immediate pressure. There was no timetable that had to be followed. It would take however long it needed. Time was not an obstacle.

However long it took.

The Chinese were masters of patience.

Experts at the waiting game.

THE LIMOUSINE NEGOTIATED the curved drive leading to the house—a large structure on two levels—and came to a gentle stop near the steps that led to the veranda. Two people stood waiting for Chan's arrival.

Dr. Luc Melier was a slender, thin-faced man with hair brushed straight back from his forehead. A recognized expert in his field, Melier was the one Chan would depend on to strip Kaplan of his knowledge. Melier was a mild, well-mannered man of good breeding and taste, and possessed a precise personality that allowed for no errors. Chan had past experience of Melier's skills and was placing great faith in the man's knowledge.

Beside Melier was Major Chosan, dressed in a conventional Western suit complete with white shirt and a neat tie. In his thirties, Chosan was a close associate of Colonel Chan; Chan had put him in charge of security and overseeing matters that required a military mindset. Chosan had a manner that was directly opposite that of Dr. Melier. He was all about duty, with no regard for the niceties of life, but he was totally dedicated to Chan and respected his authority.

As Chan stepped out of the car he felt the cool, crisp air of the Swiss environment envelop him. He paused a moment to take it in.

"It is good to see you, Colonel," Dr. Melier said.

He was dressed in a white tunic and pants, slim hands clasped against his stomach. The slight smile on his angular face was as urbane as his wardrobe.

"I hope everything is ready, Doctor."

The smile never faltered. "But of course. We have been ready for the past few days. When you have yourself settled, I will show you around."

"Good." Chan turned to Chosan. "And security procedures, Major?"

Chosan merely inclined his head. "All in order, Colonel. My people are on station as we speak. Surveillance is up and running. Nothing will be left to chance."

Chan looked around at the well-cultivated grounds surrounding the house and noted the lack of any personnel.

"I see no one."

Chosan permitted himself a brief smile. "Which is how it should be, Colonel. Rest assured my people are present. Not being seen is part of their remit. We would not wish our armed people to be seen by any of the Swiss population."

"Very good, Chosan." He became aware of Zhou's brooding presence just behind him. "You know Yang Zhou. He is here as my personal bodyguard. He will be afforded all due respect while here. Am I understood?"

Chosan inclined his head. "Of course, Colonel."

"One other thing. While I am here, you will address me as Mr. Chan. No military titles. I understand we are fairly well isolated here, but I am not prepared to make any foolish errors. It is not to be suggested we have anything to do with the military. After all, Switzerland is a peaceful country and we do not want to offend them. That is understood? Yes?"

Luggage had been taken from the car and placed on the ground. Dr. Melier called for help from inside the house and the bags were quickly picked up and taken inside. Chan was about to follow Melier inside when he turned and crossed to speak to the driver before he got back into the car. This done, he followed the others inside.

"A small matter of no consequence," he said by way of explanation. "Now, Dr. Melier, please show me around our delightful residence."

THE HOUSE WAS on a long-term lease arranged through a company based in Hong Kong, which in turn operated on behalf of the Beijing department controlled by Chan. A three-year contract, paid in full, had sent the

Swiss real estate agent away a happy man, with his calculator in his hand by the time he had reached his car, totaling up his commission. That had been four months ago. Since then Chan's people had moved in gradually, preparing for the day, now arrived, when their special guest showed up and their real work could begin.

The house, split-level, had six bedrooms, multiple bathrooms and four reception rooms. The spacious kitchen was equipped to a high standard. At the rear of the house was a study and office, already furnished with a pale wood-and-chrome desk and comfortable leather reclining seats. There were connection points for computers and peripherals. A large-screen Apple iMac had already been installed.

At the rear of the house a sweeping lawn and patio gave extensive views of the distant, snowcapped mountain peaks. Some distance away, across the rear garden area, stood a solid building that housed a large modern generator that provided the house with all the power it needed.

Dr. Melier gave Chan a full tour of the house. The colonel made no comment until they completed the inspection and ended up in the office. Chan took the chair behind the desk, swiveling it around so he could gaze out the panoramic window at the sweeping view. Melier waited, hands still resting together across his torso.

"This will suit us admirably," Chan said. "Peaceful. Isolated. No neighbors. The perfect situation for you to carry out your work, Doctor."

"I believe so."

Chan swung the chair around and fixed Melier with a stern expression. The fierce gleam in Chan's eyes was unsettling.

"Let us be clear from the start," Chan said. "This exercise will test us both, Dr. Melier. We cannot—we must not—fail. If we do, there will be no forgiveness by Beijing. The first attempt to gain control of the Zero system failed. Do you know what happened to General Tung Shan?"

"I suspect he was executed shortly after he disappeared."

Chan nodded. "Then you understand the price we both could pay if we fail. Beijing is not a tolerant master, Melier. It expects success and has no time for excuses. If you don't get what we need from Kaplan, *I* will be following *you* to the grave. I am not being overly dramatic. Simply stating the truth. If we fail, our masters in Beijing will seek to silence anyone involved."

"Col—*Mr.* Chan, I fully understand the possible penalty if I fail to get the information we need from Kaplan. I am loyal to whoever employs me, but not to the point where I fail to understand the severe price I will pay if I do not succeed. Believe me when I say I hope our mission brings us both what we want. If you were to ask if my efforts will be colored by what will happen if I fail, I will tell you truly—yes, they will. So trust me when I say my efforts will be one hundred percent."

"Then it seems we have a similar agenda. Basically, to survive. So, my dear Dr. Melier, tell me everything you need and I will provide it."

"The overriding requirement is patience. A great deal of patience, because this endeavor cannot be hurried. One misstep and any gain could be lost in a heartbeat. There must be no kind of distraction while I conduct sessions. None at all. This must be understood by all your people. Enforced without question."

"That is ensured. I will have everyone instructed of that situation."

"No exceptions, Mr. Chan." Melier stared directly at Chan. "*No* exceptions."

Chan understood and inclined his head in acceptance of Melier's demand. He understood what the man was saying. No interference. No interruption when he was working. Not even by Chan himself. It was part of the reason Chan had sent for Jui Kai. The young woman would be able to afford him some distraction while Melier worked.

"When will you begin?"

"Kaplan must be allowed time to recover from the journey and the tranquilizers he has been given. Mind and body must be rested. No distractions. No pressure. I would say that for the next day he be allowed complete freedom from any kind of stress. I am sure you want the process to begin as soon as possible, but pushing him too quickly could be a mistake."

"Whatever you say, Doctor. I was told to expect Kaplan would need a resting period after he arrives. Let me make it clear that you will be allowed all the time you need. You have my word."

CHAN GATHERED EVERYONE in the main room and addressed them as to what he would expect.

"When Dr. Melier is conducting his sessions with the American, he will not, under any circumstances, be disturbed. This applies to every member of this group. No exceptions. The work he will be carrying out is of great importance and he requires absolute privacy when he asks for it. No one will invade that privacy. I have promised him that privacy and it will be strictly enforced. Understand this. If anyone steps over the line, I will execute them on the spot."

Chan let a silence follow his words. Long enough for the gathered people to digest it. "Good. Dr. Melier will not be starting his sessions for a day after the American arrives. Carry on with your duties until told otherwise." Chan raised a hand to dismiss the group but paused to add, "One final caution. Under no circumstances will any cell phone calls be permitted. We stay anonymous as much as possible. Calls can be traced. All phones are to be switched off. Now. There will be no exceptions. Anyone who disobeys will be dealt with by instant execution. Take this as your one and final warning."

Chan dismissed them, keeping Major Chosan behind.

"Keep your people on twenty-four-hour alert."

"Are you expecting problems, sir?"

"I always anticipate problems, Chosan. The Americans will be searching for Kaplan. Since the incident with the group in America, it is not beyond possibility that they may have gained knowledge of Kaplan's whereabouts. If that is the case, they may well mount an attempt to recover him."

"You believe they would come here and strike at us?"

"In their position what would you do, Chosan?"

"Exactly that."

"Then we must be prepared. Stress to your men that they must be vigilant."

"It will be done."

"If anything happens and we are under attack, your responsibility is to protect Kaplan. I do not care how much of a sacrifice it requires. Kaplan is to be our prime consideration. Nothing else matters."

CHAPTER NINETEEN

The silver BMW SUV arrived in late afternoon. Saul
Kaplan, accompanied by Nan Cheng and Bolo, was
taken from the vehicle and into the house. The driver
joined them in the house after parking the car. Kaplan,
still partially under the effect of the drugs he had been
given, was taken to one of the bedrooms by direction of
Dr. Melier, where he was immediately put to bed. One
of Chosan's guards was assigned to stand watch outside
the room's window, while a second man guarded the
bedroom door. The arrival procedure was carried out
efficiently and with the minimum of duress for Kaplan.

Chan called for a meeting in the study he had made
his command center. He sat behind the desk as the
group came in and arranged themselves across from
him. One of the house staff brought in refreshments.
There was tea or coffee and bottled water for those who
wanted it. Chan allowed everyone to settle.

"I trust you all find the accommodation to your
tastes. Luckily all the bedrooms are large and we have
arranged for extra beds so everyone should be comfortable. It is important, because we may be here for some
time. The task ahead, which will be led by Dr. Melier,
assisted by Nan Cheng, will not be an easy one. I doubt
if we will be seeing any results for a considerable period. We must all be patient.

"I believe it has been stated before that Dr. Melier is faced with a considerable task. His needs are paramount. The breaking of the man, Kaplan, is his sole objective. I may be repeating myself, but for you who have only just arrived, let me emphasize that our only concern here is the extraction of the data for the Zero Platform. Saul Kaplan carries the secrets inside his head, and Dr. Melier is tasked with learning those secrets. Nothing else matters. *Nothing*. While we are here, our work is to ensure that Dr. Melier has no problems. That he is able to work undisturbed. If he asks for assistance, if he needs anything…he is to be given it immediately. No questions."

Chan gestured over his shoulder at the panoramic view beyond the window. "Let us be honest. We are in a comfortable area. This house is exceedingly comfortable and we are secure. As long as we keep to ourselves and create no fuss, there is no reason why our stay should be troubled."

"Do we remain within the grounds and house?" someone asked.

"Yes," Chan said. "There will be armed guards outside, so do not disturb them. I understand the requirements regarding supplies. This will be addressed. We are at least two hours from the closest town and that is where anything we require can be purchased. I want to maintain a low profile. To stay distant from anyone. If we do not create problems, I do not expect anyone to bother us. The Swiss are a respectful people. They maintain a respect for privacy, so if we do not cause them any concern, there should not be any trouble."

Dr. Melier said, "There are adequate facilities to entertain yourself during breaks. Satellite television. Recorded films. Music. It may be tailored for Western values, but much of it is tolerable."

A question came from one of Chan's men. "Doctor, have you made any forecasts on how long it may take to break Kaplan?"

"This is no textbook project. Kaplan is an intelligent man. No fool. He will resist from day one, because he understands what I will be attempting. So I will have to go carefully. Kaplan will be watching for traps even during a casual conversation."

Nan Cheng raised a hand. "If I may, Doctor?"

Melier nodded.

"I spent some time with Kaplan after his kidnap, and while we were in the safehouse I was able to converse with him. I saw from the start how clever he is. He understands his position. He knows he is at risk. That we control his life. He also is smart enough to realize that whatever we do to him must have a safeguard against ending his life. If he dies, we lose everything. He is also aware that we can do things to him that will make his life intolerable yet keep him alive. Whatever we do must not be so extreme as to destroy his mind or to put him in extreme pain."

"Nan Cheng is correct. Kaplan will fight us," Melier said. "So we must approach him with caution. Start the chemical treatment with small doses at first and then increase them. Assess him. Try to find any weakness in him we can exploit." Melier raised his hands. "It is going to be an interesting time for us all."

"Not so interesting that you lose track of why we are here," Yang Zhou said.

"We can always depend on Yang Zhou to point out the drawbacks," Chan said. "But to be serious, he does have a point. We must not forget the sole reason we are here and must not allow Kaplan to distract us. Believe me, he will try. As he will no doubt attempt to make us angry. Angry enough to do him physical harm."

AFTER THE MEETING, Melier took Nan Cheng to show him the room he had chosen for his sessions with Saul Kaplan.

It was a conservatory with a glass-paned roof, the rear wall comprising a full-width window that gave an unobstructed view across the wide lawn to the tree line beyond. After the property line, the land rose in increments toward the hazy lower slopes of the eventual mountain peaks, where snow gleamed on the highest elevations.

"An impressive view," Melier said.

Cheng nodded. "Extremely so."

"Restful," Melier said. "A view to relax a person and allow serendipitous thoughts."

Cheng stared at the curve of sky and the scraps of white cloud.

"The calm before the storm," he said.

Melier smiled. "Very poetic, Cheng. I hope we do not experience too much of a storm with Kaplan."

He gave Cheng a tour of the room. In the prime position, facing the panoramic window, was a full-length recliner; the padded leather chair could be adjusted from a sitting position to complete recline.

"For Kaplan?" Cheng said.

Melier nodded. "To make him feel comfortable and aid his relaxation."

There was a number of matching leather armchairs in the room, the leather of a light buff color. Cheng noticed that the room's walls were painted a muted shade of off-white, while the floor was covered by a beige carpet. There were also banks of lights sunk into the walls.

Melier moved to a square panel set in the wall. He activated a switch and louvered blinds were electronically drawn over the window and the roof panels. As the light was subdued another switch activated the wall lights. Melier retracted the blinds and switched off the lights as normal light returned.

"Very mood-setting," Cheng said.

"Conveniently all this was fitted when the house was rented. It was all installed by the original owner, who had the place built for him."

Melier showed Cheng the metal trollies covered by white cloth. He removed the cloth to expose the rows of neatly arranged hypodermic syringes. Next to them were small, sealed bottles holding clear liquids. Cheng scanned the labels. They were what he had been expecting, though some of the bottles held solutions he did not recognize. Others held sedatives, muscle relaxants and stimulants. His curiosity made him point at the ones he did not recognize.

"My own formulations," Melier said. "To influence Kaplan's brain functions. Manipulate his synaptic responses. I need to make him more responsive when it comes to revealing information in the deepest recesses of his mind."

Cheng must have betrayed momentary doubt.

"Do not concern yourself, Cheng. All my developed serums have been thoroughly tested. Very thoroughly. I have been conducting trials over many months. Some successful. Others not so."

"But you achieved what you set out to do?"

"I lost a few at the start, before I was able to adjust serum strengths. Fortunately not as many as I had expected. Once I had the control levels maintained, things got better, and after the initial few months we were getting a hundred percent success rate. My association with Colonel Chan allowed me to complete my work in comparative privacy. He is, if nothing else, extremely clever at arranging such things."

"Are there aftereffects?"

"Some," Melier said. "A small percentage. Again, that figure fell with experience. Each problem area, once removed, provided even more information."

"My interest is Kaplan. It would be unfortunate if he had long-term disabilities following your treatment."

"In his case I believe he could survive intact. The successful test subjects were all of a type—strong-willed and intellectually positive."

"That does characterize Kaplan."

Melier completed the tour of the room.

Cheng said, "May I ask how the colonel is about all this? The time it may take, I mean."

"Ah, Colonel—*Mr.* Chan."

"I ask because I know him of old. He is not a patient man."

"Nor very tolerant, if he suspects things are not going his way. But he has his orders from Beijing—to get results. I have impressed on him that there are no shortcuts here, that forcing the treatment could give us negative results. If Chan wants a success story, I am afraid our esteemed leader is going to have to keep a tight rein on his impulsive nature."

"Despite his rallying speech at the meeting that you are to be given unlimited freedom when working, I can imagine him reversing his promise if time becomes an issue."

"I can believe that, Cheng. But if he does renege and tries to accelerate matters, it will not turn out well."

"Not for any of us," Cheng said.

"If we fail, it will be bad for us all. Chan included. No doubt he will be recalling the previous attempt to take control of Zero and what happened to General Tung."

XIA CHAN WAS seated in the main room, his gaze fixed on the scene beyond the panoramic window. The view was of the house's generous garden and the rising slopes at the foot of the peaks. It was a tranquil scene, now made even more pleasant by the fall of snow that had started a little while ago. This close to the mountains, snowfall could be heavy, often cutting off isolated residences. Chan thought that might be helpful. If they were snowed in, it would reduce the possibility of anyone coming to bother them. He considered the matter and decided to make certain they were well provisioned in the event of a blockade. He crossed to the door and gestured to one of the security men in the corridor.

"Go find Nan Cheng. I need to speak with him."

The man nodded. "Yes, sir," he said and went to look for Cheng.

Chan returned to his comfortable lounger where he could stare out the window.

Nan Cheng appeared after a few minutes. "You wished to see me?"

Chan indicated the falling snow. "I understand snowfall here can be extreme."

"Sometimes, yes. This time of year especially."

"What provision is there if we become snowed in?"

"There is food and water for at least four days. The fuel tanks for the power generators were filled two days ago, so at normal usage we would be able to survive for at least two months. The fuel reservoir is extremely large."

Chan considered the information. "Staple food and bottled water stocks should be increased," he said. "Send a team to go to the town as soon as possible and pick up extra supplies. I would not be happy if we began to run out of food."

Cheng said, "Whatever you wish, sir."

"Simply looking ahead, Cheng." He smiled. "The military mind. Always considering the options. Maintain supplies. Better to have a little too much than not enough." As Cheng turned to go, Chan said, "So, Cheng, how is our guest?"

"Actually awake. Quite rational."

"Ready for visitors?"

"It would do no harm, sir. Dr. Melier will have no objections at this stage."

"Then it is perhaps time to introduce myself."

Chan followed Nan Cheng to the room where Saul Kaplan was housed. An armed man stood outside the door. The guard moved aside when Chan approached the door and Nan Cheng left, leaving the colonel alone with Kaplan.

"My name is Chan. I am honored to have you here as my guest."

Kaplan, resting on the lounger, glanced at his visitor. "So this is all down to you?"

Chan nodded.

"I honestly can't say I am pleased to be here," Kaplan said.

"I understand," Chan said. "However, there is no reason we should not be adult about the situation."

Kaplan managed a weary smile. "Is this where you play the good guy and shortly one of your people will come in and be nasty to me?"

"I am not sure I am familiar with such matters."

"When a suspect is being interrogated in an American movie, the police play a game with him. One police officer is nice to him. Sympathetic. Friendly. The policeman's partner comes in and he's not friendly. Threatens the suspect. It's all in order to get the man to confess. It's called 'good cop, bad cop.'"

Chan was curious until he realized what Kaplan was describing.

"Now I understand. But to put your mind at rest, there is no other person. Just me, and I have no reason to play this 'good cop, bad cop' game, Kaplan. We are going to spend time here and you are going to tell us what we need to know. Dr. Melier, who you will deal with later, will be working with you. His specialty is extracting information from people. He is extremely skilled at this. Believe me, Kaplan, it will not be a pleasant period of your life if you attempt to fight him. It will be in your best interests to give him what he wants quickly. It will reduce your suffering. Melier does not rely on violence. He uses drugs, many of which he has created himself. They are very persuasive, but unfortunately they can sometimes have unpleasant side effects. In the end, it is up to you. I suggest you think about that. Very seriously."

"I will."

Chan reached down and picked up the briefcase he had brought into the room with him.

"I am sure you will recognize this," he said.

"It's mine. You telling me you brought it all the way from the US?"

"My people have inspected the contents."

This time Kaplan's smile was genuine. "They find anything interesting?"

Chan opened it, took out a thick legal pad and showed it to Kaplan.

"Only this. And writing instruments. They have read your notes but can find nothing of value."

"If they were looking for the secrets of Zero, I can assure you they will have been disappointed."

"So they have told me."

"If you've learned anything about me, you will know that I do not record technical details in any form. Hand-written notes or digital. I keep my knowledge inside my head. I'm lucky to have the kind of brain that retains everything I create like a…an internal memory disk. It's why Zero was created the way it was. From inside my head. All you'll find on that pad are random jottings on my early thoughts for some improvements to Zero's functions. No magic formulas. No diagnostic processes. You can have your people study those notes as long as they want. They'll get nothing, because right now they don't mean a thing. They're simply handwritten muses. The drawings are nothing but doodles. Done for my own amusement as I worked. When I finally decide what I want, I store the information in here along with everything else." Kaplan tapped the side of his skull. "In here, Chan. That's where the real stuff is."

Chan sat back, his face expressionless as he studied Kaplan.

"I am trying to work out if you are serious or simply trying to antagonize me. I suggest you do not make me angry. Ask any of my people and they will tell you I can be extremely unpleasant if I feel I am being made a fool of."

"You want truth? Then I will give you truth. Your Dr. Melier is going to have to pump me full of his magic potions if you expect me to give up Zero. I will resist him every step of the way. To be truthful, Chan, I am not a courageous man. The thought of what you threaten terrifies me. But I promise I will fight Melier and his mumbo-jumbo potions. If it takes my life, then so be it. That presents *you* with a problem, though, doesn't it?

"If you push me too far and I die, then all your scheming will have been for nothing. This elaborate plan to kidnap me and bring me all the way here to Switzerland will be wasted if you simply end up with a corpse on your hands." Kaplan studied Chan's face. Saw the muscles twitch in his cheeks as he fought back the anger growing in him. "If I end up dead, Chan, your masters in Beijing are not going to be very happy. This is your big opportunity, I'm guessing. Your people screwed up once before. If you don't go home with the big prize I'm sure they are not going to cut you any slack…"

Chan rose from his chair, barely able to contain his rage. Kaplan's defiance and his cutting words had threatened to override his control. The urge to strike out at the American took Chan close to the edge. His hands were ready to curl into fists, and he was struggling to hold back his anger. He caught the sparkle in

Kaplan's eyes and realized the man was deliberately goading him. Kaplan wanted Chan to hit him. To beat him into submission. Maybe even… Chan stepped back as the thought came to him. Kaplan would have sacrificed himself to protect his secrets.

No, Chan thought, do not rise to his taunts.

"Very clever, Kaplan. You have almost succeeded in making me angry enough to use violence." Chan clasped his hands together. "I congratulate you. Had you taunted me too much, I may have injured you. Perhaps that is what you wanted. But it will not happen. I understand your tactic now."

Kaplan was seeking a way out. He was prepared to die rather than give up his knowledge. In that case Chan had to make sure it could not happen.

He crossed to the door and spoke to the armed man in the corridor.

"This man must be under twenty-four-hour watch," he said. "Someone with him at all times. *All times.* Understood? He must not be left on his own for any reason. No excuses. Do not allow him to persuade you otherwise. I want you inside that room right now. Be with him. I will speak to Captain Ling and he will make sure there are regular guards. If Kaplan tries anything he must be restrained. Keep me informed."

CHAN MADE HIS way through the house and located Dr. Melier. He spoke to the man, informing him what had happened and impressing upon him the need to have Kaplan watched over all the time.

"I mentioned he was a clever man," Melier said. "Goading us so we retaliate is a smart move. Let this be a lesson for us both. We must treat him carefully and not allow him to distract us."

"Then the sooner you commence your treatment the better, Doctor. You must make sure he is sedated and unable to do anything, to harm himself."

"I will see to it at once," Melier said.

"Make sure you do."

Chan went into the main lounge area. A log fire burned in the stone fireplace. Chan picked out a deep leather armchair and slumped down. His anger was slowly subsiding as he stared into the flames.

Damn the man. Kaplan was proving to be smarter than Chan had given him credit for. What was that American saying? Yes—Kaplan had certainly pushed Chan's buttons. And it had almost worked. Chan got to his feet and crossed the room to the wet bar. He found a bottle of expensive whiskey and poured himself a tumbler full, taking it back to his chair, where he sat and slowly sipped the drink.

Time to let Melier get to work. The sooner he had Kaplan in his hands, so to speak, the better.

He was only half through his drink when a familiar voice broke into his thoughts.

"I hope I am not disturbing you."

Chan sat upright, turning to see Jui Kai crossing the room. Chan had not realized she had arrived. With everything going on around him, he had forgotten he had sent his driver for her. He kept that to himself, not wanting to admit he had allowed her to slip his mind. But then, he thought, I do have a great deal to concern myself with.

She had changed from her flight uniform into slim-fitting black pants and a honey-colored clingy sweater, revealed as she slipped off the dark coat she was wearing.

She looked impossibly beautiful to Chan. The pale color in her cheeks was highlighted by the gleam of the flames in the hearth. It shimmered against the jet-black of her glossy hair.

"Disturbing me? No, Jui Kai, you are exactly what I need right now. And I think you look wonderful, my dear," Chan said. He indicated the falling snow outside the windows. "By the look of the weather, you have arrived just in time."

Jui Kai laughed gently. "Why, Colonel Chan, do you think we might be stranded here?"

"It might happen," he said. "And while we are here there are no military titles. Only names. It is simply a precaution so no one might let slip we are more than just visitors to this country."

"I can think of no better place to be if we become snowed in."

"I have you in my control, then, Jui Kai."

"At least the plane won't be leaving without me."

"Of course not. How would it function without you on board?"

Kai held her hands out toward the fire. Chan moved to her side, placing his hands on her shoulders. He leaned close to breathe in her perfume, gently stroking his lips across the skin of her neck.

"I am forgetting my manners," Chan said. "Would you like a drink?"

"I shouldn't while I am on duty."

"That's no problem. As of now, all flights are canceled. Therefore, you are no longer on duty."

"Then I would enjoy a drink with you, Mr. Chan."

Chan poured her a whiskey and handed it to her. Her slim fingers brushed his as she took the tumbler.

"As you are now off duty and my guest, you must call me Xia. Please. Not Chan. It sounds so formal."

JUI KAI STOOD with her back to the log fire, the tumbler of whiskey in her hand, and watched as Xia Chan crossed the room to speak with the man called Yang Zhou. He had appeared in the doorway and his hard glare showed he was not happy to see her.

She was wary of Zhou. Every time he glanced her way, she could sense his mistrust in her. As Chan's assigned bodyguard, it was his duty to view everyone with a cautious eye. She understood that, but even so there was something about Zhou she did not trust. The man was a throwback to earlier times, when allegiance to the Party was expected without question and everyone came under suspicion. Zhou was one of those who maintained that attitude and he made no attempt to conceal it. Given the opportunity, he would have taken her apart limb by limb. He was aware of her animosity. For her own part, Kai's defiant spirit refused to allow her to bow to his feelings.

He would need to be watched, she realized. If he thought for one moment that she was not who she claimed to be, he would pounce. Kai was aware of the difficulty of her position. One wrong step and she would be in big trouble, the kind that could see her arrested— or summarily executed as an enemy of the PRC. Neither prospect gave Jui Kai much in the way of comfort.

She had accepted the possibilities that came with her position. It had not stopped her from taking on her undercover role. One that she had played for the past three years, working her way through various elements of Chinese society. Role-playing had always been something Kai excelled in. She had used her skills to move from job to job, her eye always on the ball. While she passed data on to her agency in Washington she had stepped up the ladder, aiming for the prime role she was hoping to take on. Almost a year ago she had found herself in the position her game plan had been devised for, and she took her current position with the flight division that served the operations allied to the Chinese government's Special Projects Division very seriously.

By this time Kai was sending regular reports back to the US, alerting them to movements of the SPD. As the database grew, identifying members of Chinese intelligence and operations, Kai was asked for reports on a regular basis on one individual her agency was more than simply interested in.

Colonel Xia Chan.

It had taken time and patience, Kai using her skill and ability to manipulate the move closer to Chan. From the first time she had been assigned as attendant on a flight the colonel was taking, Kai had made herself known to the man. During early briefings she had taken note that Chan was a known womanizer and favored young, attractive women. Kai was both, and she was smart enough to play on his desires. She took care to make herself available during the flights, forward, without being overtly so. Her attitude appealed to Chan's vanity and over the next few months Kai found herself being assigned to his flights on a regular basis. And then as a permanent attendant, who saw to his every need, both materially and personally. It did not take long before Chan became entranced by the beautiful young woman who looked after him so well during the tedium of long flights around the country and sometimes beyond China's borders.

During her initial briefings she had learned everything there was to know about Xia Chan: his background, his entry into the military and his rise through the ranks due to his diligence and ability to seize any and every opportunity. He commanded his people with authority and never gave in when it came to completing an assignment. It was known he had personally executed two men who had defied him and protested his actions. Chan was known to the ruling body in Beijing. They had been watching him for some time, aware of his military record and rise through the ranks. They viewed his successes as exemplary and when the time came he was offered the post of heading the Zero Project. Chan had accepted with a show of humility, not revealing how he had been relishing the opportunity from the moment he had heard about it.

He was given a command, his own department within the military and the offices that went with such a promotion. Chan was allowed to choose staff from his own people and surrounded himself with intelligent and eager officers.

It was the job of a lifetime, one that placed him in the spotlight. Chan was astute enough to understand the responsibility placed upon him—and the penalty that would come if he failed. He took that as part of the price, and told himself he would not fail. The first few months of his new command were taken up by organizing his team, making contact with everyone he would need.

Chan was given carte blanche for anything he required, including foreign mercenaries in America who would carry out the actual kidnapping of Kaplan and hand him over to Chinese members of the organization. Those same Americans would be paid to carry out diversionary hits against Zero Command to—hopefully—put it out of action, even if for only a short time while Chan and his group, assisted by the recruited Dr. Melier, would work on Kaplan. Melier had already been working for Chan, finalizing his mind drugs for the time he would use them on the captured American. In seclusion the doctor had perfected his drugs and when word came that Kaplan was to be apprehended Melier was more than ready to make the trip from Paris to Switzerland.

There were many meetings Chan had to chair as he met and discussed what would be done when they took over Zero. In Chan's mind it was never *if* they took Zero over, it was always *when*, so strong was his conviction he would succeed.

He traveled around to his meetings by one of the Gulfstream jets assigned to him as part of his military commission, and it was on these interminable journeys that he pursued his affair with Jui Kai. He had long been attracted to the beautiful young woman, and she, it seemed, reciprocated. He had no idea she was simply playing the part she had cultivated and Chan was her target. After their initial meeting, it was easy for her to continue in her role. Kai had known that if Chan had a weakness it was for a pretty face and everything that went with it. He had a string of conquests behind him and, once bitten by the promise of interest, was easily seduced. If the high command knew of his peccadillos, and they most likely did, they made no comment. Someone like Xia Chan had strong emotions, and his attraction to the opposite sex, as long as it did not interfere with his work, was viewed as a minor flaw.

Over the weeks Chan and Kai met on a number of occasions as he took increasing flights to his string of meetings. Her willingness to return his attentions flattered the man. He made sure she became a permanent member of his flight crew. It allowed them time alone together and Chan used those meetings to entertain his young admirer. He was not an unattractive man. In his early forties and in excellent physical shape, he possessed a strong sexual drive and his trysts with Kai allowed him to demonstrate this to the younger woman. Kai, for her part, endured the liaisons and displayed the right amount of satisfaction to keep Chan happy.

Jui Kai took the intimacy in her stride. She was not particularly enjoying what happened, but her long training had forearmed her. The role she had undertaken had from the start implied that sexual liaisons might occur. She took it on board and when it happened she put up with the indignity. Her one consoling consideration was that Chan, though virile, was not an adventurous lover. It was straight, unimaginative sex. For that she was grateful, glad that Chan had no perverse demands.

She was his attentive romantic partner and used whatever chances she saw to gain the knowledge she needed to pass on to her US base.

The detailed information Kai gathered, mainly due to the listening mechanisms she had planted in Chan's clothing and briefcase—tiny devices developed by the electronics department of her agency—had revealed his deep involvement in the Zero operation. On a number of flights where she had served as flight attendant Chan had been in the company of military personnel and the

Zero plan had been discussed a number of times. The data recorded by Kai had been transmitted to Washington and deciphered by the linguistics teams there.

They'd learned of the increasing Chinese interest in Zero once more, which only served to further the interest of the intelligence community. The listening posts scanned every pickup source they could, from internet to Echelon, scanning and recording scraps of chatter coming to and going out of China.

Despite the earlier suggestions of something happening, the data came too late and the agency was caught off guard. They had believed something was brewing, but their attention had failed to grasp the closeness of the operation.

Saul Kaplan had been taken before it was realized the Chinese were already well into their plan. Incoming information stopped being transmitted in the days before Kaplan was kidnapped, catching everyone by surprise. By the time alerts were being sent out, the abduction had already happened.

"WHAT IS SHE doing here?" Zhou had asked on Kai's arrival at the house, ignoring any kind of protocol. "She is nothing but a flight attendant."

"Very clever of you to have noticed, Yang. To answer your question, she is here as my guest. My guest. As such, she will be treated with respect. I asked her because she will provide me with the conversation I miss. A brief distraction from what we are doing here."

"I do not—"

"Yang Zhou, please do not force me to remind you who is in charge of this operation—complete charge. I do not have to explain myself to you. Whether you like Miss Kai or not is something that does not interest me."

"Your safety is my concern."

Chan smiled. "My dear Yang Zhou, do you think she has come here to harm me? Perhaps you should search her to see if she is carrying a weapon. The young lady had no idea I was going to bring her here, so I doubt she has a devious plan she intends to carry out. Perhaps you would like to follow her around the house? No? Then I am going to sit over there with her and have a drink and talk. Just keep me informed about Dr. Melier's progress."

Chan returned to where Kai was standing near the fire, watching him with a faintly amused smile on her lips.

"Your bodyguard does not care for me," she said. "I am sure he believes I will teach you bad habits."

"Zhou does not care for anything but his work. I suppose that should please me, but at times he becomes an irritant. Devotion is one thing—obsession is another. Although I must admit I do have something of an obsession myself, Jui Kai." Chan offered her a seat. He sat across from her. "Let us not concern ourselves with Zhou. I would rather spend my time with you."

"I must admit to being a little embarrassed by all this attention. I am just a flight attendant. Flattered, of course, that you pay me such an honor, but I feel out of place here. I much prefer when we can be alone. Away from prying eyes. Even though it has to take place in the confines of your aircraft."

"I will not allow that," Chan said. "I insist that you enjoy yourself. In fact I will make it an official order. And stop being so coy. I know you are playing one of your little games. Not that you will find me ungrateful for that."

Jui Kai saw the smile on his lips as he spoke. Chan was making an effort to lessen her discomfort, so in her role as his subordinate she made a play of lowering her gaze and returning his smile.

"Then I will do as my superior requests," she said. "May I get you another drink?"

"Just a small one. I must not allow myself to have too much. Our work here is of great importance so I must devote much of my time to it."

"Of course. I am quite happy to enjoy the comfortable surroundings and wait until you are free."

"But nevertheless, we will eat together tonight. That I promise. In the meantime feel free to look around. My only word of caution concerns the room down the hall. You will find it guarded. No one is allowed to enter. Apart from that, the house is yours to enjoy."

Jui Kai found his words ironic.

Looking around and listening were matters she hoped to achieve. She thought about the high-tech sat phone in her pocket and hoped she might get the chance to send a message. She thought of Yang Zhou. Whatever she did would need to be done with care. If she was caught, her situation would alter drastically. Chan's bodyguard would react quickly if he suspected her of anything underhanded. He looked more of a real threat each time she was in his presence. She would need to be on her guard around him.

"To return to your comment about our relationship being tied to that aircraft—I am considering how we can be together more often. Outside your duties during my flights. Give me time, Miss Kai, and I will resolve our problem."

"I did not say it was a problem, Xia. Just that being restricted to the plane does not give us as much time as I wish for."

"I can make things happen, Kai."

Xia Chan felt good saying that. It was true.

He was Colonel Xia Chan of the SPD. He could make things happen.

Kai watched the increasingly heavy snowfall.

"Don't worry," Chan said. "We will be safe here. I am sending three of my people to the nearby town in the morning to increase our food supplies in case we do become stranded. You see, Jui, I think of everything."

A little while later Kai excused herself to go to the bathroom. Behind the locked door, she took the chance to send a coded text, informing her base of the situation. There was little she could do herself. If the snowstorm continued, she was going to be as cut off from the outside world as Chan and his group.

THE SNOW CONTINUED through the night. The fall was constant and, aided by the ever-present wind, snow piled up around the house.

As much as Chan wanted to be with Jui Kai, the way matters were developing with Kaplan, his night was spent observing Melier's treatment. He contented himself with the knowledge she was here in the house, and her presence pleased him. There would be time later for him to be with her.

Kai was forced to remain in the background, watching and listening to the events taking place. There was little else she could do for the present. She had managed to send her text and all she could do now was wait.

She slept fitfully in one of the empty bedrooms. She rose once she heard increased movement and refreshed herself in the bathroom before making her way to the kitchen and helping herself to a hot drink.

When she returned to the lounge again she found it deserted. The fire was burning, throwing welcome heat across the room.

Some time later Chan appeared. He looked tired, having spent most of the past few hours observing Melier at work. He had found the session interesting but tiring. He wanted results and he wanted them quickly. His earlier promise that Melier should have as much time as possible plagued him. It was immature of him to expect speedy results, he knew it, but the need to please his masters in Beijing forced him to expect too much, too soon.

He had arranged for a three-man team to prepare to leave, taking one of the large SUVs and setting out to collect the provisions they might need if the severe weather maintained its grip. A minor matter, but a necessary one.

He checked the deployment of the sentries patrolling outside. He knew they were not happy, now the weather had become so bad, but he remained indifferent to that; everyone had his duty and would be expected to perform it.

He spoke with Yang Zhou, who had inexplicably teamed up with the nearly silent Bolo; the pair prowled the house like a pair of Rottweilers.

Chan had a brief conversation with Kai, apologizing for the fact he was having to pursue his operations rather than spend more time with her. As usual, she was accommodating and told him she would wait until he was free.

Still, Chan experienced a feeling of disquiet. He did not know why.

CHAPTER TWENTY

Valens's phone vibrated and she took the call. Though disguised, she recognized the caller ID as her contact at the agency assisting their investigation of Saul Kaplan. Following a brief greeting, she listened to the update from Price.

"Okay, we'll handle it," Valens said. "This could be a direct threat aimed at Zero Command. Thanks for the intel."

"Watch your backs," Price warned. "It looks as if there *is* a leak. If the perp thinks he's been made, he might decide to make a fight of it."

"Noted," Valens said before she hung up. "If it's true, I look forward to getting my hands on that son of a bitch."

Valens collected Brandon and they headed out of doors, going for their SUV.

"You drive," Valens said.

"Be nice to know where we're going."

"Larry, you want everything to be made so easy for you," Valens said. She allowed him a leery grin then gave him the address. They drove out of the base, Brandon following the route displayed on the GPS.

"Don't these people understand the concept of the internet and having their banking details looked at?"

"They always believe they're the exception," Valens

said. "Rosen has taken the bait, accepted the money and tried to hide it. Like most, he's not as smart as he thinks he is."

"What amount are we talking about?"

"Totals up to almost a quarter mil in his account."

"And he never imagined that would be spotted?" Brandon shook his head. "It's like he wants to be caught. He's made it too easy. Almost takes the fun out of it."

"Don't get too sloppy. Sometimes these things turn around and bite you on the ass."

"Listening to your delicate turns of phrase is so uplifting, Agent Valens."

"Comes with experience."

They reached Rosen's address twenty minutes later. It was a small house on a quiet residential street. Being midmorning, it was quiet. No parked cars apart from those in driveways.

During the drive, Valens had contacted Detective Zeigler. He had agreed to keep his team out of sight initially, while Valens and Brandon made first contact.

"Pull over," Valens said while they were still a distance away.

When the car stopped, Brandon turned off the engine and they sat studying the area.

"You have that look in your eyes," he said. "Tell me what I can't see."

"Nice quiet street," Valens noted.

"Does that have to mean trouble?"

"Not necessarily," Valens said.

She opened her door and got out of the SUV. As Brandon followed, catching up with her long stride, he noticed she had opened her coat and had her right hand resting on the butt of her issue pistol.

That, he decided, did not bode well.

A small lawn fronted the house and ran alongside a concrete drive where a three-year-old Ford sat. Valens laid a hand on the hood. It was cold. She flicked a signal for Brandon to check the side and rear of the house. She took the front door, drawing her Glock as she passed the window. The blind was down, so she was unable to see inside.

"Doesn't have to be a warning sign," she said quietly to herself.

The front door was closed. Valens spotted the bell push. When she pressed it she heard the faint chime inside. They waited. Nothing happened. She hit the bell a second time.

Be patient, Claire.

Her cell vibrated in her pocket. She checked it. A text from Brandon: Come around back. Not good.

Brandon was waiting at the door, Glock in his fist. The look on his face told Valens she would have been waiting a long time for someone to answer the front door.

The back door led into the kitchen.

A body lay on the tiled floor. Facedown. The back of the man's head was a shattered mess. Among the splintered bone and torn flesh the mass of the bullet-impacted brain could be seen. A large blood pool spread across the tiles from under the side-turned head.

"Damn," Valens swore.

Even through the glass of the door she could recognize Harry Rosen's face. She pushed her pistol into the holster and reached into her coat to pull out latex gloves, working them on. She tried the door and found it unlocked. She pushed it wide. Before she did anything else, she took out her Glock again, nodding to Brandon. They cleared the door quickly, staying well clear of the body.

Valens keyed her cell and told Zeigler he could move in.

Brandon worked his way around the edges of the kitchen, moving to the door leading through. He vanished from sight. Valens looked around the kitchen. Nothing out of place except for the body. She crouched and put fingers against the side of Rosen's neck. No pulse and the flesh was already cooling.

Brandon said, "Clear."

Valens stood. She wished things were, but in reality the day was far from being clear.

Zeigler and his team appeared.

DETECTIVE JERRY ZEIGLER, hands deep in the pockets of his topcoat, stared around the living room of Rosen's house.

"Nice place," he said.

Valens smiled. She knew that statement was far from what Zeigler was really thinking. This was the second time they had met recently, and, as with the first time, a body was involved.

Behind them the kitchen was full of Zeigler's investigative team. They were checking for evidence. Measuring. Photographing. Taking down every detail that might help in them reach some kind of conclusion.

"Are we going to have the same dance, Agent Valens? Please tell me it isn't so. No disclosure? No names?"

"As far as I'm concerned, *Jerry*, this is all yours. Harry Rosen is a civilian. Murdered in his own home on your turf."

Zeigler glanced around. "Let me find a chair to sit in. I'm not used to shocks like that this early in the day."

"I told you last time," Valens said. "When the time comes I would hand over to you."

"So what else can you tell me?"

"Rosen was a civilian contractor working at the base. He handled computer maintenance. Been doing it for almost a year. Good worker. Did his job, came and went. Never any problem."

"But something was off?"

"While we were running checks following the recent incident, it was found Rosen had been getting large cash deposits into his bank account. Way above anything he could earn from his day job. We came to have a talk with him. The rest you know."

"Looks like somebody didn't want Rosen saying too much. My instincts are telling me you left something out, Valens. It's been a good visit up to now. Do not spoil it."

"I can tell you the money Rosen received came from a suspect source."

"Hmm…"

Valens smiled. "You have a sharp nose, Jerry. The money came via routes we sourced back to a foreign agency. We believe it has a connection to the previous matter."

"Your dead Air Force guy and his missing passenger?"

"It's becoming extremely complicated."

"So complicated you can't let me in any further?"

Valens took a breath, considering what she was about to say. Zeigler was a solid guy. He was a cop ready to do his job, and drawing him in a little further might get Valens more information.

"Detective Zeigler—Jerry—if I lose my job over this I *will* blame you. Right now my investigation is stalling. So I will give you what I can. The kidnap victim is Saul Kaplan. Works out of the base where I'm assigned. He heads a department involved in work that comes under the umbrella of national security. The project is vital to the country's defense capability and we are in the know that the people who took him are attempting to coerce him into giving away his knowledge."

Zeigler took in what Valens said with a weary smile.

"Makes a change from the usual crimes I deal with. What can I do?" Zeigler asked. "I don't suppose you want to tell me exactly what it is this Kaplan is working on?"

"No can do, Jerry. My generosity with giving away information has to stop there."

"Dumb of me to ask."

Larry Brandon joined them. "One of your techs says he's pretty sure the slug is a 9 mm. It'll be confirmed when he gets the autopsy done." He glanced at Valens. "How is this going down?"

"Local police will run the main investigation and we'll work our part in tandem." Valens sensed Brandon might come up with an objection. "As I explained to Zeigler, this is an urgent case, so any help they can offer will be gratefully received."

BRANDON COULD HAVE said something, but he had noticed the expression in Valens's eyes so he stayed silent. Regardless of her slipping over the official line he could see she was doing her best with a difficult situation. Brandon understood Valens's driving force. She had been through a bad enough time on the earlier incident. It could not have been enjoyable for her to be faced by a similar occurrence.

CHAPTER TWENTY-ONE

Switzerland

By morning, with the snow still falling, the house was essentially isolated. There was a thick blanket of white over everything beyond the window and Saul Kaplan had tried to fix his attention on the fall, but Melier was doing things close by and distracting him.

"I hope you are not going to say this will hurt you more than it hurts me," Kaplan said.

"Then I will not," Melier said.

He held out a hand and Nan Cheng passed him a hypodermic.

Kaplan watched with concern in his eyes. He winced slightly as Melier inserted the slender needle into his arm and depressed the plunger. As the contents were injected into his arm, he felt a slight burning sensation that caused him to take a quick breath.

"Unfortunately for you," Melier said, "this is the first of many, I am afraid. Unless you wish to end this and give me the information I require."

Kaplan ignored him, focusing on the snow falling beyond the window at the far end of the conservatory. He imagined the flakes touching his skin. Cool and so light they had no weight to them. He tried to push aside the warm flow of the solution Melier had put in his body, but it was difficult to dismiss it so easily. It was almost as if he could track the course of the chemical as it traveled. Could feel the insidious way it crept up to his brain, fingering its way into the core of his being. He sensed movement at his side and saw Dr. Melier move into his line of sight. The man's expression was neutral as he stared down at Kaplan. Beyond Melier the rest of the room had become a soft blur, everything slightly out of focus. Kaplan blinked his eyes. It made no difference.

"Please do not try to fight the effects, Kaplan. It will not help," Melier said.

Kaplan wanted to speak. When he tried, his speech was already slurred, his mouth not obeying. Confused thoughts overlapped inside his head. He wanted to tell Melier to go to hell—he found he was unable to form the words. Coherent thought was slipping out of his head. He attempted to concentrate, to make sense of what was happening. Nothing happened. He might have panicked but he couldn't understand why he wanted to.

"*Is...it...working?*"

Nan Cheng's voice came from a distance. Although Kaplan managed to make out the words, he failed to understand what they meant.

Melier nodded. "Far quicker than I expected."

"So much for his resistance."

"I believe Kaplan's intellect is allowing the chemical to be absorbed faster. His brain is able to interpret the chemical signature so much quicker because it needs to learn what is happening on a higher level. If it goes on this way, Kaplan will find himself overwhelmed, even though his brain function operates on a speedier level." Melier felt a surge of excitement. This was working far better than he had hoped for. "Pass me the second dose," he said.

As Cheng picked up the syringe, he glanced at Kaplan's rigid expression. His eye moving back and forth as he struggled to resist.

"Is it safe to give him more so quickly?"

"I assessed the dosages during my trials," Melier said. "My results told me a follow-up injection into healthy individual was not liable to create any untoward effects. Kaplan is an excellent subject."

Cheng watched as Melier delivered the second injection. Reaction this time was slower in coming.

Kaplan's body curved up off the couch, eyes wide. A sheen of perspiration glistened on the taut flesh of his face. He began to mumble in a low monotone, his words meaningless. Cheng moved closer, but Melier reached out a restraining hand.

"Leave him," he said. "This will pass." He led Cheng across the room. "We must leave him while the chemicals work on his nervous system. He will rest, and when he wakes he will be ready to talk to me. Answer my questions."

"YOU REMEMBER ME? Dr. Melier. We spoke earlier."

Kaplan looked at him, eyes searching Melier's face. His expression was bland. Empty. He ran his tongue over his dry lips.

"I'm thirsty."

"Bring him some water," Melier said.

Cheng tipped cold water from one of the insulated jugs and handed it to Kaplan. He drank hurriedly, spilling some water down his front.

"Not so fast," Melier advised.

Kaplan held out the tumbler for more. This time he drank slowly until the tumbler was empty.

"Better?"

Kaplan nodded.

"Good. Now, where were we… Oh, yes…you were giving me details of the encryption codes for Zero. The operating procedures."

Kaplan faced him, brow furrowing as he made to recall what he had supposedly been telling Melier.

"I don't remember…"

"Take your time, Saul. There is no rush."

Kaplan slumped against the chair back and stared over Melier's shoulder at the falling snow.

"It must have been falling for a long time," he said. "The ground is covered quite deeply. How long have I been here?"

"A while, Saul. Now let us go back to what you were telling me about Zero's codes."

Melier looked across at Cheng, then at the recording device, as if to convince himself it was still operating. Cheng nodded gently.

Over the next couple of hours Melier spoke quietly to Kaplan. His voice was low, coaxing, drawing words from the American. His persuasive tone had a soothing effect on Kaplan, who kept reaching across to gently rub the spot on his arm where he had taken the hypodermic needles as he responded to Melier's questions.

When Kaplan showed signs of fatigue, Melier allowed him to rest. Kaplan closed his eyes.

"Pause the recording," Melier said.

Cheng did so. He shook his head as he looked from Kaplan to Melier.

"It is amazing. He shows no resistance to your questions. Answers most of them without a struggle. And his vital signs are giving normal readings."

"More than I had hoped for at this stage," Melier said. "Tell Chan we have some answers he might be interested in. I believe he is going to be extremely pleased at what we have learned so far."

WHEN CHAN ENTERED the room, Melier presented him with the digital recorder.

"What you have been waiting for," he said. "Only a small amount of data, but enough, I believe, for you to attack the Zero system."

"My congratulations, Dr. Melier. My faith in you has not been wrong." Chan glanced at the resting man. "Will he be able to give you more?"

"I believe so. Now he needs to rest. Later I will administer more of my formula and talk with him again."

"If you will excuse me," Chan said, "I must deliver this to my technician. He is as anxious as I to make some headway."

Chan made his way through the house to the room that had been designated for the purpose. It was equipped with high-end electronics, the computers extremely powerful and the internet connections of the highest caliber.

Seated at the main station was Tien, the man Chan had selected himself many weeks previously. Tien was considered one of the brightest techs available. He swung around in his chair when Chan came into the room.

"Something for you, Tien. What we have both been waiting for."

He passed over the digital device. Tien, young, his

eyes bright with anticipation, took the recorder and quickly made the connections that fed into his tower. His fingers flashed across the keyboard, inputting instructions.

The monitor in front of him flashed alive, codes and numbers scrolling across the screen. Chan understood very little of what he was seeing. He held back his impatience as Tien continued manipulating the on-screen display. Finally he sat back and laid his hands on the desktop.

"What are we waiting for?" Chan said.

"To see if Zero accepts the input. The codes from Kaplan should integrate with the mainframe on the platform. It may take some minutes. At this moment it is all down to the two operating systems. Mine and Zero's."

"If you have a few minutes to spare," someone said behind Chan, "there is something important you should be aware of."

Chan turned and faced Zhou.

"What are you talking about, Yang Zhou?"

Zhou held up a slim black device. "This," he said. "An extremely efficient signal tracker. It can locate any cell phone being used."

"I gave orders that no calls be made," Chan said.

Zhou raised the tracker.

"Then let us see who has defied you. Shall we?"

Something in the almost triumphant expression on Zhou's face told Chan he was not going to like the answer.

CHAPTER TWENTY-TWO

Jui Kai had learned that much of her time during an assignment would be spent simply observing. It was something she had forced herself to accept. Making sudden, impulsive moves would more likely lead to her exposing herself than to achieving anything of use. Resigned to waiting for Chan, she relaxed in the comfort of the lounge chair, stared at the fire in front of her and thought about her consignment.

Since taking on her shadowing of Colonel Chan, that need had grown. Over the past months, since her deliberate action at making herself always available to him, Chan had become more amenable. That worked in Kai's favor. He called on her frequently, and always when he took yet another of his flights. The man had an involved lifestyle, taking him back and forth across the country for endless meetings and discussions. Since becoming the man in charge of the Zero affair, his workload had increased. Kai took advantage of this, making herself totally available when he wanted to see her, and his influence meant there were no problems in her life.

In the fairly regimented Chinese society, Jui Kai was able to move around freely. That suited her needs, because being able to come and go meant she had free time for reporting to her control, keeping them up to date.

Even Jui Kai had had no idea about the plan to kidnap Saul Kaplan. The matter had been kept very secret; Chan had kept the operations close. There had been no hint of anything untoward even when she was with him. She had to give him full marks for remaining silent in that respect. The first time she'd learned about the abduction was during the flight to Switzerland; she had overheard the colonel and Zhou talking.

Zhou had seemed alarmed at the way Chan discussed the operation in front of her. Chan had simply waved away his displeasure.

"The deed is done, Zhou. Please do not worry yourself."

As she'd returned to her position in the galley, Kai had already worked out how to pass on the information, knowing she could not risk using her cell phone while they were in flight. Once in her room at the hotel, she'd sent a short text to her US contact, advising that she would follow up with additional information if and when she gained any.

It had come as an unexpected surprise when Chan had sent his car to pick her up from the Swiss hotel. She'd gathered a few things, made a quick change of clothing and gone quickly down to the waiting car. It had already started to snow as the car left the hotel and followed the road that led into the surrounding landscape. Kai had had no idea where the car was heading and, though curious, she'd asked no questions so as not to arouse any suspicions with the driver.

Arriving at the isolated residence, she'd known immediately that Chan had chosen well. If this was where he had brought Kaplan he had picked the right place. There were no other houses anywhere near. The place was surrounded by wooded areas, the terrain behind the mansion rising in a series of slopes to the snowcapped mountains. Kai remembered hoping there would be a signal for her phone if she had the chance to send out a location.

Chan had been his usual charming self, making her feel welcome. The interior of the house was stylish, well appointed and expansive. In fact the only fault was in the shape of Yang Zhou; the man exuded hostility. He'd made no secret of the fact he hadn't approved of her presence, but Chan had overruled his objections.

The logs in the fire pit crackled, breaking into her thoughts. Kai shifted and slipped her cell from her pocket to check the signal, relieved to find the bars were at maximum level. She always made sure the phone was kept fully charged, too.

Slipping the phone back into her pocket, she stood and crossed to the wet bar to add ice to the tumbler. It allowed her to pass the arched opening that gave access to the passage beyond.

Zhou was there, talking to the man she knew as Bolo. They showed no indication they had noticed her, but their presence was simply enough to alert her.

For a moment she wondered if they had seen her check her phone. She dismissed the idea. She had been on the far side of the wide lounge, her back to the arch and hidden by the rear of the armchair. Despite that, she reminded herself to be wary in their presence and not give them any reason to become suspicious.

Kai returned to her seat and sat back. She had to admit it felt good, seated before the blaze in the hearth while beyond the double-glazed window the snow continued to fall; the Swiss certainly knew how to protect themselves from the extremes of the weather.

She felt herself becoming slightly drowsy, and started when Chan suddenly appeared at her side, his approach silent on the thick carpeting.

"I believe you could become used to this comfortable life," he said, taking the armchair close by. He held a filled tumbler in one hand.

Kai smiled. "It would be easy," she said.

"We should take advantage of it while we can."

"That sounds as if everything could change quickly."

"The needs of the state come first," Chan said. "But not for some time yet. I have arranged for a meal to be brought here for us."

"You spoil me."

Chan smiled. "Let me enjoy these small pleasures, Jui Kai."

"Of course." Kai sipped her drink. "I could not help but overhear your conversation on the plane. This man, Kaplan? He is important to our country?"

Chan drank. "He has information that could be of great use to us. I decided to bring him here where we would not be disturbed while we talk to him."

Kai raised her glass. "Then I wish you success, my dear Chan, in whatever you do."

"At least my time here will be spent in your enchanting company."

Kai indicated the heavy snowfall. "That may be a long time."

"Something we had not anticipated," Chan said. "Though at this time of year, and this being Switzerland, perhaps a little insight might have been called for."

Kai laughed, partly for Chan, but just as much for

herself. If they became cut off here, her opportunity
to let her US control know became more of a reality.

That need became paramount when Zhou came into
the room and called Chan to his side, speaking quietly.
Kai deliberately pretended to concentrate on the snowfall beyond the window, though she was able to see the
reflection of Chan and Zhou. The low murmur of Zhou's
voice reached her in the otherwise silent room and she
picked up on a little of his conversation.

"Melier…needs…speak with you," Zhou said.
"…Urgent…breakthrough…with Kaplan…"

"Excuse me, my dear," Chan said, returning to her.

"Business first," Kai said, her tone casual.

Chan followed Zhou from the room, leaving Kai
alone. Though not entirely alone. She spotted Bolo still
in the passage, standing motionless.

As solid as a block of granite, she decided.

She recalled the names Zhou had used.

Melier, the chemical interrogator.

More significant was Kaplan.

Here in the house. Under Chan's control, with Dr.
Melier attending.

Not, Kai realized, a very good combination.

Saul Kaplan had the Zero data inside his head.

And Dr. Luc Melier stole information from inside
human minds.

And they were all here, heading for a shutdown on
travel if the weather stayed the way it was.

As far as Kai was concerned getting another message out had become imperative. She needed to inform
home that all the Beijing players were here, gathered
under one roof.

Where was a superhero when you wanted one?

She reminded herself of Zhou's hostility and was forced to consider his observation of her since coming to the house, even though it had been at Chan's invitation. It had been a break for Kai, but she needed to stay alert because Zhou seemed to be taking more of an interest in her. Especially now that he had apparently recruited Bolo to stay around while he accompanied Chan.

She needed to warn her agency that Kaplan was here and obviously under some kind of pressure. The sooner she did that the better. Waiting any longer would not work in her favor. Jui Kai was starting to get the feeling she was on a short leash.

She rose and crossed to stand closer to the open hearth, moving so that she could observe Bolo; as a watcher he was less than discreet. Kai went to stare out the window, fingering the compact cell in her pocket. The reflection in the window showed Bolo was still observing.

She made her decision and returned to her earlier position in the armchair, which placed her with her back to the corridor, hidden by the high back of the chair. She slipped the cell from her pocket and held it in her lap, fingers quickly powering it out of sleep mode. As soon as the bars showed, Kai brought up the call list and accessed the texting facility.

Checking the number she needed, she put in the text and pressed the send key. The message sat for what seemed a long time. Kai breathed relief when the message was sent. She left the cell open, using it as a signaling device, and slipped it down between the seat cushion and the back of the armchair. Hopefully the cell would transmit until the battery ran down; she hoped there would be a pickup of the signal. Kai accepted that there might not be anything her home base could do, but sending the text made her feel as if she was still carrying out her mission.

With the message sent, there was little else she could do. There was no way she was going to be able to get close to Saul Kaplan. Chan would have the man under strict guard and she was without any kind of weapon. All she could do was monitor the situation.

Chan was gone for a long time.

Kai waited. Inactivity unsettled her. She understood her delicate situation. She was alone in the enemy camp, so to speak, with no kind of backup.

YANG ZHOU CAME into the lounge unannounced sometime later, his face flushed with anger. Bolo was close on his heels.

Kai could see Zhou's image in the window. He appeared to be holding a compact black object in his left hand and was moving it around, as if searching for something. The determined way he crossed the room in her direction warned her something was wrong. She turned in the seat, catching the expression in his eyes. Before she could fully react, Zhou reached out and closed his right hand around her arm, yanking her from the seat and dragging her to her feet.

Over his shoulder she saw Chan in the background, watching.

"Traitorous bitch," Zhou said.

"What have I—?"

She got no more of her words out. Zhou's powerful backhand caught her across the side of her face, the blow landing with brutal force. Kai felt her head snap to the side and as Zhou released his hand from her arm she stumbled to her knees. The side of her face burned from the blow and Kai tasted blood in her mouth where her teeth had cut flesh. A hand, Bolo's, took hold of her hair, yanking her upright so that her face was fully exposed when Zhou struck her again. This time a hard-fisted punch tore her lips and drove her to the floor on her back. Zhou stood over her, his face flushed with rage, eyes raking her with undisguised revulsion. He slammed a foot into her side, over her ribs. The blow was full-on, the pain unbearable, and Kai cried out.

Bolo moved into Kai's line of vision and she stared at him through eyes misted by tears. He leaned over and took hold of her, lifting her to her feet as if she was a child. He held her while Zhou struck her again and again until she was limp in Bolo's hands, head hanging. Zhou hit her face and body with powerful, well-delivered blows. Her blood dripped in steady streams from her mouth and the torn flesh of her cheeks.

When the beating stopped, Zhou stepped back. He held up the object in his hand. It was some kind of electronic device. It produced a low, steady sound as he moved it back and forth, the decibels increasing when he moved to stand beside the chair she had been using. Zhou extended his arm, the signal getting louder, steadier. He leaned forward, reaching down with his right hand and when he raised it again he was holding Kai's cell phone. He turned the phone to show the still-open setting.

"Switched on to maintain an active signal. Colonel Chan will be most disappointed when he learns you are a spy," Zhou said.

Kai could barely hear him. She was only just conscious. Her left eye had already swollen shut and she was in agony. She tried to move her jaw but it had been hit so hard it felt dislocated. Her entire body burned with crippling pain and it was hard to even breathe. Her only coherent thought was centered on the text she had sent, hoping it had really gotten through…if it had then it would confirm where Kaplan was being imprisoned.

She was unaware that Chan had come all the way into the room.

He brought up short when he saw the state of the young woman with whom he had been spending time.

"Is it true?" he asked Zhou.

"Yes," Zhou said. "Our scan showed a cell phone signal in the house. We traced it. It came from this room." He showed the phone to Chan and allowed him to see the open signal. "I think it is time we turned this off," he said.

Zhou shut the phone down. He opened the back and removed the power pack and SIM card.

Chan sighed tiredly. He refused to look at Kai. "Then I owe you an apology, Yang Zhou. I should have listened to you when you raised your concerns."

Zhou shrugged. "Let us hope we have done enough to prevent any further interference."

"My own vanity," Chan said. "I allowed it to cloud my judgment."

"Now that it is clear again, what do you want to do with her?"

"Let us decide that later, Zhou. For now lock her in the cellar. It will allow her time to reflect on her errors."

"It is extremely cold down there," Zhou said. "She may not survive for very long."

"That would be a shame. I hope you can hear me, Jui Kai. Instead of a warm bed, you will spend the night in the cellar. Bolo, take her away. If she resists, make her aware how we treat traitors."

Bolo half carried the young woman from the room.

"Has the American given away any useful information yet?" Zhou said.

"Actually he has," Chan said. "Hopefully there will be more to come. Dr. Melier's potions have worked with surprising swiftness. Even he is surprised at the speed in which Kaplan gave up some of his secrets."

"Melier is extremely proficient. So what have we learned?"

"Enough to allow us to infiltrate a section of the ordnance system."

"Missile control?"

"One of the auxiliary pods apparently. It would be enough to launch a single missile if we wish to demonstrate our capability."

"Only one?"

"My dear Zhou, do not forget that Zero is an extremely sophisticated platform containing hundreds, maybe even thousands, of electronic functions. We have barely scratched the surface here. Far less than we need. The cryptic codes that will unlock more and more of Zero's operating procedures are not to be broken easily."

"If the Americans become aware we are attempting to break through the codes, won't they simply change them?"

"A valid point, Zhou, but remember we have the one man who can override any changes. Kaplan retains master codes that can break through any cyber walls thrown in his way."

"And they are the harder ones to reach?"

"Exactly. Kaplan is the master key needed to unlock Zero's cyber vault. Dr. Melier is attempting to go further into Kaplan's mind to reveal more of Zero's secrets."

CHAPTER TWENTY-THREE

Phoenix Force traveled overnight from the US on a charter aircraft organized by Barbara Price with her usual efficiency. By the time McCarter and company had showed up at Stony Man Farm, Price had had their paperwork ready, including passports, entry visas and the usual credit cards made out under the group's cover names. When they touched down, there was a smattering of snow across the Alps and a forecast of heavy falls—imminent—with a wide bank of viscous, darker cloud that appeared to be moving slowly into the general area.

As the five trooped out of the Lear jet, hauling their gear, they felt the cutting chill of the wind. In his luggage each man had extreme-weather gear Price had informed them they would need.

"Didn't anyone understand when I said I was a Florida man," Encizo complained.

"Yeah, we understood," Hawkins said, "but we chose to ignore it."

"Thanks for the support."

"You're welcome," Hawkins said, offering a dazzling smile.

They moved into the arrival area and presented their paperwork at the desk. McCarter told the officials they weren't there for pleasure but rather for business. That they were a research group looking into climate conditions for an American organization. He presented a folder that held paperwork to that effect, including official visas that Stony Man's documentation section had prepared. The uniformed officials processed their entry quickly and without fuss, stamping passports and offering the usual greeting.

From there the five went to the rental desk and McCarter told the blonde, blue-eyed young woman they had two vehicles already booked. The procedure went smoothly and with lots of smiles from the young woman. She handed over the paperwork and the keys and directed Phoenix Force to the exit door. An identical pair of Volvo SUVs stood waiting, already fully fuelled and ready. McCarter and Manning took one. The others piled into the second vehicle. The first thing Manning did was tap in the GPS coordinates for the hotel Price had arranged. The heater started to circulate warm air around the interior as Manning drove out of the lot.

The road they traveled led them higher up into the mountain slopes. The scenery was inspiring, with forested acres and the majestic rise of the Alps ahead. Even now they could see the snow sitting deeply on the higher elevations of the mountains. The wind was pushing scraps of falling snowflakes back and forth.

"So, do we have a plan?" Manning asked.

McCarter, stretched out in his leather seat, considered the question.

"Good one, Gary. Straight to the point and putting me on the spot."

"Thought so. You have no plan. I guess this is going to be one of your 'plunge in and see where it goes' schemes."

"Assess the situation and develop a strategy," McCarter said. "Right now that's what I'm doing."

McCarter glanced through the windshield.

"If we get snow it could help when we make our move," he said. "Provide cover. Come on, Gary, you're from the frozen north. Don't you see the advantage?"

Manning grinned. "That's your strategy?"

McCarter shrugged. "Could be."

"Brother, we could be in trouble."

It took almost an hour and a half to reach the hotel.

Barbara Price, with her usual skill, had booked Phoenix Force into a resort some twenty miles from the target house. It was the closest she could get the team. The Swiss countryside was pretty isolated after that. The rising mountain slopes, thick with swaths of trees and foliage, had few houses, and even these were all widely spaced across the landscape. The hotel parking lot was empty except for a single, powerful-looking Porsche.

"Barb said not to be surprised if the area is quiet," McCarter said. "We're a few weeks shy of the skiing season."

"She got that right," Manning said.

The circling mountain range, showing white on the high peaks and upper slopes, was overhung by a blue sky that held scraps of white cloud. The air was sharp, cold, but the dark mass of heavy cloud they had seen earlier was being driven in their direction by a rising wind.

"I wouldn't be surprised if we had snow any time now," Hawkins said, humping luggage out of the SUV.

"You know what you're talking about?" Encizo quipped. "Son of the plainsman."

Manning said, "He could be right."

"Canada mountain man talks with slippery tongue," James said, a wide grin on his face.

Hawkins wagged a finger at him. "You won't be laughing when you're butt deep in the drifts, brother."

Phoenix Force trailed inside the spacious lobby and crossed to the desk.

The interior was all pale wood, high beams and polished floors. Behind the reception desk a middle-aged man in dark shirt and pants waited to greet them.

"Mr. Coyle and party, yes?"

McCarter took the man's outstretched hand.

"I am Bertran Yudell," he said. "I welcome you to our humble establishment."

"This is the kind of humble I could get used to," James said.

"So, let us get you all booked in," Yudell said. "I have the cards for registration here. Your very nice lady who arranged the booking has provided all your details and your account is open for you."

The formalities took only a few minutes. Key cards were handed over.

"Do you wish for help with your luggage?" Yudell asked.

"No, thank you," McCarter said. "We'll be fine."

"A package was delivered for you, Herr Coyle. It is in your room."

"My camera equipment," McCarter said. "I'd hoped it would arrive safely. There was some delay with the correct models. Let's hope we received what I asked for."

"The young woman I spoke to assured me everything was in order. A very pleasant young lady."

"I'll be sure to let her know," McCarter said.

"Is there anything I can get you?"

"How about some hot coffee?" Manning suggested. "Give us ten minutes to settle in and we can take it in the lounge over there."

"Of course, gentlemen. I will arrange that."

Taking their luggage, the members of Phoenix Force followed the indicator board and climbed the stairs to the next floor. Locating their rooms, they settled their luggage, including the locked cases.

Alone in his room, McCarter made sure the door was locked before crossing to inspect the package Price had arranged to be delivered. When he lifted it he found it to be solid. Opening it, he discovered the reason. Beneath the layers of foam and insulation were five 9 mm handguns and the same number of Cold Steel Tanto tactical knives in sheaths. The handguns comprised four Beretta 92FS models and one Browning Hi-Power, McCarter's favorite. Each pistol was accompanied by a pair of loaded magazines and a shoulder rig. Identical screw-on suppressors for the pistols had also been included. At the base of the package lay a row of flash-bang canisters that, McCarter knew, could be used as an entry diversion.

"Everything except the kitchen sink," McCarter said. "One day, love, I'm going to find out how you work these bloody miracles."

McCarter knew that Stony Man, with the long-term expertise of Mack Bolan, had set up a number of ordnance suppliers in certain areas of the globe. These clandestine outfits provided matériel for select clientele and the Farm was one of them. In the case of Stony Man, contact was made under highly secure covers, all transactions carried out via cash and with no paperwork attached. Purchases were delivered by carriers who were discreet and highly professional.

Once he had checked the weapons, McCarter closed the package and placed it at the back of his closet, locking it and pocketing the key. The weapons would be distributed later to his teammates.

THEY MET UP again downstairs, making their way to the lounge area, where comfortable armchairs were placed around the log fire burning in the generous hearth. One wall of the lounge allowed a wide view of the slopes beyond. As soon as Phoenix Force was settled, a young woman pushed in a wheeled trolley with the requested coffee as well as platters of cuts of cold meat and cheeses. There was also sliced bread and Swiss butter.

Herr Yudell appeared standing to one side as he watched his guests help themselves.

"Please do not hesitate to ask for anything else you require, gentlemen."

"At the moment it's fine," James said.

"I hope you enjoy your stay while you are here. Business or pleasure, we will endeavor to make your time in my country an enjoyable one."

"So," Manning said after Yudell had departed, "are we geared up for business, or only pleasure?"

"Something tells me fun and games are not likely to be on the agenda," McCarter said. "But we now have the necessary tools. Thanks to our guardian angel back home."

Phoenix Force was alone in the lounge. No other guests were around as they drank their coffee and sampled the food provided.

"We'll need to send Barb a thank-you card for all this," James said.

"That we will," McCarter said, refilling his coffee cup. "Spend too much time here and we'll forget why we came."

Encizo said, "Somehow I don't think so."

James had brought his laptop with him. He opened it and powered up. He tapped in the coded sequence for a secure connection to the Farm's satellite and waited. Within minutes, he was able to log in and video connect with the Zero Command site.

Claire Valens came on screen.

"Good to see you," she said.

"And you," James said. "Any news?"

"You're pretty up to speed," Valens said. "We're just waiting for a report from you."

"As of now we're at the hotel, where they serve bloody good coffee."

"And snacks," Hawkins interjected.

Valens smiled. She didn't deny them the right to their moment of relaxation. Once they moved out to engage the enemy, the lighter moments would fade quickly. Thrust into the unpredictable and violent heat of battle, any comfort they might gain would be swiftly torn away.

Her brief attachment to the team had already showed her their level of professionalism. They tackled matters head-on, using speed and force, and had no qualms when it came to handing out terminal justice. They handled violent situations with a determination that might have shocked someone not used to such efficiency. Valens had had her share of encounters and she was no beginner, but she admired this tight group of men who worked as one combined unit. They acted on impulse, each seeming to know what the other expected. It was a bonding that could not be learned from a training manual; it was born and developed through extremes of combat, where each man looked out for his brother in arms. There would be nothing that would split these men apart. Nothing that could break the affinity they had going. There did not seem to be any awkwardness in their actions. They were, she knew, true professionals.

Claire Valens felt a faint shiver of reaction as she listened to the brief reports from McCarter and Manning. They relayed the information in direct, unemotional tones that told her she was in the presence of real professionals. Valens understood their way and in no way criticized how they operated. They were soldiers who lived in a different world than most.

The enemy they were facing now was determined to wrest control of Zero from America and they would show little compassion as they made that attempt. In Valens's eyes the struggle she was part of had become as close to a war situation as she had ever been. She understood the need to push aside conventional tactics and to take the struggle to the enemy. Here and now, like it or not, they were engaged in a battle to deny an enemy their spoils.

The undeclared battle for control of Zero was under way.

"You have everything you need?"

"A squad of battle tanks and a platoon of combat troops wouldn't go amiss," Manning said.

"I wish I could conjure them up," Valens said.

"One thing you could do," McCarter said. "Access Zero and check out upcoming weather conditions for our location."

"That I can do."

Valens called up Zero and Doug Buchanan on a video link as Phoenix Force listened in.

"Our team in Switzerland needs a weather update, Doug. Can you guys deliver that?" She was aware of her collective request. Without even being deliberate she was seeing Buchanan and Zero as a combined entity; it was becoming an easy option.

"We will consolidate our data and offer a prediction," Zero advised.

"He means yes," Buchanan said.

"I figured that."

Valens could see one of Buchanan's wall monitors showing a time-lapse sequence of weather over the Swiss landscape, the image changing and overlapping as Zero's computers relayed the images.

"It's looking like a big snowfall sliding in," Buchanan said. He worked the touch screen in front of him, bringing up more data. "Coming down from the north. It should hit any time now. It's going to be massive."

"That isn't what we want to hear," Valens said.

"The prediction is accurate," Zero said.

"I don't doubt you're right. Okay, I'll pass that along."

"Keep us in the loop," Buchanan said.

Valens's face reappeared on the Phoenix Force laptop screen.

"Looks like you're in for a big snowstorm anytime," she said. "That going to be a big problem?"

"One of our talents is being able to work around problems like this."

"We'll try to keep you advised."

"Okay," James said. "We'll come back once we make our plans."

He shut down the laptop.

Encizo, who had been standing at the lounge window, pointed with his coffee cup.

"It's over the peaks," he said, "and heading our way."

McCarter joined him and they watched the dark mass gathering. Trees closer to the hotel were swaying as a wind swept in from the higher slopes. The first big flakes began to appear, swirling in toward them. The intensity of the wind snatched at the first flakes as the fall began in earnest.

McCarter muttered something under his breath and returned to his seat. He poured himself another coffee. His mind was working overtime as he assessed what was happening on the other side of the glass. He viewed it from both angles.

Falling snow could give Phoenix Force cover as they moved in on Chan's lair. That was a plus. Adverse weather would make it harder for the opposition to see anyone coming. On the negative side, it could work against Phoenix Force if the fall became really heavy—which was likely in this part of the country. Operating in the middle of a snowstorm, in low temperatures, could turn out to be restrictive. There was, McCarter decided, no alternative. The team would make their move and rely on experience and sheer nerve to carry the strike through. Either way the assault on the site might become a less than attractive deal. Not that the Briton had envisaged it being a walk in the park.

Just another obstacle to overcome. McCarter smiled.

What the hell was he expecting?

Going up against Colonel Chan and his force was never going to be easy. The Chinese had their prize and they weren't about to give it up without a fight.

"We rest up overnight and move in the morning. Snow or not, we have to go for it," McCarter said. "Weatherwise we don't have any choice. No way of knowing how this bloody bloke Chan is going to push things along. The longer we wait, the less chance Kaplan has."

He picked up the laptop and waited for the secure connection to Zero Command, informing Valens that the snow had arrived.

"You watch yourselves," she said. "Chan isn't going to cut you any slack, I'm sure." She was distracted by the signal from her cell phone that a text had arrived. Turning back to the screen, she said, "You might want to hear this text from Jui Kai. Chan is sending a three-man team to pick up extra provisions in the morning. He's convinced the coming snowfall might lock them into the house, so he's making sure they have backup supplies. That's three less for you to have to deal with."

"Only if we stop them from returning. Thanks for the intel, Claire. We'll get on that."

The Phoenix Force leader ended the link, his thoughts on what the morning would bring.

With evening coming on and the sky darkening quickly around the area, McCarter advised Phoenix Force there was little else they could do now. There was no argument when he suggested they turn in. They needed the rest a few hours of sleep would offer, helping them shake off the lingering effects of jet lag. The flight had not been as long as some Phoenix Force had experienced, but adjusting to the new environment was a wise move. They would need the reserves the coming day would expect.

CHAPTER TWENTY-FOUR

They were up at first light.

McCarter handed out the weapons and other ordnance as Phoenix Force gathered briefly in his room. The others returned to their own rooms to check the pistols, load and secure them.

Each Phoenix Force veteran geared up. Because of the severe weather they all had insulated inner and outer wear, including gloves and headgear. Along with extra magazines of 9 mm loads, the team carried the screw-on suppressors and sheathed Tanto knives. There were small backpacks to hold items they didn't carry on their person, which included the flash-bang grenades. In addition they had lightweight goggles to protect their eyes in case the heavy snow interfered with vision. Each man had a compact short-range com set complete with ear buds. As standard they all carried fully charged sat phones that would allow them to maintain contact with Stony Man and Zero. They donned the winter clothing, the weatherproof boots. The shoulder rigs were worn beneath the zippered, proofed jackets.

McCARTER LOGGED ON to Zero and spoke to Buchanan.

"We've been monitoring the house the past couple of hours," he said. "Right now the weather has effectively put paid to that. The storm has moved in over the area, so you're looking at heavy snow for the next few hours. Sorry I can't promise better weather. Our last decent image did show a car leaving. Three men inside. Managed to zoom in and get a look at the license plate. Sending it through. Then we started to lose the pictures."

"Doug, thanks for the update," McCarter said before signing off. "Keep us in the know if you get anything else."

"Stay sharp, people," Buchanan said in closing. "If I can get any signal on those three in the car, we'll send you the word. Right now I'm being blocked by the storm. We keep losing transmission pictures over the area."

"This data about three of Chan's crew going on a road trip," Manning said. "Reduces the odds a little."

"Maybe this sounds crazy, but how about we go for them?" James said. "Stop them going back to base?"

"Not so crazy," McCarter said. "Gary, you and Cal take one of the SUVs and track that crew. Anything you can do to stop them tying up with their mates back at the house…"

"You sure you want to do it this way?" Manning asked.

"The way that snow is coming down," McCarter said, "we're going to have one go at this. Cutting the odds should help. If you can disable that crew, join us at the house. We're only going to get this one chance to spring Kaplan. I don't intend to lose it, so let's go."

As they made their way downstairs, heading for the parked SUVs, Herr Yudell met them in the lobby, expressing his alarm.

"You are going out now? The forecast is for exceptionally severe weather," he said. "Look how heavy it is now. I have just heard on the radio weather band that this is going to be an exceptionally bad storm. I know the signs. Not just the snow but heavy wind. Very risky to go outside."

As the others carried on outside, McCarter calmed the agitated manager.

"We are more than used to dealing with such extremes, Herr Yudell. We have done this kind of thing many times before. Our research demands we experience such climatic conditions. Don't concern yourself. We've sat phones and com sets and we will be in regular contact with our home base."

"Research?"

"Why we are here," McCarter said. "Part of a long-term program on global weather conditions we are involved in. Storm flow patterns. Wind speed and such." He patted Yudell's shoulder. "We know how to deal with this kind of weather."

Yudell watched them leave, shaking his head.

"Crazy Americans."

McCarter made his way to the waiting SUV, Encizo behind the wheel, Hawkins in back with his laptop. The SUV with Manning and James in had already moved off, picking up the coordinates supplied by Zero and entered into their GPS.

Hawkins, sitting behind McCarter, had the laptop showing a download from Zero that displayed a map of the area, the subject house online.

Encizo had picked up a local map from the hotel reception. He spread it out so the others could see, using it in conjunction with the satellite display. He traced the area with his finger.

"This is our current position. We need to follow the

road north, then curve around to the east. It follows in the general direction of the target house. Along this line here. We should come in well behind the house and make our final approach by foot."

"What distance are we talking?" McCarter asked.

"Roughly a twenty-mile route from where we're sitting now. Last stretch, once we leave the car, will be around two miles."

"That's going to be fun," Hawkins said, staring out the window at the swirling snow.

"Couple of miles should be manageable," McCarter said.

Encizo started the SUV and they eased out of the hotel lot, rolling out along the road and following it up the gentle incline.

"This Colonel Chan is going to have sentries," Hawkins said. "We figured that in our itinerary?"

"If he's anywhere near as good as he's supposed to be, he will have sentries," McCarter replied. "He's military, so security of his area is going to be part of his strategy."

"Isolated location. Under his control," Encizo said. "He chose well, but this change in weather wouldn't have been part of his overall scheme."

"Won't be the first time weather change has interfered with a military plan," McCarter said. "Bracing walk will do us all good."

"Unlikely we'd be able to walk up to the front door and ask for a cup of sugar," Encizo said.

"Never thought of that old trick," McCarter said.

He used his sat phone to check in with Manning and James. The connection was spotty in the weather conditions.

"According to Zero, the suspect vehicle left a short time ago," Manning said. "We have the plate number so we should be able to ID it."

"Sharp eyes on this," McCarter said, ending the call.

Encizo had the wipers on full. The blades were having a hard time keeping the windshield clear. Already the fallen snow was building up on the road and the surrounding landscape. Above the topmost peaks the sky showed dark with the steady fall and the wind was picking up stronger now.

"This is what you call real cover," Hawkins said. "We should be able to walk right up to the door before anyone sees us."

"It's what goes down when they do spot us..." Mc-Carter said.

McCARTER WATCHED THE increasingly heavy snowfall with a less than happy expression on his face. Doug Buchanan's forecast from Zero was living up to his predictions. That left Phoenix Force with an added concern.

"Is this going to cause you problems?" Claire Valens said as she connected via her sat phone and McCarter brought her up to date.

"There are usually problems of one kind or another," the Briton said. "This just goes on the list."

"I'm guessing right at the top."

"Not far wrong there, love," McCarter said. "For sure we won't be dressing in T-shirts and shorts."

"Hey, we have a connection with Zero again," Hawkins said.

He positioned his laptop where McCarter could see it. Doug Buchanan's head and shoulders filled the screen, though the connection was less than perfect due to the heavy snow.

"The way the bad weather is building around you," Buchanan said, "I may be about to lose the signal completely. Snowstorm is a doozy. Even our scanners are losing out so I'm not going to be able to give you any more backup for a while. Sorry, guys."

"We're grateful for what you've already done for us, Doug," McCarter told him. "Once we hit that house we're going to be on our own, so you stay hard, mate. We'll give you a buzz when we have good news."

Hawkins broke the connection.

"Nothing like being upbeat, boss," he said.

"You said it." McCarter was fervently hoping any future news would be just that.

Upbeat.

That wasn't the case. When he received his next call from Valens, the news was more on the downside.

"Zero has been hacked—in simple terms," she said. "An outsider has broken through some of the system into one of the weapon circuits."

"Bloody hell."

"Don't ask me how they did it. Doug tried to explain but he lost me after half a dozen technical words. It tells me Chan must have got some data from Saul and he's using it against Zero."

"Chan must have a top man running his computer system," McCarter said. "Smart enough to be able to use what he's been given. Claire, what's Doug doing?"

"I'll let you know when I know."

CHAPTER TWENTY-FIVE

Virginia

"Can't you block the intrusion?" Colonel Corrigan asked.

"We're trying," Buchanan said. "Part of the system has started to block us out. It's overriding the encryption protocols. Someone has gotten in."

"Kaplan must have been forced to give up information," the colonel concluded.

"Kaplan's locks have been breached," the voice of Zero said. *"We are attempting an emergency shutdown of the weapon controllers."*

Next to Corrigan one of the technicians, Paul Shelley, said, "Nothing is working from here, either, Colonel. I'm attempting to cut through the block but nothing seems to be online."

"It looks as if whoever took Saul has forced him to reveal part of his protocol codes," Buchanan said.

"This was a disaster waiting to happen," Corrigan said. "Kaplan having his own set of codes into Zero was a mistake."

"The sat phone system hasn't been breached," Buchanan noted. "If Valens's people are close to where Kaplan is…"

Corrigan snatched up a sat phone and punched in the number. He waited as the call rang through.

"What's your situation?" he said when Valens answered. "I hope you have good news for me, Valens, because we are in deep."

"The team is heading for the target," Valens said. "Right now they're knee-deep in a snowstorm. It's not helping their progress."

"Put Coyle on."

Valens transferred the connection through to McCarter's sat phone.

"Corrigan wants to talk to you."

"Talk to me, Colonel."

"We have a big problem here," Corrigan said. "Zero is losing part control of the weapons. Someone is interfering with the systems. Buchanan is unable to shut down and we're blocked out, as well."

"We heard."

"If we can't get back in, we could be facing the chance of a strike from the Zero missile banks."

"We're close to the target area," McCarter said. "Bloody weather has turned hellish. We've encountered some of the perimeter guards and spotted others. Couple of my team are on an intercept with some of the opposition. They left base to pick up supplies, so I'm fingers crossed my guys will stop them coming back."

"Do you have an estimate of how many are in the house?"

"Our asset managed to get a message out. Says it's hard to gauge. Some are inside, others exterior guards. But since the text we haven't heard any more from her. I just hope she hasn't been caught out."

"We'll do what we can at this end, Coyle."

"Corrigan, I hate to ask…but if everything else fails could you take out Zero?"

"Don't think that hasn't crossed my mind. But we designed Zero to defend itself. It's tied in to the Slingshot system. It can detect a hostile missile coming its way and blow it out of the sky before it becomes a danger. You can be sure that whoever succeeds in taking over the weapons system will make sure that facility is still online."

"I thought I'd ask," McCarter said.

"If we make any headway, Coyle, I'll let you know."

Corrigan disconnected, which pushed the call back to Valens.

"I got your end," she said to McCarter. "Comes down to you getting inside that house and closing down whatever our Chinese friends are playing at."

"Said like that, it doesn't sound too bloody hard," McCarter said.

"I didn't mean to downplay it. I can't even begin to imagine what you're having to face out there."

"If I get the chance I'll take a picture on my phone and send it to you, love. Just update me when you get the chance."

McCarter ended the call before Valens had the chance to say any more. She was grateful for that because she had no idea what to say to him at that moment.

DOUG BUCHANAN PASSED his hand over the touch pad, bringing up a display on one of the large view screens, and watched as the image came into focus. What he was seeing did little to alleviate his feelings of unease. He spoke quietly, knowing the permanently activated sound sensors would relay his words to his unseen partner.

"Number three launch silo is ignoring my commands," he said. "Again."

"Confirmed."

Buchanan smiled. The Zero response, as usual, was brief and to the point.

"Nice to know you're on the ball."

This time there was a slight pause before Zero responded.

"Ball?"

"It means you are aware of the situation."

"Of course, Douglas. My collective sensors keep me alerted to any deviations of the safeguards."

"The problem is number three will not retract. And that's my worry," Buchanan continued.

"A complete diagnostic has determined an outside influence."

Buchanan activated his com station and came face-to-face with the duty man at Zero Command.

"Any update on Kaplan?" he asked.

The Air Force man, Paul Shelley, shook his head. "Ongoing situation, Major."

"Let's talk about this malfunction," Buchanan said. "We still have number three online as activated. Nothing we've tried will bring that damn thing back inside its pod."

"We have the same situation here, sir. The thing just won't respond."

"All circuit checks give us the same feedback," Zero confirmed. *"It appears we have no input to that section of the platform."*

Colonel Rance Corrigan's face came on screen. For once he didn't appear as smart as usual. His uniform was slightly rumpled and his regulation tie hung off center.

"I just came from Diagnostics. There is an unknown signal that has wormed its way into the system," he said.

"Damn thing has overwritten our code and has made its way through every safeguard we have. I can confirm it has intruded into the activation commands and frozen us out of pod three."

"I believe what we have here is a highly sophisticated update based on the Remote Access Trojan," Shelley said.

"I agree," Zero said. *"But, as you state, Officer Shelley, this is a much more powerful version. Far more invasive than the basic RAT virus."*

"Tell me about that," Buchanan said.

"RAT allows someone other than the owner of a computer to take control of the machine," Shelley said. "Operate the mouse function. Add data or delete. Tell the system what to do. Basically it becomes the controlling hand."

"The only good thing is pod three is one of the short-range defensive missiles. Fired from here, it doesn't have the range to get to any earth target," Buchanan noted.

"What if next time the intrusion gets into one of the long-range missile pods? That's my worry," Corrigan grumbled. "Somebody triggering one of the big ones."

"Saul is the only man I know who could sort this," Buchanan conceded.

"And the only one who might have given away the system override."

Buchanan didn't have an answer for that. Mainly because he had the feeling Corrigan was right.

"There may be an interim solution," Zero said. *"What you would term as* drastic.*"*

"Right now drastic sounds good," Buchanan said. He ran some more online checks, confirming the intrusion thread. "This is awkward. We built this platform. We installed the programs and hardware, and now someone is hacking our system to work against us."

"We won't give up without a fight," Corrigan said.

Zero spoke again; the same modulated tone that never altered. *"Douglas, did you not understand what I said?"*

"Yes. I heard but I'm not sure I want to hear your definition of drastic, pal."

"You should have faith."

"I have faith. Plenty of faith in you. The only thing is my life is finite so I'm not too curious about your version of drastic."

"At least we should hear what's being proposed," Corrigan said.

"That's easy coming from someone based on Earth," Buchanan said. "Begging the colonel's pardon."

"The colonel is correct," Zero said.

"Tell us."

"A total shutdown of the entire system," Zero said. *"Power down everything. Turn the platform off, in simple terms."*

Buchanan took a breath. Stared at his reflection in the view window behind the monitor banks.

"Wouldn't that close you down, as well?" he asked.

"I did say a complete shutdown, Douglas."

"We would be dead in the water. No air. No light. No computer connection."

"Exactly."

"You don't need air to breathe," Buchanan pointed out.

"Have you forgotten the emergency breathing apparatus? Flashlights? And you can survive in your biocouch for a number of hours without power. It contains extended-life power cells."

"Are you convinced that procedure would work?"

"We purge everything. Set the computer system to reboot after a period of time."

"And that will break this intrusive link?"

Zero paused before replying. *"That is the theory."*

"Only drawback is theories don't always work out."

"I can understand your reluctance, Douglas."

"Comforting you can see that."

"I could quote you the percentage of it being successful."

"Rather not go there," Buchanan said. "What do you think, Colonel?"

"It's not me sitting up there figuring the odds," Corrigan said. "I can understand the logic behind the reasoning but not what you would be risking, Doug."

"If we had Saul here he would tell me to take that risk, because he'd have worked out the survival rate to the minute."

"Your decision," Corrigan said. He focused on the operator who had been sitting listening to the conversation. "What's your feeling on this, Paul?"

Paul Shelley cleared his throat. "Based on probabilities, shutting down and rebooting offers the best chance of clearing the intrusion. But…"

"I hope you weren't going to say 'I wouldn't bet my life on it.'"

Shelley managed a quick smile. "I was going to say there isn't much else we can do. The weird thing is Saul and I were positing this very same concern only last week and it was our next project. A system firewall that would preclude anyone hacking in from another site. Sitting down and creating the program. Sorry, Doug."

"Saul getting kidnapped wouldn't have been on the

cards, so we have to get around that," Buchanan said. "Let's do what we have to do before something really heavy goes down."

"Shall I initiate the sequence, Douglas?" Zero asked.

"Is my couch ready for standby?"

"Of course. Your sustainable backup will come into play once the power goes off."

Buchanan reached to the rear of his biocouch and checked that the emergency air tank was in place.

"The readout shows your air supply is fully ready," Zero said. *"A conservative estimate gives you at least eight hours' breathable oxygen."*

"Doug, are you sure about this?" Corrigan interrupted.

"I live on borrowed time on my best day. What the hell, Colonel? Let's kick these bastards off the field."

"Initiating platform shutdown in thirty seconds," Zero said.

"Just make sure you keep your eye on the clock," Buchanan said.

Buchanan watched the vid screen. Colonel Corrigan and Shelley were doing the same.

The readout clock in the corner of one plasma screen counted down the seconds.

Eighteen seconds...seventeen...

Buchanan decided this was a hell of a way to make a living.

Ten...nine...eight...

Somewhere in the platform a warning buzzer sounded.

Four...three...two...one.

The Zero Platform went dark.

CHAPTER TWENTY-SIX

Switzerland

The increasingly heavy snowfall added to their journey time. The four-wheel-drive SUV handled the thickening fall well due to Encizo driving with care as he negotiated the steepening road. He would have been the first to admit that without the direction aids of GPS and the Zero feed, the trip would have been harder. By the time they reached the cutoff and moved east to bring them in behind and above the target location, the snowfall had increased even more. The wind sloughing down from the high slopes buffeted the slow-moving SUV.

They were driving through an all-white world. The snow dominated everything, layered it in smooth folds that grew with every passing minute. The deep drifts that were formed by the wind changed the landscape utterly. The wind added its own mark to the snow, creating shapes and concealing the outline of the terrain. The line of the narrow road and the verges on either side began to vanish so that there was simply a smooth run of snow without any defining limits.

Encizo finally pulled the vehicle to the side of the road and under the cover of a stand of trees that were heavy with clinging snow. He came to a stop and cut the engine. The moment he shut off the wipers, the windshield became quickly covered, almost shutting out daylight.

"Close as we can get," he said. "Now we walk."

"When it snows in this piece of real estate, it really snows," Hawkins said. "It's just like a blizzard back home in Texas."

"I suppose you're about to tell us Texas has the biggest snowfalls around," Encizo said.

"Not a word of a lie."

They geared up, checking hardware, even though they had done it back at the hotel. They never let anything go by chance. Especially the weapons they might have to depend on. The Tanto knives in their sheaths were looped onto their belts under their coats.

"Now," McCarter said, "I feel properly dressed."

They ran checks on the com sets, inserting ear buds.

"Okay, ladies, shall we dance?" McCarter said.

The trio of Phoenix Force commandos went EVA. They set their position and began the trek for the house, shoulders hunched against the persistent and heavy fall of snow spinning down out of the leaden sky, shoulders hunched against the unending slap of the wind.

Their progress was slow, hampered by the deepening layer of snow underfoot. Talk was kept to the minimum. There was little to say now.

Soon enough they would be facing the enemy; there was no doubt that the people behind this affair were enemies of America. Chan and his group as a whole had already showed their intentions: out-and-out theft of the Zero technology by kidnapping Saul Kaplan and attempting to put Zero Command out of action with hostile intent. It was not a wild stretch of the imagination to class it as an act of war. The way China coveted

Zero had led them to pursue a deliberate intent to carry through their scheme. Once Phoenix Force came into contact with Chan's group, there would be no negotiation. No stalling while sides deliberated what to do.

David McCarter. Rafael Encizo. T. J. Hawkins.

Three of Hal Brognola's covert warriors, ready to carry out their mission with little concern for their own lives. This was what they did. Wherever they were sent. To face their nation's enemies and go against the odds.

Gary Manning and Calvin James would undertake their own part of the mission by confronting more of Chan's force.

Each man was thinking about what lay ahead. The mission they were undertaking had the possibility of working against them. Phoenix Force had enough experience to be aware of the way things might go. They were not being pessimistic, simply accepting that life was finite and any one of them might fall to an enemy bullet. As good as they were, the Stony Man combatants were just as likely to be injured as the next man. It was that realization that kept them on high alert, ready to face down whatever was thrown at them. Once that had been assimilated, they trudged on through the storm, staying close and concentrating on their destination.

Almost before they knew it they were crouching in the shelter of close-spaced trees, with the house in front of them, almost obscured by the snowstorm.

The wind-driven snow swirled and eddied around them. They had been forced to pull their goggles in place to protect their eyes.

With the house in sight McCarter had made a final call to Valens, informing her of their arrival and advising her they would be going dark for the foreseeable future. Sat phones were switched off and stowed away. The last thing they needed was an unexpected call to come through at a difficult moment.

Valens, understanding what they were about to do, offered a last few words of encouragement before signing off.

McCarter switched on his com set and ran a quick check before he parted company with Encizo and Hawkins. Each man moved out in a different direction as they began their final approach to the objective.

McCarter, Hawkins and Encizo had scoped out the layout of the house while at the hotel. The image projected via Zero had showed them the overhead outline of the building, which had allowed them to assign sections to each of them when they were in place. It would stand them in good stead now. They could not depend on Zero to offer them further help at the moment. The inclement weather had effectively sealed off their contact with the platform.

"Don't lose contact," McCarter said to his teammates through his com set. "Hit a snag, call for assistance. We help each other. Don't bloody forget that. And keep your eyes open for outside patrols. Chan will definitely have someone on the lookout. I guarantee that."

They used the tree line to cover their individual approaches to the house. The snowfall covered their movements, but also hindered their field of vision. Layered snow had to be wiped away when it began to coat the goggles. It lay on their clothing and even though they wore insulating layers, a degree of the chill temperature got through. It became necessary to keep their fingers flexed under the gloves, the movements helping to hold back any stiffness. And the deeper the snow became the slower their movements, each footstep requiring an effort.

No time limit had been set. Moving in on the house decreed they move with a degree of caution, watching out for any roving sentries.

THEIR FIRST OBSTACLE was the stone-built structure that housed the generator supplying power to the house. It was a solid building, squat, with a heavily secured door. Some electrical cables were showing, which suggested they were below ground. There was a fleeting moment when the thought of trying to disable the electricity supply crossed Phoenix Force's minds; common sense told them it was out of the question. They had no explosive devices with them, and any strike against the building would raise every alarm in the house. Cutting power might put Kaplan in danger because they had no idea what he was being subjected to and they were going to need light for their attack once they reached the house. It was a frustrating choice but one they had to accept.

McCarter was on his own as he closed in on the stone building, pushing his way through the deepening snow and finding his vision reduced by the wind-driven flurries. He almost missed the dark-clad armed Chinese who appeared from around the side of the building.

It became a shock moment for both men.

McCarter recovered quickly and lunged for the Chinese sentry. He was reluctant to fire his Browning; even with the wind, the sound of a shot might carry and alert the other sentries.

The Briton didn't waste time thinking. He simply acted. He reached out and caught hold of the Chinese guy's shoulder, yanked the man toward him and headbutted him. The sodden crunch attested to the accuracy of McCarter's action as the sentry's nose was crushed flat, blood squirting in twin streams. Before the dazed man could recover, McCarter hauled him around and slammed him face-first into the pale stone wall of the power building. He caught a handful of the Chinese guy's hair and repeated the blow a few more times until the man stopped resisting and slumped to his knees. He rolled sideways, his face a crushed and bloody mask, bone splintered and exposed where the rough stone had ripped at his flesh. When McCarter let go, the guy fell facedown in the blood-spattered snow. There was a glistening deposit of blood on the stone wall.

McCarter blew air through his lips as he bent down and claimed the subgun the Chinese had dropped. He checked it and made sure it was ready for use. He delved into the sentry's coat pockets and found a couple of spare magazines.

"Bloody handy," he said.

Rafael Encizo had disengaged with McCarter as he spotted movement off to his right. Someone moving through the trees close by. He remained where he was, his keen gaze searching the light and dark shadows close to ground level. He was rewarded by the fleeting sight of a bulky figure clad in a padded coat; he made out the features of a Chinese sentry as the guy moved into a clear section. He was carrying a squat black SMG and the way he was holding the weapon, Encizo could see the man was no amateur.

Encizo was aware he needed to keep any action as silent as possible. If they were going to breach the house, the less fuss they made the better. Any noisy action would alert those inside the house, which could have serious repercussions for Saul Kaplan. Kaplan was the reason they were here. His safety was paramount. It meant Phoenix Force's approach to the house had to be kept quiet and not put the Chinese group on the defensive too soon.

The moment Phoenix Force was discovered, the peaceful Swiss landscape was going to be disturbed.

Encizo eased his Beretta from the shoulder rig. After checking the load, he slipped out the suppressor and screwed it in place. He barely took his eyes off the Chinese sentry as he went through the pistol's prep.

Easing himself into a comfortable position, he raised the Beretta and settled his sight on his target. He never figured out what made the man turn, staring directly at Encizo, but the Phoenix Force pro knew he had been made. It was one of those moments that could have gone either way. He didn't let the moment faze him. Already on the way to targeting the sentry, Encizo continued his move. In effect he simply realigned the Beretta, eased back on the trigger and fired.

The subdued *chug* of sound was lost in the closeness of the trees and the noise of the wind. A dark hole appeared in the Chinese guy's forehead, slightly left of center. The head was snapped back under the impact and the close range gave the 9 mm slug enough penetrating power to traverse the skull and blow out the back in a spurt of grainy red that spotted the white snow. The sentry stiffened and toppled backward, his body rigid. He slammed to the ground, limbs shaking for a few seconds before he became still. A final breath escaped his lips, pluming briefly in the cold air.

Encizo moved quickly. He holstered the Beretta and

crouched over the dead man, picking up the SMG. He checked the body for any other weapons. Found nothing except a backup magazine. He did find a neat black com set in one of the pockets and a quick smile edged his lips when he saw it was not even switched on.

Encizo touched his own throat mike and said, "Scratch one." He didn't wait for a response, simply turned and picked up his continuing approach path to the house.

TEN MINUTES ON and McCarter had worked his way closer to the rear of the house. He could see lights shining through the windows ranged along the length of the wall and even spotted a faint outline as someone passed by. The images were broken up and distorted by the falling snow.

He crouched next to a thick-trunked fir, checking for movement. He hadn't seen any other patrolling sentries but McCarter was convinced they were around. The Chinese would be covering themselves and with the increased intensity of the storm they would be taking even more precautions in case of intruders. McCarter's suspicions were confirmed when he spotted the armed figure trudging through the snow off to his left. The guy was moving with head down against the wind-driven snow, subgun held tight to his chest. He wore a padded coat and had the fur-edged hood pulled up.

McCarter had his man spotted and was set to deal with him. He decided he was definitely too close to the house to risk a shot. Apart from the sound carrying, the swirling snow could easily cause him to miss. The Phoenix Force leader decided it would have to be up close and personal. Not something he relished but they were going to get one chance at this rescue and screwing up right at the start was not something the Briton wanted.

Almost as if on cue the Chinese sentry turned and moved in McCarter's general direction, still plodding determinedly through the deep snow and still approaching. The man was wide and stocky, legs on the short side, which made moving through the drifting snow difficult.

McCarter pulled back into the shadows and watched the Chinese sentry close in on his position. The guy was moving with a cautious tread, his eyes constantly on alert though he had no eye covering and was being forced to squint against the drifting snow. He plodded on to within three yards of the tree concealing McCarter and took a long, slow look around. The man was being as thorough as weather conditions permitted.

Not taking any bloody chances, the Briton thought.

The man was doing his job. McCarter couldn't fault him for that, but he had no ideas about cutting him a break. The situation called for swift action and McCarter was geared up for it.

McCarter strap-hung the subgun from one shoulder and reached to his side, gripping the knife sheathed on his belt. It slid clear of the leather, McCarter maintaining a solid grip on the textured surface under his fingers.

The sentry took a moment to check his surroundings as he drew level with the tree. His head moved back and forth as he checked out the area. His caution made McCarter wonder if the guy suspected anything amiss. The sentry stepped forward again, seemingly satisfied he was alone.

And then he moved past McCarter, presenting his back to the Phoenix Force commander.

It was one of those moments that might have made McCarter reconsider what he was about to do. The sentry was oblivious to anyone near him—which left the Briton with a decision to make. He either bypassed the guy or made his play. If he left the guy alive he became a wild card, liable to show up again without warning. McCarter took no longer than a breath to reach his decision. This was not the first occasion McCarter had needed to silence and remove a possible threat to the mission, and any enemy combatant left capable of responding added to the risk for McCarter's partners. It was a reason why he did not hold back.

McCarter turned slightly, coming up behind the man. His left hand reached out and around, clamping over the sentry's mouth, fingers digging in to maintain his grip. The Chinese made a convulsive movement, but McCarter jerked him tight against his own body. His hand maneuvered the man's head back, exposing a few inches of his neck, and in that moment the Chinese must have realized what was intended for him. McCarter felt the guy flex his body, attempting to break free.

In that moment McCarter swept the ultra-keen blade of the Tanto around, coming into contact with the tight flesh of the guy's throat. He cut from left to right in a deep slash that sliced through everything in its path. Hot blood burst from the suddenly gaping gash, spilling down the front of the victim's padded coat, soaking through to the shirt beneath. In the seconds that followed the man felt the onset of pain and he began to kick in protest. He would have cried out if he had been able.

McCarter's hand remained in place, an effective gag

that reduced any sound to a low mumble. The Briton held his position, his strength overwhelming that of the stocky Chinese, and as the blood flow continued and lethargy began to take hold, the struggles lessened. When the man lost control of his legs, slumping against him, McCarter lowered the body to the ground and bent to check for a pulse. There was none.

McCarter sheathed the Tanto, took hold of the dead man's coat and pulled him deep into the surrounding foliage. He picked up the subgun the Chinese had dropped and checked it for a full load. He rifled through the guy's coat pockets and located a second magazine, which he dropped into one of his own pockets. Then he double-clicked his com set to transmit an update signal to his partners.

A moment later Encizo's voice came softly through the ear bud.

"You made contact?"

"At the moment, just the one. I have a feeling there are going to be others, so watch your arse."

Encizo simply clicked an affirmative reply. David McCarter understood that to mean the Cuban had become otherwise engaged.

SNOW WHIPPED ACROSS the slope, the flakes chill against Hawkins's face. He felt the cut of the wind through his clothing; insulated or not, the protection being offered was not as good as he might have expected. He flexed his gloved fingers around the Beretta. The solid feel of the pistol gave him a little comfort.

McCarter's voice came through his com set, the ear bud working well and muting the sound of the wind.

"You set?"

"In position, boss. Rarin' to go before I freeze my butt to the ground."

Hawkins picked up one of the circling sentries. The guy was off to his left; bulky in a thick coat, a hat pulled low over his head. He carried a squat SMG in his hands, the weapon held close to his body to protect it from the falling snow. The Chinese was on the short side and he was finding moving through the deep fall of snow difficult, having to lift his legs high.

Crouching, Hawkins raised the suppressed Beretta, two-handed, and took a sighting. He held off from firing. The distance was too far to be sure of a solid hit; the drifting wind might easily disturb the slug's passage. Hawkins opted for a closer shot. He was a good marksman but saw no need to take too much of a risk. The weather conditions suggested caution.

He lowered his weapon and moved through the deep layer of snow, still behind the sentry, and kept coming. He was aware that the Chinese might decide to turn and check the immediate area. If he did, Hawkins knew he would be seen. He chose to keep advancing, preferring to close the distance.

The Texan's target paused, raising his head from its chin-down position to begin a slow check of the area.

Hawkins's opportunity to get even closer looked as if it was about to taken away. He pushed forward, increasing his pace. The depth of snow hampered his movements and he muttered to himself as he watched the target twist his upper body, the guy's head coming around in a slow turn.

In a few seconds the Chinese would be looking directly at Hawkins. The seconds dropped away.

Take the shot.

Hawkins could see the guy's face in profile. Time was running out.

Take the shot.

He dropped to one knee, raised the Glock and slipped his finger over the trigger.

No more time.

The Chinese sentry's face was full-on, eyes scanning the whiteness of the layered snow. Seeing the dark bulk of the armed man, the guy moved the sub gun, pulling it away from his body.

Do it, Hawk, take the shot.

And Hawkins squeezed the trigger.

He felt the Beretta jerk but barely heard the subdued sound as it fired into the hiss of the wind.

The 9 mm slug hit above the Chinese guy's left eye. His head snapped back. The fur hat flew off, black hair exposed. Hawkins saw a dark burst fly from the back of the guy's skull as he dropped. He landed in the soft bed of snow, a fan of red misting the air as he went down.

Hawkins closed in on the guy, reaching to tuck his Beretta away and retrieve the subgun from where it had fallen. He knocked snow from the weapon, quickly checked the magazine, reloaded and made sure the subgun was ready to fire. He crouched and searched the pockets of the dead man's coat, locating an extra magazine. He slid it into one of his own pockets, pushed upright and spoke into his com set.

"Target down. Moving on."

How many more? McCarter wondered.

He advised his team to stay alert in case there were other outside sentries. They were engaging an unknown number of the enemy. There had been little opportunity for Phoenix Force to scope out just how many Chinese there actually were patrolling the area. It would have been a better option if they could have counted the exact number, but time and circumstance had placed the Stony Man force directly into the conflict. The rescue of Saul Kaplan had been undertaken in a less than ideal situation.

McCarter had to pose questions to himself as he crouched in the snow, his eyes scanning.

The number of sentries?

Were the sentries supposed to call in using the com sets? If so, how often? If there was a call schedule, the missing reports were going to be noticed sooner or later.

How soon?

And if that happened, how many more would be dispatched to find out what was happening? Advance knowledge of enemy strength would have been a preferred option, but that wasn't the way this mission had played. Phoenix Force had to make this strike using what information they had. Success or failure would depend on how well McCarter and his partners could handle what lay ahead.

Any extraneous backup from Zero appeared to be limited to outside statistics and that had been badly affected by the severe weather conditions. Zero's online imagery had been compromised by the wind-driven snow, fragmenting any details and presenting the feedback as a pixilated mass. McCarter would have liked that kind of backup. He accepted that the orbiting platform was having its own problems and needed to concentrate on those.

It had come down to human observation. To the practiced eyes of the Phoenix Force commandos. It was not the first time they had been left to their own devices when landed in a less than perfect battle zone. Left to fend for themselves, they would handle the setbacks and push the fight to the enemy.

Battle zones were flexible. Perimeters could change quickly. The fluid motion of combat had its own peculiarities, and any soldier involved had to be able to adjust to those needs. Blind charging ahead had the habit of costing lives where changing with the tide allowed advance and retreat and hopefully a better outcome. David McCarter had done his share of combat. In all conditions, on multiple continents. He'd made his mistakes, luckily survived, and he liked to believe he had learned from his errors.

Like today. Here and now.

Phoenix Force was facing an unknown force and the only way to come through it was to assess the situation and try to outthink the enemy.

It was, McCarter had decided before today, a hell of a way to make a living.

Somebody had to do it, and he was as likely a candidate as the next bloke.

HAWKINS HAD MOVED to the rear corner of the sprawling house. Up close it was far larger than he had realized. He huddled against the wall, feeling the hard drag of the wind against him. It tugged at his coat, the near-frozen flakes scratching at the fabric. He moved along the wall, keeping one shoulder in contact with the structure. In the swirling snow mist it would have been easy to lose direction and wander away from his line of travel. Disorientation could easily occur in such conditions. The last thing Hawkins wanted was to get lost. A number of times, Hawkins had to sink to a crouch as he came to windows set in the wall.

His target was the main entrance. When he reached it, he would wait until he received McCarter's go signal. The three of them would make their entry at the same time, using their flash-bang grenades to clear a path.

The swirl of snow just ahead formed and re-formed. Hawkins flicked at the scattering of flakes on his goggles.

Damned if it didn't look like a solid formation in front of him.

Almost like…and Hawkins realized it *was* a human figure no more than a couple of feet ahead. Now he could make out the head, shoulders. The extended length of arms. Hands gripping a subgun. The Chinese starting to shift the weapon.

Hawkins reacted with no further thought…

His months of training kicked in and directed his actions, relying on the techniques drilled into him at boot camp and at further intensive sessions at those grueling days and nights when grim-faced instructors pushed him to the limits and beyond.

Hawkins was measured in his response. No using the subgun; shots would betray his presence, put the enemy on alert and possibly put his partners at risk. He was calf-deep in clinging snow, so no fancy footwork. That left his upper body and arms free. He was gripping the subgun and Hawkins used it.

He swept the barrel formation down across the guy's right forearm, midway up from the wrist. Hawkins put every ounce of his strength into the blow. He felt it thud down across the limb and the bone snap. The guy gasped against the sudden shock of pain and his fingers slackened around the hand grip. The subgun sagged.

Hawkins caught a glimpse of the pained expression on the sentry's face. He had already reversed the sweep of his weapon, slashing it around and driving the bulk of the subgun into the Chinese guy's face. No hesitation. No remorse. There was only the need to put the guy down hard. Bone and flesh collapsed inward under the brutal impact. Nose and mouth turned to bloody red flesh.

Hawkins pulled back the subgun and struck again, putting in deadly force. The already crushed face became even more a mask of bloody, ruined flesh. The Chinese fell back against the side of the house, semiconscious.

Hawkins reached his right hand under his coat and slid out the Tanto. He leaned forward and thrust the blade deep into the side of the guy's neck, withdrew and repeated the thrust, severing the main artery. Blood began to pump from the wounds, thick and red. It arced away from the body, spattering the house wall and falling onto the snow. It looked starkly bright against the pristine white.

Hawkins stepped back. He pushed the Tanto back in its sheath, picked up the guy's subgun and ejected the magazine to join the other ammunition in his pocket.

The Chinese slid over sideways, facedown in the bloody snow, his body still trembling. Hawkins turned away and moved on, not looking back. He didn't need to see the dead guy again.

He gripped the subgun in his hands.

It had to be done. No time for regrets. A kill in cold blood was never a pleasant matter. It always came down to a choice. Him or you. Hesitate and the victory would go to the enemy. It still didn't mean it was easy to contain. The image lingered. The look in the guy's eyes as he went down...the shock...the onset of death. A man couldn't kill that way and not feel the moment...

Hawkins felt for his com set and tapped the button.

"Almost on target," he said quietly.

"Wait for my signal," McCarter said.

"Waiting."

Hawkins clicked off.

He came to the edge of the wall and pressed against it to check the house frontage. It was clear. He followed the length of the wall to the front entrance. His goal.

His next stop...

CHAPTER TWENTY-SEVEN

Gary Manning picked up the Saab 9-3 as it pulled out of the parking area and made a slow turn onto the street.

"Target vehicle is just leaving the supermarket parking area. Vehicle identified. Three Asian occupants. License number just like Buchanan said."

"Copy that," James said. "Okay, I see it. On the main street and heading out of town. He's driving slowly. Pick me up just beyond the traffic lights."

Manning turned along the main street and cruised until he picked out James's tall figure at the curb on the far side of the lights. He slowed the SUV and pulled in to allow his partner to join him. James dropped on the passenger seat, slamming the door. He shook the snow off his cap and shoulders.

"Bro, next time it's your turn. Man, it's chilly out there."

Manning rolled the SUV forward, two vehicles behind the Saab.

"I thought you were from Chicago," he said. "Used to cold weather."

"You think I ever got used to it?" James grinned. "Hell, Gary, that's rich coming from a Canadian."

The com set in James's hand clicked a couple of times. He raised it and made contact.

"You picked up the opposition?"

"We're tracking them out of town right now. We'll wait until we're clear before we engage," James replied.

"Just make sure they don't show up back here."

"Understood. We'll attempt to link up once we deal with our trio of Chinese perps. Problem is this damn snow is coming down like never before."

"I just heard from Valens. Zero is experiencing some interference with missile control. No idea how serious yet but hearing something like that is bloody scary."

"More than scary," James said. "This is the one thing we don't need to hear. We'll see how fast we can shut this end of the deal down."

The connection closed. James turned to Manning, who had been listening in.

"I guess we have the best of a bad situation," Manning said. "At least for the moment."

With the small town falling behind and the road snaking up into the hills, the looming crags of the mountains always in the foreground, the traffic thinned out gradually until the Phoenix Force vehicle was the only vehicle behind the Saab. The snowfall showed no sign of slacking off. As they traveled the wind intensified, pushing at the side of the SUV.

"That guy behind the wheel is going to spot us in his mirror sooner or later," Manning said.

James had drawn his 92FS from his shoulder rig. He ejected the magazine and the bullet already in the breech. He snapped the slide back a couple times to dry-fire the weapon. Satisfied, he replaced the lone shell in the magazine and inserted it into the pistol. He worked the slide again to load, put on the safety and dropped the weapon in his lap. He held out his hand for Manning's weapon and repeated the check procedure for his partner.

"What's going to be their reaction? Grin and bear it—or figure they've been made and try to discourage us?"

Manning said, "I have a feeling it's going to be the latter."

GWANG CHI HAD been studying the side-view mirror for some time. Although the falling snow obstructed his overall picture, he was convinced the SUV behind them was following. Chi had a suspicious nature and, with the mission as it was, he refused to relax his stance.

"The SUV behind us. Gray. It has been there since we left the town."

In the back seat Deng Woo craned his neck to check the rear window. "I see it. But this is a public road, Chi."

"I am aware of that."

In the driver's seat, the third member of the trio, Gok Kwai, asked, "But you are still unsure?"

"Only a feeling," Chi said. "I am sure it fell in behind after we left the parking lot."

"Let us assume it *is* following us," Woo said. "Is it going to remain there all the way back to the house? Are we going to lead it there?"

"Good question," Kwai said.

"Chi, you are in charge," Woo pointed out. "You need to make a decision. Colonel Chan would not be best pleased if we led anyone back to the house."

"They could be enemy agents," Kwai said. "Maybe even Americans looking for the man Kaplan."

Gwang Chi took out his phone and tapped a speed dial number. He waited for the pickup.

"Mr. Chan. This is Chi. We may have a problem. It appears we could have someone tailing us."

"They followed you from town?"

"Yes. And they seem to be taking the same route we have taken. With the condition of the road, there is no way we can outrun them."

"You must confirm who they are, and if they prove to be an opposition group they must be stopped. Matters here must not be interrupted. Do you understand?"

"Yes, sir."

"This is in your hands, Gwang Chi. Do not fail me."

Chi put away his phone.

Woo asked, "What does he want us to do?"

"If they are the enemy, Chan wants us to stop them."

Kwai was unable to hold back a snort of annoyance. "Just as easy as that?"

"No one said this was to be a holiday," Woo said.

Gwang Chi slipped out the pistol he wore under his coat. He carried an 8899 in 88 caliber. His favored weapon.

Woo took out his own identical make and caliber.

Kwai deliberately slowed the Saab to see if the car following would pull out and pass. It did not. Instead it reduced speed to match the Saab.

"He is following us. You see…if I stop, so will he."

Chi said, "That sign ahead shows a turn. Take it and stop so we can get out. If that car follows then we will engage."

Kwai took the turn without slowing or indicating. He felt the Saab slide a little as it hit the turn. He corrected and as the car straightened it was under his control again. He ran forward a couple hundred yards and then braked. The Saab skidded to a stop and both Woo and Chi began to exit the vehicle as Kwai saw the other vehicle make the turn.

"Two GOING EVA," Manning said, braking the SUV.

"Maybe they're lost and want directions," James quipped, reaching for his door handle.

"I love a funny guy," Manning said.

He watched the pair of suited Chinese jump from the Saab and turn to face the SUV. Regardless of the falling snow there was no mistaking the handguns the pair was carrying.

"Damn," he said, "these guys are not funning."

James worked the handle and pushed his door open, swinging his lean body around as he prepared to exit. His action became the trigger that galvanized the Chinese.

One of them let loose a pair of shots that hit James's open door. He heard the solid thump of the slugs, dropped to a crouch and leaned around the edge of the door to return fire. Three fast shots from the 92FS blasted out window glass that showered the Chinese guy. He ducked low, making a quick move to retreat the length of the Saab, and as he exposed himself for a second James fired again. A single shot this time, from a two-handed grip. The retreating Chinese jerked as the 9 mm slug caught him in the shoulder, blowing a bloody hole through the flesh. The man went down on his knees, freezing for a couple of seconds that gave James his follow-up shot. It slammed into the back of the guy's skull, took his left eye on the way out and pitched him bloody-faced to the snowy ground.

DENG WOO FELL, his face awash with blood from the exit wound.

Bending forward, Gwang Chi took hold of the sub-gun lying on the floorboard between the front seats. He cocked the weapon, pushed open his door and stepped out. The subgun crackled with fire, slugs whipping up gouts of snow as they struck the ground feet from Woo's killer.

Chi adjusted his aim and raised the line of fire. He raked the SUV where the American still held himself under cover, blowing out the window glass and gouging the panel. He made to fire again. The subgun jammed. Chi worked the cocking lever, raking it back and forth until it spit out the offending bullet.

JAMES FELT LESS protected as the autofire blasted his door. He dropped prone in the snow and rolled clear, angling his Beretta up as the shooter moved the length of the vehicle, frantically wrestling with his subgun.

Out of ammunition?

Or simply jammed?

It made no difference because it allowed James a thin window of opportunity.

He took it.

Fixing his target, James rose to his full height and fired, putting two slugs into the man.

The Chinese jerked under the impact, his grip on the subgun allowing the muzzle to drop. His finger reflexed on the trigger and, with the jam cleared, sent a long burst into the side of the Saab. The slugs tore through the side panel and punctured the fuel tank. In a freak combination one of the slugs ripped through a cable feeding power to the gauge on the tank. Exposed fumes from the gasoline ignited. The reaction was instantaneous; the fumes reaching back into the tank and setting off a blast that rocked the Saab off its rear wheels, fire spreading out and up into the air.

The flames caught the Chinese, setting his clothes

alight. Already in shock from the slugs, the Chinese slid to knees, barely able to beat at the fire eating at him.

GARY MANNING TOOK the opportunity to break clear and head for the Saab. He was watching the guy who had emerged from behind the Saab's wheel.

The driver, his autopistol in his hand, used his free hand to fan at the flames as he swiveled his lean body around, desperate to move away from the burning Saab.

Manning knew the driver had spotted him coming into position and watched as he attempted to gain a target. The Canadian fired first, triggering a trio of shots that ripped into the man's chest, opening ragged holes in his coat. The Chinese went down, bumping against the side of the Saab as he fell. He landed on his side, spilling bright blood on the snowy ground.

"Cal?" Manning shouted.

"Here." James appeared, slapping at the snow that clung to his coat.

He joined Manning and they checked out the scene. The rear of the Saab was a mass of flames. Glass had popped under the heat and they could smell burning rubber where the fire had consumed a tire.

"No chance of coming to an agreement with those guys," James said.

They stood and watched the smoke rise from the vehicle. The swirl of gray ashes mingled with the snow that still dropped over the scene. The car would burn for a while until the gasoline was used up.

"Time we weren't here," Manning said.

James nodded. "Let's bug out."

They climbed back in their SUV. Manning started the vehicle and reversed slowly to the road.

"Barb is not going to be happy when she has to explain the bullet holes to the rental people."

"Think so?"

Biting wind and snow blew into the SUV through the shattered window, making the drive even more of a problem than it already was.

Manning and James only had one concern about that. Being able to reach the rest of the team in time...

CHAPTER TWENTY-EIGHT

"The connection is gone," Tien, the tech, said. "Our link to Zero has been broken."

"I suggest you get it back," Chan said.

"I am trying, sir."

"What has happened?" Zhou asked.

"There appears to be a break in our link to Zero. Let us hope it is temporary."

"Perhaps the Americans have restored their control."

"Thank you for those encouraging words, Zhou."

"Everything has gone. Zero is completely off-line," Tien said.

"How could that happen?" Yang Zhou challenged.

The colonel looked at him. "An obvious answer would be that the Americans have shut Zero down."

"Can they do that?" Zhou asked the technician.

"I imagine they have done so," Tien admitted. "If my thinking is correct, it is an attempt to reboot the platform. A full close-down can have the effect of clearing away problems in the system and allowing a clean restart."

"Does it always succeed?"

"There are times it fails," the tech said. "If a particularly powerful virus has been allowed into the system, a reboot cannot override it. But we have not introduced a virus. Simply an electrical diversion into the operating system and even that is not powerful. That was why we were only able to take command of a single missile pod. Until we achieve control of full protocols, our intrusions will be weak, sir."

"There are times I am glad to be a simple soldier," Zhou said. "All this technical discussion is above my head."

"We all have our limitations," Chan said. "Zhou, go and check our defenses. When it comes to that… I am in your hands."

YANG ZHOU WAS pleased to be away from the crowded room. He was not comfortable with the electronic paraphernalia, much preferring the feel of a gun in his hand. That was something he appreciated.

He made his way to the rear of the house, meeting up with one of the interior security men. The expression on the man's face alerted Zhou.

"Is there a problem, Deng?"

"The perimeter sentries are not responding. Their communication sets are silent."

"All of them?"

Deng nodded. "All four."

"Inform Major Chosan. Tell him what has happened and that I am investigating. Have all the security personnel alerted," Zhou directed as he reached for one of the thick coats and shrugged into it. He pulled on weatherproof pants and worked his feet into boots. He also made sure his personal weapon was placed in one of the large pockets in the coat before he closed the zip.

"It may be the temperature," Deng said. "Severe cold can sometimes affect the com units. Do you want me to come with you?"

Pulling on a wool cap, Zhou raised the hood on the coat. "Just make sure everyone is in a state of readiness in case this is more than just equipment malfunction." He checked his own com set and heard it connect with Deng's. "Keep your channel open. Your task is to protect the inside of the house."

With his pistol in one hand, the com set in the other, Zhou waited as Deng opened the door. Snow drifted in as he went outside, feeling the tug of the wind against his body. The snow was cold against his face. The door closed with a solid thud behind him and Zhou stared around the area.

Where were the sentries?

He knew the general positions they were patrolling, but with the swirling snow and the buffeting effects of the wind it was difficult to locate exact positions. Zhou knew that it would be a waste of time calling out. The wind would simply take his words away.

The thought crossed his mind that perhaps Chan's scheme was turning out to be less successful than he had hoped it might be. They were here, in a foreign country, with only a small contingent around them. If things turned sour, they would have less than the full protection of the home country. Bringing Kaplan here had been a diversionary move, a scheme to cover what Chan was doing. If his presence here in Switzerland had been compromised…? Seclusion and privacy were concepts that went only so far. Zhou was beginning to see that Chan's operation was not as clever as he had been anticipating.

Zhou only had to think about Jui Kai. Exposed now as a traitor. How much information had she given out before her capture? Was she working for the Americans? Perhaps already having sent out details of where Kaplan was? That could be why the patrolling sentries were failing to report in. Maybe there was already an American presence in the area. Armed commandos closing in to mount an attack?

This was not good, Zhou decided.

What if there were already armed men surrounding the house? Waiting to make their attack. As much as he did not like them, the Americans had a reputation for this kind of operation. Hard and fast retrieval of their own people. Insertions into a hostile environment.

Zhou gripped the pistol, moved away from the house and began to look for his men. Surely they had to be around. The snowfall. The wind. They conspired to reduce his vision greatly. He blinked his eyes to clear away the clinging flakes.

Zhou felt the snow slip under his boots. He caught his balance and cast his eyes around to see if he could pick up any movement. Nothing. The snow-covered ground, with the trees and bushes, presented him with shadows. Zhou knew that shadows could conceal both friend and enemy. And the falling snow provided additional distractions.

The sooner Colonel Chan made headway with Kaplan, the better for them all. Gaining information about Zero was the prime objective here. Yet it was not working as smoothly as Chan had anticipated. Too much could go wrong. The less than successful operation in America had proved the point. The expected strike against Zero Command had not happened. Zhou had never been fully convinced of its viability. The idea itself, to cripple the ground-based contact with Zero, had been neat. It would have severed Zero from earth and given China that extra fillip once they had Kaplan in their hands. Such an idea had merit—if it worked— but that one had not.

Zhou pushed the negative thoughts to the back of his mind. He was here to do what he was ordered. Nothing more. The clever thinking was left to the likes of Colonel Chan and Dr. Melier. They created the plans. Zhou preferred his skills in another field. And that was why he was here, in the snow and wind, searching for the sentries who had disappeared or were huddled together in some sheltered spot. That would have suited Zhou. If he found them shirking their duties, he would be able to vent his anger for having made him come out into this damned storm. The frustration he was feeling over this entire affair would boil to the surface if he was provoked, and a reluctant sentry would find himself shriveling beneath the incandescent rage of Yang Zhou.

He had been moving on, treading carefully across the snow, aware that he might stumble over a rough piece of ground he was unable to see.

When the toe of one boot nudged something that yielded soft at his touch, Zhou paused. Stepping back, he made out a bulky shape under the snow and before he did anything else he knew what he was going to find. He traced the outline with his boot, followed it until he realized his assumption had been correct. Zhou bent and used his hand to scoop away the piled snow.

It was a body.

He found the head, cleared the snow and recognized the face of one of his men. There was a bullet hole in the forehead, a ragged and bloody hole in the back of the skull.

Zhou had the feeling the other sentries would also

be found dead. If they were still able to operate, some alarm would surely have been raised.

His com set alerted him.

"Zhou? This is Deng."

"I have found one of the sentries," Zhou reported. "He has been shot. He is dead."

"Major Chosan has put everyone on alert."

"Be prepared in case there is an attempted breach."

"But—"

"I believe it is the Americans. Searching for Kaplan."

Yang Zhou spotted movement on the fringe of the trees. It was a tall figure clad in a thick coat and wielding an SMG. He reacted quickly, snapping up the pistol and firing. He knew he had not made a hit as the slug impacted against a branch, tearing at the wood and throwing up a spurt of settled snow. He adjusted his aim and fired again, a fraction too slowly as the man pulled to the side then stepped from full cover.

Zhou saw the subgun move and settle. The man had moved so quickly he had caught Zhou off guard.

Aware of his open position, Zhou turned away, his movements hampered by the clinging, deep snow. He didn't hear the chatter of the weapon but did see the spear of flame from the muzzle. He felt solid blows to his middle. Oddly no pain. Just the tearing sensation as the slugs buried themselves deep in his body.

Zhou stumbled to his knees. He dropped the pistol and the com set. Through the swirl of driven snow, he could see the figure moving in his direction.

In the final moments of his life Yang Zhou recognized his killer as a *gweilo*, a foreign devil, and it was that more than anything that made him sad. To be killed by one of the enemy he was here to defeat…

Zhou fell face-first into the deep snow, already spotted with his lifeblood, and realized he would never know if Colonel Xia Chan's grand plan would be a success.

THE SLUG HAD chunked against the tree, throwing up shards of wood and snow that brushed McCarter's face as he sidestepped and returned fire from his borrowed subgun. He saw the slugs strike the Chinese in his chest. The man stumbled and went down. Despite the wind causing noise McCarter had a bad feeling the sound would be heard by others, and when he saw a door open ahead of him he didn't need to second guess himself.

He keyed his com set and threw out the warning to Encizo and Hawkins.

"Heads up, mates. I just announced our presence. No more hiding in the shadows. Time to show our hand. It's a go!"

CHAPTER TWENTY-NINE

Hawkins, still crouched at the main door, was relieved when he heard McCarter's order. He was tired of waiting and slowly turning into a snowman. He pushed to his feet and shook the layered snow off of him and the subgun. He slipped one of the flash-bang grenades from his pack and snagged the pin. He reached the front door, worked the handle and felt the door give. Hawkins pushed the door partway open, let go the canister and lobbed it through the gap. As it landed inside, he heard a raised voice shout a warning. The words were in Chinese.

Instinctively Hawkins pulled to the side. Autofire sounded and slugs ripped through the door, filling the air with wood splinters.

"Son of a…"

The grenade detonated, Hawkins protected from the intense glare of the explosion and the harsh crack of sound by the door and his hunched position. The second the effect fell away, Hawkins leaned in and pushed the door wide.

He saw a doubled-over, armed figure in the wide hallway, only feet away. The man's weapon stuttered loudly as Hawkins appeared, the stream of slugs bypassing him and thudding into the wall. The Phoenix Force warrior returned fire, his subgun issuing a burst that hammered into the target's chest and dropped him instantly.

Somewhere in another part of the house, Hawkins heard another flash-bang detonate. He heard glass shatter, followed by a third detonation coming from another direction.

Autofire reached his ears.

It was an indication his partners were making their own insertions.

Ahead of him Hawkins spotted moving figures erupting from a door, subguns turned in his direction. One started to fire and Hawkins went flat on the floor, angling his weapon up at the yelling figures. His finger stroked the trigger, the subgun adding its sound to the increasing noise as autoweapons began to fire throughout the house.

The pair of shooters was caught in Hawkins's intense fire, bodies punctured by the 9 mm blast. They fell back, punctures in their clothing blossoming red.

On his feet, Hawkins moved along the corridor, the muzzle of his subgun tracking. He paused long enough to pick up one of the abandoned subguns and sling it over his shoulder by the strap.

ENCIZO HEARD THE thump of sound as the first flash-bang activated. It was his signal to go. He raised a booted foot and kicked open the door in front of him, tossing in his own grenade and then pulling back to cover his ears. The second the detonation faded Encizo swung around and went in through the door. He saw a man down on the floor, crawling aimlessly, shaking his head. Encizo hit him with a short burst that snapped the guy's head to the side, a bloody geyser erupting from the skull's exit wound.

The Cuban crossed the room and checked the corridor beyond. It spread to the left and right.

A subgun opened up, ripping chunks from the wall. Encizo turned and triggered a burst in the direction of the muzzle flash. He picked up the shooter's cry. The guy slumped to his knees, still hanging on to his weapon. A second sweep from Encizo's subgun slammed the guy back against the wall, leaving a bloody imprint from the shots.

A scream of sound came from behind Encizo. He half turned and saw a heavyset figure barreling at him, massive fists swinging. The guy smashed bodily into Encizo, the impact taking the Phoenix Force warrior off his feet. Locked together, the pair slammed to the floor.

Encizo felt the subgun jar from his grip and skitter across the timbered floor. He didn't have time to worry about it. His immediate concern was fending off the attack of the powerful figure clinging to him, and attempting to loosen the arm that had snaked around his neck. Initially it was all he could do to pull his chin down low to prevent the encircling limb from shutting off his air.

Encizo hunched his powerful body and raised himself off the floor, planting his hands flat and using his considerable strength to try to dislodge his opponent.

The Chinese resisted as Encizo attempted to rise, but the Cuban pushed hard and gained his knees. For a moment his attacker held his advantage, though his feet had cleared the floor.

Encizo felt his opponent lean forward to press his hand against the adjacent wall. His move gave Encizo enough momentum to push full-up off the floor, still with the man clinging limpet-like to his back.

His attacker pressed the side of his face against Encizo's. He had been unable to encircle the Phoenix Force warrior's neck so now he reached around with his free hand to clamp it over Encizo's face, clawing with his thick fingers. Encizo turned and faced away from the wall, then pushed back, using the strength in his legs to drive the Chinese against the wall. The man grunted from the impact but refused to release his grip. Encizo repeated the maneuver, increasing the force each time. Despite his initial refusal to concede, Encizo heard the man's ribs creak under the relentless thud of his body against the solid wall.

Encizo knew his position was untenable. If another of the Chinese showed up, he was going to be deeper in trouble.

He couldn't get at his holstered pistol because his opponent had it blocked by his solid body. But the sheathed Tanto knife on Encizo's left side was clear. He dropped his hand, grasped the handle and yanked it free. He swept the keen blade up and razored it along his attacker's arm at his neck, feeling the steel slice through cloth before it went into the flesh.

The Chinese expressed a pained sound as the open wound began to spill blood but his grip on Encizo did not slacken.

Encizo reversed the knife and stabbed backward at the bulk of his assailant's body, feeling the Tanto sink into his opponent's side. Encizo pushed harder and the knife slid in deeper. This time the Chinese gave a gasp and his grip around Encizo's neck and face withdrew.

The Phoenix Force commando pulled away, withdrawing the knife and spinning on his toes as he passed it to his right hand. He caught a glimpse of the man's angry face as the Chinese lunged at him with unexpected speed, big hands spread.

Encizo stepped back and swept the Tanto in a move that caught his attacker unprepared. The blade sliced across the man's face, side to side, cutting deep and opening a gash that traversed the Chinese's right cheek, crossed the bridge of his nose and cut across the left cheek. As the soft flesh opened, a wash of bright blood erupted from the wounds and flooded down the man's face, spilling across his front.

The Chinese gave a shrill squeal. Encizo followed through with a powerful thrust that sank the Tanto blade deep into the man's neck, just under the left jawline. It went in up to the hilt. Encizo yanked it back and forth, extending the wound, then stepped back, leaving the man clasping both hands to the spurting wound as he fell back against the wall. The flow of blood from severed arteries would result in a bleed-out that would end his attacker's life within a short time.

Encizo quickly sheathed the bloody knife and snatched up his subgun. He picked up the sound of autofire coming from different directions in the house.

Phoenix Force was on full dispersion. He made a quick check of the subgun as he made his way along the corridor in search of fresh targets...

McCARTER DROVE HIS subgun stock at the closest window, shattering the glass, and tossed in his flash-bang. He took a protective stance and as soon as the effect had dissipated he turned and cleared the sill, dropping inside what looked like an office-cum-study. Expensively furnished with a huge desk where a large-monitor Apple iMac computer sat, the screen saver throwing colored bands across the desktop. Across the far side of the room double doors stood slightly ajar. McCarter could hear the rattle of autoweapons coming from deep inside the house. He crossed the room in long strides and yanked the doors open, peering into the wide corridor.

Yards along, he came face-to-face with a Chinese dressed in dark pants and a cream shirt. The guy had a pistol tucked into his belt.

McCarter had no idea who the guy was, but he did see the move for the weapon.

"Not on your best day," McCarter said and triggered the subgun. The burst chewed into the man's chest, knocking him off his feet and spinning him against the wall, where he lay kicking in silent agony.

The slam of boots on the wood floor sounded behind McCarter. He turned and saw a pair of shooters coming at him. They were moving fast, bringing the subguns they carried on line.

McCarter leveled his weapon.

He had the advantage because the pair was running as they headed for him and were having to compensate for the movement of their weapons.

McCarter was motionless, his weapon directly aimed at the pair, and when he fired his aim was on target. The Chinese pair caught the full brunt of McCarter's burst. The 9 mm slugs caught them center mass, piercing flesh and cracking bone as they struck. McCarter held the trigger and let the subgun run dry. The pair went down in a bloody tangle, crashing helplessly to the floor.

McCarter tossed aside his empty weapon and calmly went to the two men he had just put down. He picked

up one of their dropped weapons, checked the load and
turned around, heading in the direction of what appeared to be a furious firefight.

ENCIZO AND HAWKINS had teamed up, exchanging fire
with armed occupants of the house. Smoke was still
lingering from the flash-bang grenades and the effects
were causing slow responses from the opposition. It
gave the Phoenix Force team an advantage that they
made use of it as they moved from room to room, corridor to corridor. The rattle of autofire responded as the
Phoenix pair took on the opposition. As skilled as the
Chinese were, they were facing a pair of battle-hardened
professionals who exercised their unique fighting prow-
ess without letup. This was a fight to the death, with
no quarter asked or given. The Chinese fell back under
the heavy autofire, which was added to when McCarter
joined his partners. They fought with only one goal in
mind—the removal of the enemy force.

Extra magazines for the subguns were liberated from
enemies already down and the trio pushed hard, their
fire directed at anyone who moved. Shell casings littered the floor. Splinters gleamed white where fired
shots hit the timber structure of the house. Snow blew
in through shattered windows. The house echoed to the
unrelenting sound of autofire.

"We need to find Kaplan," McCarter said over the
harsh rattle of gunfire. "If Chan decides the game is
over, he might decide to cut his losses and kill him."

"Cheerful thought," Hawkins said.

As the enemy fire slackened, Encizo turned to check
out the corridor that angled off from where they were.
He spotted an open archway and moved to check it out.

It was a wide, open lounge area with a blazing fire in the big hearth. No one seemed to be in the room, but Encizo did spot a woman's coat lying on the floor next to a leather armchair.

He immediately thought about Jui Kai.

Where was the undercover woman?

HAWKINS CHECKED FARTHER along the corridor. He spotted a flicker of movement at a door and moved in on it. The door moved again as Hawkins edged closer. He angled his subgun at the door, his gaze fixed on it.

When the door was jerked open, Hawkins was ready as the muzzle of a subgun was pushed into view, a lean-faced Chinese wielding the weapon. The guy missed Hawkins. The Phoenix Force warrior didn't miss. His subgun only a couple of feet from the guy's head when Hawkins pulled the trigger, he sent a crushing burst into the skull. Flesh and bone blew apart, the exiting slugs taking out a flash of blood and fragments of brain.

The Chinese toppled backward into the room, Hawkins following.

He took in the wide window configuration and the glass roof, and picked up on a lounger holding the motionless form of Saul Kaplan. To the side, the man Hawkins recognized as Luc Melier was bent over Kaplan, doing something with a hypodermic needle. On the other side of the lounger a second guy was holding a metal instrument tray. His head snapped around when he saw Hawkins.

"Hey!" Hawkins said, his voice raised.

Melier looked up from his position, the needle still in his hand, his face draining of color as he saw Hawkins.

There was a look in Melier's eyes that warned Hawkins

the doctor was not ready to give up. It proved out when Melier turned back to Kaplan, the hypo in his hand offering threat.

"I will kill him."

The Texan didn't hesitate. He centered the subgun and put a burst into Melier's chest, knocking him back and away from Kaplan.

As Melier went down, the man holding the instrument tray let it drop. He turned around and took a couple of steps, reaching for a pistol resting on a cabinet. His fingers had barely touched it when a subgun clattered just beyond where Hawkins stood. The burst ripped into the guy's narrow back, knocking him forward into the cabinet, sending it flying as the man dropped, body arching in agony.

Hawkins glanced over his shoulder to see McCarter moving into the room.

"I know," the Briton said. "You had the situation in hand."

"Only partly," Hawkins said. "Thanks, boss."

At the door Encizo said, "See to Kaplan. I'll go look for Chan."

McCarter and Hawkins shouldered their weapons and moved to stand on either side of the lounger. Saul Kaplan stared up at them, his gaze flicking back and forth between the dark-clad, armed pair.

"I would like a glass of water," he said. His voice was weak, trembling, but there was a definite toughness lurking behind the drugged cloak.

"Agent Valens has been worried about you, sir," McCarter said.

"I'll bet she had a hand in arranging all that shooting I just heard."

"In a manner of speaking, yes."

"If I was a younger man," Kaplan said, "I would ask her to marry me. But at my age I don't believe I could handle her."

"No way," Hawkins said. "After what you've been through there isn't anything you couldn't handle."

ENCIZO HAD MOVED along the corridor, looking and listening. Now that the shooting had died down, the house had taken on an odd silence.

Or so Encizo thought until he picked up on a ragged voice calling out. Close by but muffled. He tracked the sound, following the voice until he reached a single door at the end of a side passage. The door was bolted shut. Encizo could hear the voice louder now.

It was female.

Rising and falling as though it was an effort for the speaker.

Encizo shouldered his subgun, worked the sliding bolts at the top and bottom of the door and pushed it open. He saw a faint light and steps leading down into what was plainly a cellar. A wave of freezing air reached him. Encizo drew his handgun, though he had a feeling he wasn't going to need it. He descended the steps to the cellar, where he found the badly bruised and bloody figure of who he took, correctly, to be Jui Kai.

She had undergone a severe beating. Her face was a swollen, discolored and bloody mask. Blood had spilled down the pale sweater she was wearing and had dried to dark stains. The cellar floor, filthy and damp, had soaked and stained her black pants. When Encizo crouched where she sat slumped against the cellar wall and gently raised her head, she stared at him through her right eye. Her left one had swollen shut.

"I'm getting you out of here," Encizo said.

She barely nodded. Encizo saw where the side of her jaw was pushed out of shape and realized it had been dislocated; it must have hurt like hell for her to call out.

Encizo bent over and scooped up her slim form in his arms. Kai leaned against him, one arm slipping around his neck as he moved toward the cellar steps. As he carefully climbed, Encizo felt her body start to tremble as she began to cry.

"All you want, honey," he said. "Cry as much as you want."

He took her to the big lounge where the log fire burned and lowered her into a leather armchair. He then covered her with the coat he'd picked up from the floor.

Kai beckoned him close.

"Is Kaplan safe?" she asked, her words muffled, her voice cracking.

"I'm safe," Kaplan told her as he was led into the lounge by Hawkins. He was weak, only just able to support himself as he stood and looked down at the young woman, his own suffering forgotten as he stared at her bloody, swollen face. "What have they done to you, child?"

Kai had to speak out of the side of her mouth.

"Nothing a good makeover won't fix," she said, her words slurred and soft. "And thank you for the *child*."

Kaplan crossed over and slumped down on one of the other armchairs. His body was still under the effects of the drugs Melier had been putting into him. He seemed to alternate between coherence and sudden lapses of weariness.

"Is that a drink cabinet?" he asked.

"Is that a good idea?" Hawkins said.

"Son, after what they did to me, you really think a glass of whiskey is going to kill me?"

Hawkins brought him a tumbler of whiskey and he took a long swallow.

"Now I know I'm in heaven."

"Where's the boss?" Hawkins asked his partner.

"He's gone to find Chan," Encizo said. "That *cabrón* is still loose somewhere."

CHOSAN HAD STATIONED himself at the door. He had it open a few inches so he could keep watch on the narrow passage at the top of the flight of stairs. The eruption of automatic fire had faded and the house had fallen silent. No one came to report on what had taken place and when Chosan tried to raise a response on the com set there was nothing. So he remained at his post, gripping the subgun he carried. Behind him he could hear Colonel Chan and the cyber technician in deep conversation. While the tech remained calm, explaining things, Chan seemed to become more and more agitated because things were not going his way.

The situation was serious, Chosan had decided. The house had been breached—most likely by some American strike team—and from the engagement it had become highly aggressive. Chosan was no coward. Nor was he a fool. In his estimation the strike force had overcome Chan's group. The fact that he could not contact any of them and no one had come to reassure them suggested the fight was over, in the Americans' favor.

Chosan glanced back over his shoulder. Colonel Chan and the tech were huddled together in front of the sophisticated computer setup. From what he could gather, the Zero Platform, their ultimate target, had been briefly attacked via the computer system, taking control of a small section of the platform's weapons system. He had overheard the tech explaining that the information extracted from Kaplan by Dr. Melier had let him make an incursion into the system, but only on an isolated piece of hardware. Even though the success had been limited, it had pleased Chan. He had seen it as the start of a complete takeover of the Zero Command Centre and once more information had been taken from Kaplan, the Chinese would be able to control even more.

But when the Americans shut down the whole platform, akin to switching off a light bulb, Zero had become a lifeless hulk, orbiting the Earth as a silent, dark mass of metal. Zero offered nothing to Chan. He wanted it all. Complete control over the platform, weapons and technology. Shutting the platform down had denied Chan that. All his ranting and raving at the tech made no difference. Zero had been removed from any influence and Chan's grand strategy had burst like the proverbial bubble.

His dream had been ended—but, being who he was, Colonel Xia Chan refused to accept the facts.

"They will have to power it up again," Chan said. "When they do, we can make another attempt."

"By the time Zero comes back online, our connection will have been broken. They will reboot using different protocols, so that what we used will no longer be recognized."

"Are you being deliberately obtuse?" Chan snapped. "It is as if you are obstructing me."

"Colonel, it is the Americans who are causing the

obstructions. I will admit that the way they have chosen to work against us comes with risks, but I feel once they turn Zero on again, they will return the platform to a safe mode. We will not have the time to penetrate their electronic safeguards again. And how long can we hold out here, Colonel?"

"There has been a great deal of gunfire," Chosan said from his position at the door. "Now that it has ceased, I can no longer make contact with anyone…"

CHAN STRAIGHTENED, STRIDING back and forth as his mind worked furiously. He refused to allow the word *defeat* to form in his mind. After everything he had achieved, he could not allow the matter to die.

He had kidnapped Kaplan and brought him all the way from America.

His gathering of his team here in Switzerland, here in this house, had gone well.

Dr. Melier, well known for his skills with drawing out information, had been summoned and had gone to work on Kaplan.

No, this could not be allowed to end. Must not be allowed.

Somehow he had to salvage matters. To keep things—

There was the sound of autofire. Chan spun around and saw the door shielding Chosan blown to pieces under a sustained burst of fire. The wood panels splintered and chunks of wood and slugs spit into Chosan's chest and head, tearing his flesh and bone apart. He fell back from the door, bloody and shredded.

The door was kicked wide and a tall, lean-faced *gweilo* came into sight, his subgun turning in Chan's direction.

The tech swiveled his chair around, already fisting his handgun. Even at this decisive moment he retained enough courage to stand against the intruders. The intruder let go another burst and the tech was dropped facedown over his keyboard, his blood spattering the monitor screen.

"No," Chan said. "I will not give in to you. This must not end here."

The intruder raised a hand.

"SAVE IT, CHUM," McCarter said. "Not interested. You have caused a lot of grief one way or another, Colonel Chan. But that's it. You had your chance, you son of a bitch."

The muzzle of the subgun lined up as the colonel reached for his sidearm. McCarter eased back the trigger and stitched Colonel Xia Chan from groin to chest. He kept the trigger engaged until the magazine emptied and the weapon fell silent.

Chan hit the floor in a bloody heap, his body weight settling under the sodden suit. He might have been a high-ranking soldier of the PRC, but he died wearing a civilian suit on the floor of a Swiss house in the middle of a snowstorm.

McCarter reloaded and turned the subgun on the computer setup, raking it with the full stack of 9 mm slugs until it was a shattered wreck. Then he walked out of the room and made his way back to where his teammates were gathered.

"Okay," he told himself. "All we have to do now is get out of bloody Switzerland and make it home."

CHAPTER THIRTY

"We need an extraction," McCarter said. "Seven people. ASAP. Out of Switzerland and over the best border you can find. Medical assistance is needed for Jui Kai and Saul Kaplan."

"Let me think about this," Price said via the sat link. "One question. Can you drive to the border if I arrange a pickup? Are you still socked in by the snow?"

"We'll make it, Barb, even if we have to get out and push."

"I'm going to call you back. I need to talk to the cyber team."

The sat phone shut down.

"We'll use one of the vehicles parked outside," McCarter said. "Check which SUV has the capacity and has fuel. Then get Kai and Saul settled."

Manning and James, having returned to the location a half hour earlier to find the battle over, had joined them in the lounge.

He looked at Calvin James but used his code name in front of Kaplan and Kai. "Landis, you're responsible for looking after them."

"We could have waited in town," Manning said. "You obviously have this all in hand."

"We struggled," Encizo said. "But we managed."

Phoenix Force abandoned all the subguns they had acquired during the firefight, keeping only their handguns.

Hawkins had found the kitchen, where he busied himself making coffee for everyone. They all took a filled mug. James located bottled water in the large refrigerator and loaded them into an empty backpack.

Manning had gone outside to check the parked vehicles. He came back in, stamping snow off his boots.

"Big SUV out there. Plenty of room and the tank is close to being full."

"Let's load up," McCarter said. "Sooner we move out the better. How's the snowfall?"

"Still coming, but a good driver should be able to push us through."

"That's you," James said, looking at McCarter.

McCarter had test-driven vehicles for some high-production British auto companies over the years.

"Bloody hell, mate, I don't get much chance of that these days," he said.

"It'll be good practice for you," Encizo said.

BARBARA PRICE CALLED back twenty minutes later.

"I'm looking at a map right now. Your best bet would be the Swiss-Italian border. It's going to take you five, maybe six hours. Maybe longer if the weather holds you back. An Air Force Pave Hawk helicopter from Aviano will rendezvous with you at the border and take you into the base. Medical assistance will be on board and when you get to Aviano the base hospital will take over. From there the Air Force will bring you guys home."

"I'm impressed," McCarter said.

"And so you should be."

"Whose arm did you have to twist to get all that organized?"

"Do not ask."

"Okay, do not tell."

"Aaron has worked out your route," Price added. "Coordinates on the way. Now keep in touch. I want to know where you are at all times."

WITH MCCARTER AT the wheel, the SUV eased away from the house and headed south, following the coordinates sent to his phone by the Farm.

The first couple of hours were the slowest. The snowstorm showed no sign of letting up. The powerful 4x4 plowed effortlessly along the narrow road. The afternoon was slipping away by the time they reached the lower slopes and found the landscape leveling out a little.

There was little talk. They were all simply grateful to be riding in the comfort and warmth of the SUV. After the rush of combat, coming back down left each man drained to a degree though none of them would relax fully until they were out of the country.

The roads, even when they got to the main routes, were quiet. Only a few vehicles showed. McCarter drove steadily, aware that the road surface was dicey. They stopped once to pick up hot drinks and on the second stop McCarter took the opportunity to fill the gas tank. He wanted no unexpected problems this late in the game.

By the time full dark fell they were all relieved to see that the snowfall had lessened. So had the wind that had followed them down from the higher ground.

Price called and Manning answered.

"How is the road trip going?"

"Pretty good," Manning said. "Weather has let up a little. We've made pretty good time."

"Your ride, courtesy of the US Air Force, will be with you in a couple of hours. You'll liaise at the end of your route. Any problems, call me and I will guide you to the pickup point." She paused before asking, "How's your designated driver doing?"

"Pretty well for a novice," Manning said.

"I heard that," McCarter said.

Price's laugh could be heard through the sat phone.

THE SWISS BORDER lay close. Lake Maggiore was glinting in the early dawn light as McCarter rolled the SUV to a stop. Here there was no sign of the snow that had covered the landscape they had left behind. The area was quiet. A breeze rolled in off the lake and the temperature was chill.

They made the rendezvous with twenty minutes clear to spare. The meet had been set for 4 a.m.

Since Price had enabled a sat phone connection with the incoming Pave Hawk HH-60G, McCarter contacted the pilot.

"We can track your signal from the phone," the co-pilot said. "When I give you the word, hit your lights."

"Got that," McCarter said.

The call came minutes later and McCarter switched on the headlights for the incoming chopper.

By the time the helicopter appeared Phoenix Force had everything ready. They had stowed their weapons in a duffel bag and stripped off all their combat gear. Encizo took charge of the bag.

The dark configuration of the Pave Hawk swept in out of the pale light and sank to the ground yards away.

The moment it settled, the side hatch opened and two figures clad in flight gear dropped to the ground. They took charge of Jui Kai and carried her to the helicopter. The others followed, James assisting Saul Kaplan. The transfer was fast and silent. Once they were inside, the hatch was closed and the helicopter geared up and lifted off. It gained height and swung around, powering into Italian airspace and away.

The Air Force medics immediately went to work on Kai, assessing her injuries and giving her something to help her settle. The agent reached out and took Encizo's hand.

"I didn't get a chance to thank you properly," she rasped. "All of you."

"You did a lot yourself," Encizo said. "Managing to send those texts. Keeping us informed. We should thank you."

It still hurt her to speak, but she had to ask. "Did you shut down Chan's operation?"

Encizo nodded. "We did. And to save you asking, Colonel Chan has been retired permanently."

"Zhou? Bolo? Melier?"

"They are all dead," McCarter said. "Now, just relax, young lady. Try to enjoy the ride. Bit noisy, but it was the best we could get under the circumstances."

"It's wonderful," Kai mumbled. Her eyes dropped and she went to sleep.

"She going to be okay?" Encizo said.

"Yes," the medic said. "It will take time, but she'll get there."

WHEN THEY REACHED the Air Force base, it was full light. The Pave Hawk put down gently. A medical team was waiting and took charge of both Jui Kai and Saul Kaplan. He kept insisting he was fine but he was overridden by the Air Force doctor. Phoenix Force watched as they were whisked away to the medical center.

After thanking the chopper crew for their help, Phoenix Force was escorted to facilities where they were able to shower and change into fresh clothing, courtesy of the Air Force. Someone had paved the way for them and they were treated with quiet politeness. The cafeteria was next and the five found themselves enjoying a cooked breakfast that was more than they might have imagined.

McCarter took a call on his sat phone. This time it was Brognola.

"Air Force looking after you guys?"

"Like bloody royalty," McCarter said. "I got three eggs with my breakfast."

Brognola chuckled.

"Mission accomplished?"

"Mission accomplished. Maybe now the Chinese will stop trying to get their sticky fingers on Zero. This time around it cost them enough."

"As soon as you are ready, there'll be a flight laid on to bring you home."

"Jui Kai may need to stay here on the base until she's fit enough to travel."

"No problem. She will be well looked after. That is one brave young woman. What about Kaplan?"

"Insists he's fine," McCarter said. "But I'm guessing it's going to be a while before he is off that junk Melier was pumping into him."

"Hope he's fine," Brognola said, "because he's

needed. Zero is still off-line and they're having a difficult time bringing it back."

"That isn't going to make the doc very happy."

It didn't and he wasn't...

SAUL KAPLAN REFUSED to stay away from Zero Command. On the flight back from Italy he was on the phone to Zero Command as attempts were being made to reboot the platform. During the protracted session, despite his condition, he was giving instructions to Paul Shelley, the tech on duty. The man seemed to be unstoppable.

"If nothing else works he'll take a shuttle and go up there and kick-start it himself," Manning said in an aside to his team.

"I can believe that," McCarter returned.

"Guy is a walking wonder," Hawkins said. "I can see how he got that platform built."

Kaplan spoke with the duty tech.

"Are we ready, Paul?" Kaplan said.

"All set, sir."

"Key in that sequence I just sent you."

There was a protracted silence after the tech had applied the numeric code.

"Might take a while before you get a response," Kaplan said. "Anything on the screen yet?"

"Nothing, sir. Still blank."

Kaplan sighed. He glanced across at McCarter. "Nothing done in a rush is worth it," he said.

"How are you feeling, Saul?"

"To be honest, after all the excitement it's something of an anticlimax."

Minutes dragged by. Kaplan stared at the laptop

James had placed in a position for him to view the Zero Command Center.

Claire Valens appeared on the screen.

"You should be taking things easy," she said. "A teenage hacker you are not."

Kaplan smiled across at McCarter.

"She worries about me," he said.

"If you say I'm like a mother hen… Saul, remember I carry a gun—"

"We have something," the tech's voice cut through and Valens moved aside.

The screen changed to show what was coming up on the monitor at Zero Command. The blank screen began to scroll with columns of coded numbers. Long streams of text came and went. More numbers. The monitor erupted with colors and an endless display of code. It went blank again and this time for a full two minutes before the monitor jarred and showed a fragmented image.

Doug Buchanan's face appeared on the screen. The image froze and then returned, this time sharp and clear. He was speaking but there was no sound…and when it did come through it was full-on and sharp.

"…your time. You people been out partying?"

"Doug?"

"That you, Saul?"

"I'm here, Doug."

"Jesus, Saul, you gave us a fright. Are you okay? Did they hurt you?"

"I have to admit they gave me some headaches. But I'm fine. We're on our way back now. Few more hours in the air and we'll be landing."

"Thank God."

"Nothing to do with God, just these men who came and took me out of Colonel Chan's hands. Now, tell me, are you fully back online? Have all the systems rebooted? How are you doing?"

"It was a little hairy while we were in the dark. We got through by having some meaningful conversations about the meaning of life and the universe."

"We are almost fully operational again," Zero said. *"I am running full diagnostics as we speak. The shutdown has succeeded in clearing the recent intrusion."*

"That's a start," Kaplan said.

"What about our Chinese friends?" Buchanan asked.

"Beijing got a bloody nose," McCarter said.

"Good to hear. Saul, what did you think about Switzerland?"

"I didn't get a chance to see a great deal. What I did was very cold and snowy."

"Guys, do you think the Chinese will try something like this again?" Buchanan asked.

"We already discussed that. Never say never," McCarter said. "But I have a feeling they'll be having a bloody long think about it."

"We have a lot of work ahead of us, Doug. Safeguards to initiate so no one can repeat what just took place," Kaplan said.

"The missile silos have been retracted and locked," Zero said. *"We have already put fresh coding in place."*

"Doug," Kaplan said, "if you don't mind, I do need to rest for a while. All this action has left me a little weary."

"Saul, there's nothing else you can do for the moment," Valens said over the link. "Take a break. This time it is mother hen talking."

LATER, BROGNOLA SPOKE to McCarter over his sat phone.

"We're waiting for the you-know-what to hit the fan," the big Fed said.

"You think it's going to come?"

"A Swiss chalet full of dead Chinese? What do you think, David? The Swiss are going to be well and truly pissed about that. They are going to want answers."

"Going to be a pile of diplomatic shuffling taking place," McCarter agreed. "The Swiss are going to find those bodies when the snow backs off. Which could be some time away. I'm sure they'll do some identifying and get some answers Beijing is going to have to answer for. Chinese nationals found dead in a Swiss house? Weapons spread around? Let the buggers get on with it. Going to be hard for them to own up to kidnapping an American citizen and transporting him to Swiss territory. The Chinese aren't about to make too much fuss unless they want to broadcast what they've been up to. If there's any backlash in our direction I'm sure the President will field some pretty sharp answers. He sent us into Switzerland with his backing and we followed orders to the letter."

"I already spoke to the man. He's ready for any comeback. His thinking is on a par with yours. On the plus side he's sending his thanks to Stony Man for our input."

"Hope he remembers when it's time for a pay raise," McCarter said. "And he shouldn't forget Josh Riba. Agent Valens. Or Jui Kai—that girl should get a bloody big Presidential commendation."

"How is she doing?"

"Cal did what he could with his limited medical supplies. Right now she is sedated and sleeping in the Aviano medical center."

"They've been told to look after her," Brognola confirmed. "She'll be given whatever treatment she requires."

"What's the news on Gadgets?" McCarter asked, having heard about the Able Team commando's injuries.

"It looked worse than it was. Some bruising and superficial wounds. A little R and R and he'll be fine."

"It's always a close one," McCarter said. "We'll get in to see him as soon as we can."

"This was a rough ride all round," Brognola said. "But we came through."

"That's for now," McCarter said. "I hate to be a damper on things, but the bad guys don't quit." The Briton paused. "Then again, neither do we."

Brognola couldn't argue that point.

He knew there would be a next time...and Phoenix Force would stand up to be counted.

EPILOGUE

The Zero Platform was back on full stream. Outwardly nothing had changed. For Doug Buchanan the routine picked up its pace again. Zero had been scanned and scanned again. Every facet of the platform had been checked so that there was no doubt that the problem created by Colonel Xia Chan had gone away.

Buchanan scanned the readouts, analyzed the constant stream of data flowing in from the probes and the external listening devices. The events of the past day or so were already fading. He had his future to look to. With Saul Kaplan back, there was going to be plenty to occupy both him and Zero. By the time Kaplan finished, Zero would be on an even higher level of protection.

The voice of his unseen partner broke the silence.

"Douglas, I have been thinking. I believe you were saying some time ago that I should develop a sense of humor."

"I did?" Buchanan recalled his rash comment and realized it was going to come back and bite him.

"You cannot have forgotten. I can give you the exact time from my files."

"No, that's okay. So what was it you wanted?"

"To understand more fully what it means to humans—this sense of humor."

"That could take a long time, pal. A very long time."

"That presents us with no problem, Douglas. Let's face it—neither of us is going anywhere—and we do have all the time in the world."

* * * * *

COMING SOON FROM

GOLD EAGLE®

Available November 3, 2015

GOLD EAGLE EXECUTIONER®
DARK SAVIOR – *Don Pendleton*

Cornered at a mountain monastery in the middle of an epic winter storm, Mack Bolan will need both his combat and survival skills to protect a key witness in a money-laundering case from cartel killers.

GOLD EAGLE DEATHLANDS®
DEVIL'S VORTEX – *James Axler*

When a group of outcasts kidnaps an orphan with a deadly mutation for their own agenda, Ryan and the companions must protect her without perishing in her violent wake.

GOLD EAGLE OUTLANDERS®
APOCALYPSE UNSEEN – *James Axler*

The Cerberus rebels face a depraved Mesopotamian god bent on harnessing the power of light to lock humanity in the blackness of eternal damnation.

GOLD EAGLE ROGUE ANGEL™
Mystic Warrior – *Alex Archer*

Archaeologist Annja Creed must face down a malevolent group of mystic warriors when she discovers an ancient document that could lead to lost treasure.

COMING SOON FROM

GOLD EAGLE®

Available December 1, 2015

GOLD EAGLE EXECUTIONER®
FINAL ASSAULT – *Don Pendleton*

When the world's first self-sustaining ship is hijacked and put up for auction, terror groups from around the world are scrambling to make an offer. Mack Bolan must rescue the hostages and destroy the high-tech floating fortress before it's too late.

GOLD EAGLE SUPERBOLAN™
WAR EVERLASTING – *Don Pendleton*

On a desolate ring of islands, Mack Bolan discovers that a reactive volcano isn't the only force about to blow. A Russian mercenary and his group of fanatics are working to destroy America's network of military bases and kill unsuspecting soldiers.

GOLD EAGLE STONY MAN®
EXIT STRATEGY – *Don Pendleton*

One reporter is killed by a black ops group and a second is held captive in Mexico's most dangerous prison. But when Phoenix Force goes in to rescue the journalist, Able Team learns that corruption has infiltrated US law enforcement, threatening both sides of the border.

DON PENDLETON'S
THE EXECUTIONER®

"An American patriot and Special Forces veteran determined to extinguish threats against both the United States and the innocents of the world."

The Executioner® is a series of short action-thrillers featuring Mack Bolan, a one-man protection force who does what legal elements cannot do in the face of grave threats to national and international security.

Available *every month* wherever Gold Eagle® books and ebooks are sold.